UPON A
WAKIN
DREA

TWELVE TALES OF MAGIC AND MISADVENTURE

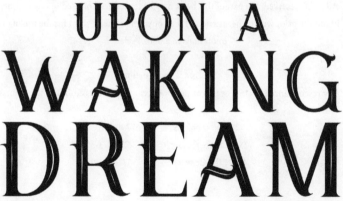

UPON A WAKING DREAM

J.S. BAILEY

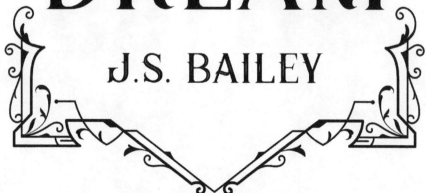

UPON A WAKING DREAM

Edited by Kelsey Keating
Cover Design and Interior Formatting by We Got You Covered Book Design
WWW.WEGOTYOUCOVEREDBOOKDESIGN.COM

ISBN (ebook): 978-1-7367790-2-6
ISBN (paperback): 978-1-7367790-3-3
ISBN (hardcover): 978-1-7367790-4-0

THIS COLLECTION IS DEDICATED TO

G. S. JENNSEN

WHOSE STORIES HELPED ME DREAM AGAIN.

TABLE OF CONTENTS

INTRODUCTION

GROWING UP, THE FICTION I consumed consisted primarily of mysteries, fantasy, science fiction, and the various volumes I was forced to read in school. I'd begun writing at a *very* young age, and it was my dream to someday become a science fiction author like the many I had looked up to.

There was just something magical about traveling to Pern and flying around with Anne McCaffrey's dragons, rescuing missing fathers from Camazotz with Madeleine L'Engle's Murry kids, and fighting epic space battles in the many dozen *Star Wars Expanded Universe* novels that have tragically been retconned.

I wanted to write like those authors because they had inspired me and taken me away to new worlds that I found far more interesting than my own. I created my own alien languages. I drew solar system maps of alien worlds. My bedroom walls were bedecked with star charts, maps of the moon, and *Star Wars* posters. I wrote a complete novel about shapeshifting lizard people called Solorthians who were hiding out in the Amazon Rainforest. (It's saved on a floppy disk and some outdated CDs, for anyone who may be interested.)

My future career in science fiction seemed to be taking shape rather nicely. Time has the tendency to change all things, however, including one's aspirations and choices of reading material. When I was introduced to Dean Koontz's large volume of work at the age of twenty, I quickly fell in love with the supernatural genre and ended up writing novels featuring vengeful yet remorseful ghosts, exorcists, and humans with special powers. The aliens of my childhood became a distant dream.

It had been years since I read a science fiction novel, but in 2015, the premise of G. S. Jennsen's *Aurora Rhapsody* series intrigued me so much that I ordered myself a copy. I was quickly sucked into a futuristic universe where the Milky Way galaxy is being invaded by alien armadas that arrived through a portal cleverly hidden in the heart of a nebula. Just like that, my love of science fiction was reborn.

In a way, writing this collection of stories was like revisiting an old friend I hadn't seen in a while. If you're looking for ghosts and demons, you won't find any of those here. What you will find includes a woman so desperate to change her life that she literally alters time, a Flat Earther who finds himself abducted by aliens, a broke college student who gets a little more than what he bargained for when he takes on a mysterious job, and a peculiar stranger who arrives in town and affects everyone he meets in somewhat unsettling ways.

Disclaimer: some of these stories fall under the fantasy umbrella, rather than the science fiction one, and one of them even turned out to be dystopian flash fiction. I hope you won't hold it against me.

Enjoy!

— J. S. Bailey

LETTER FROM
GLOMSUET

DEAR STACY,

I sure hope this message reaches Earth. They say it will, but I don't know if I can trust my couriers. They're a ragtag bunch of miners headed off to Trgskpik so they can drill for some special ore that powers their electric toothbrushes. Not the miners' toothbrushes, per se. The people of Glomsuet's toothbrushes. That's where I've been all this time. They're very particular about their teeth.

I begged to go with the miners, of course, but they refused, saying they didn't like my accent or my smell, and when I offered to pay them twenty thousand *opkik* for passage, they laughed in my face. For thirty thousand *opkik*, they agreed to take this message to Earth along the way to Trgskpik, but for all I know, they've decided to use the envelope as a scorepad in a game of *ongjit*. Which is sort of like chess, but not really, because they use a scorepad, and the loser has to serenade the winner for the rest of the day whether they can sing or not.

You're probably very confused at this point. I'll rewind a bit and start at the beginning.

Remember that convention I went to back in 2015? The one where Flat Earthers like me gathered from near and far to celebrate our planet's beautiful flatness and laugh at all the scientific "elites" who've duped everyone into thinking we were living on a big ball floating in space with a bunch of other balls? I'd asked if you wanted to go with me, and you said you didn't want to be seen hanging around with the tinfoil hat crowd, who couldn't use common sense to see that the Earth was, in fact, round, and I told you to give me proof that it *was* round, and we got into that silly argument again.

That was the only problem with our relationship. We got along swell until good old Mother Earth came up, and we'd turn blue in the face trying to convince each other we were right.

Well, that's the night it happened. I don't know if you know that or not. Since we'd argued, you might have thought I was purposely ignoring your calls, but if you did try to call me, I was much too far away at that point to get any reception.

If you remember, they held the convention out in the big field just down from the high school. There were lots of tents and RVs set up since folks came from all over for the gathering. I'd finally peeled myself away from the rows of vendor booths so I could walk home along that trail that winds around the duck pond and cuts through the woods over to my street. The route was a mile and a half, tops.

If I'd gone home using the sidewalk that goes into town and went up and around the other way, you and I would probably be sitting out on my back deck right now, looking up at the stars and arguing whether or not they were immense, hot spheres of gas many light-years away or small, cosmic LED fixtures designed to make the night sky look pretty.

You'd probably say, "Emilio Bustamante, you wouldn't believe the sky was blue unless you saw it yourself," and I'd point to the night sky and say, "It looks black to me."

I left the crowds behind and passed one couple making out near the duck pond. They were the last humans I've ever seen. It feels weird thinking that. If I'd known what was about to happen, I might have tried to appreciate that brief moment a little bit; maybe gazed at the couple as they continued to grope each other and told them that even though I didn't know them, they meant the world to me, and I held them in the highest honor because I would never see any other members of our species again after them.

Not that the people of Glomsuet look much different from us. But they're from Glomsuet, not Earth.

About five minutes after I passed the couple, I heard a noise off to my left. I hadn't quite reached the edge of the woods yet, and I saw a large shape looming in the twilight, about the size of my house. I'd never seen a structure there before, and I shone my flashlight toward it to get a better look and saw a metal-hulled craft parked in the meadow grass like a UFO from one of those old Twilight Zone episodes. It was stereotypically disk-shaped, with round portholes spaced evenly around the edge. To my delight, the hatch was open, and a metal plank had been lowered to the ground. A faint glow issued from inside. This was brilliant! I thought someone must have made this for the convention and was going to charge admission for anyone who wanted to go out into the dark field and climb aboard.

I didn't see anyone around, so I made my way up the ramp into the craft to give myself a personal tour. The attention to detail was astounding. Screens mounted on the inner walls displayed alien glyphs that didn't mean anything to me. I expected to see dummies of little green men manning the controls, but instead, on a nearby wall, hung a framed photograph of a dark-skinned couple with a little girl standing in a garden full of bright plants I didn't recognize. I say dark-skinned, but they didn't look African-American. The bone structure was all different—their cheekbones seemed more pronounced than in most people I'd met, and their faces were a little longer—it's hard to explain properly when there isn't anyone on Earth to compare them to.

I moved through the craft into a different room that contained two sets of bunk beds. It was then I noticed the smell. Not a bad smell, but one I couldn't place. The whole craft smelled like it—it reminded me of honey mixed with coconuts mixed with motor oil.

I later learned that this is what the people of Glomsuet smell like. To them, I smell like something the *igrikki* dragged in through the flap. I have to shower twice daily in order to be socially presentable.

Anyway, I continued to explore the craft until I came to a door propped open a few inches, and I saw the woman from the photograph on the wall standing behind a desk addressing someone I couldn't see in a language I couldn't understand. It wasn't Spanish, which I can't speak but would know the sound of anywhere since my grandparents all came to the U.S. from south of the border. It definitely wasn't French, either, and I was starting to think it was maybe something like Russian when I realized the whole craft had begun to vibrate.

I had the sudden feeling I wasn't really supposed to be there at all, and when I made a hasty retreat toward the hatch, I found it locked tight.

"Hey, let me out!" I cried, unable to find the knob or lever that would open it. Heavy footsteps raced toward me, and the dark-skinned woman appeared around the curve of the ship, followed by a man who seemed to be her subordinate. Both wore plain white cotton-like clothing. The top two buttons of the woman's shirt were unbuttoned, and against her skin lay a silvery pendant in a shape I would later learn is their letter for the "V" sound as it appears before the letter for the long "E" sound. Their alphabet contains many oddly-specific glyphs.

They both started shouting at me in that unknown language, and I felt my face heat in embarrassment. "Don't you speak English?" I asked as my heart raced. What exactly had I gotten myself into?

Instead of answering me, they turned to each other and started jabbering away again, throwing gestures at me periodically that left me no doubts in regard to the subject of their conversation. While they seemingly argued, my gaze went to the nearest porthole. I detected movement outside and, curious, I went to the round pane and saw, in horror, the ground—very, *very* far below. Tiny lights of towns twinkled like stars, and my stomach sank as my brain registered the rate at which they were shrinking.

I got up in the woman's face and pointed toward the floor. "You take me back down, now!" I yelled. My meaning should have been obvious, yet all she did in reply was place her left hand atop her head in a gesture whose meaning I couldn't intuit.

I began to feel sick as I glanced back to the porthole. We were so high now that I could see the eastern outline of North America lit up like a Christmas tree from a million city lights, bordered by ocean black as pitch.

It occurred to me that the curving shape of the continent did not look like the North America that appeared on the flat-Earth maps I'd adhered to my entire adult life. It looked like the North America I'd seen on every classroom globe, curved as it clung to the side of a sphere.

We drew even more distant from the only place I'd ever known. I could see the sun now, burning bright off to the left, and as we changed course a few degrees, I spotted the line where day turned into night, right over the Rocky Mountains.

I staggered back a step. The entirety of the Earth was visible to me now, and in that moment, I realized you were right, Stacy. Everything you believed about our home was right, and I was the stubborn dunce who'd let myself believe the Earth was some cosmic paper plate floating in the void while a tiny sun waltzed about above it.

A hand landed gently on my shoulder, and I whirled to face the woman, whose eyes were full of curiosity. "Veeven," she said, pointing at herself. She pointed to her subordinate. "Pridip."

"Emilio," I sighed, pointing at myself. Tears rolled down my cheeks. I couldn't figure out why Veeven and Pridip wouldn't take the ship back down and let me off, and at the time, I thought they were being cruel. (I later learned that their ship ran entirely on autopilot, and they had no way of returning me home unless they overrode their system, which would have shorted out their autopilot, leaving them stranded on Earth since they were scientists, not navigators, and wouldn't have been able to find their way home.)

They disappeared from the main room for a few minutes and returned with two more members of their crew, whose eyes went round when they saw me. Unlike Veeven and Pridip, the woman had a sort of Caucasian skin tone, with high cheekbones, yellow eyes, and an entirely shaved head, and the short, stocky man's skin was pale and had a faintly bluish tinge that made him look a tad low on oxygen. His closely-cropped hair was blonde. It felt jarring to see such alien combinations of features, but heck, I probably looked just as alien to them.

I don't remember all the details about that day, but I do know they gave me a bottle of some liquid that soothed my nerves, and the next thing I knew, I was opening my eyes lying on a bunk bed. Dismayed that my little adventure had not been a dream, I rushed to the bedroom's porthole and saw that all the stars had vanished from space. Apparently Glomsuet ships travel quickly through space via the use of artificially-generated wormholes, which we had now entered.

I noticed that my skin felt squeaky clean, and when I reached my arm up to sniff it, it had a vaguely chemical odor. I think they must have decontaminated me while I was unconscious. Smart move, probably—they wouldn't want to annihilate their planet with my Earth germs.

The bluish man I'd met before entered the room then, pointed at himself, and said, "Limmik." He turned his finger to me. "Emilio."

I nodded. "That's right. Emilio. Um, do you have a restroom on board?"

Limmik stared blankly until I demonstrated my need using crude sign language. He laughed and made a gesture for me to follow, and he led me to a room that looked like it could have been a bathroom on the starship Enterprise, with gray fixtures and a little pump bottle of soap that smelled like garlic.

It took about two days until the ship left the wormhole and a bright planet appeared in the porthole. The oceans looked blue just like Earth's, and I could pick out three continents on the side visible to me: two a deep green, and one a sandy brown. Despite my unhappy circumstances, I began to grow excited. I would be the first human to

visit another planet! I pulled out my smartphone to snap a picture, but the battery was dead, and my charger was a zillion billion miles away on my kitchen counter.

The land loomed ever nearer. It looked like we were headed right toward the greenest continent, which was shaped a bit like a squirrel riding on a big jellybean. There were mountains near the coast, and to my delight, the ship's trajectory angled right toward them—you just don't see too much of mountains when you live in rural Indiana, you know.

Veeven had come up to my side. She pointed out the porthole and said, "Glomsuet," and even though I couldn't understand her, I got the feeling she was welcoming me to this mysterious new place. I smiled at her and said, "It's beautiful."

The ship landed on a sort of helipad in the middle of a bustling city where the buildings were white and silver and red and every other color under the suns. Limmik and Harnash, the pale woman with the shaved head, emerged from an inner room in the ship holding clay pots of wildflowers that looked like the ones that had grown in the field by the woods near my house. So this had been a botanical expedition. No wonder these folks seemed so peaceful. Ordinary aliens probably would have vaporized me already.

When we stepped out of the ship onto the landing pad, two dark-skinned women in green cottony uniforms greeted the crew, and then all eyes went to me. I felt very small and wished I could explain myself, but all I could do was shrug.

Then the fear kicked in. I was an alien here. An honest-to-God alien. And knowing what a lot of humans would love to do to any hapless aliens who landed on Earth, I had the feeling I was about to be sent to a lab to be dissected.

Veeven said something to one of the other women and grabbed my arm, then led me into the nearest building and into a cool reception area. The bluish-skinned woman behind the reception desk was flipping through a magazine and barely looked our way when Veeven led me past her down a long, echoing corridor to a door marked with several glyphs in their language.

We went inside. A wide window spanning almost the entire length of the far wall looked out onto a lush garden where vines climbed trellises and a hundred different kinds of flowers were in full bloom. Made sense, if these were botanists. Maybe some of those plants out there came from other worlds, too.

Veeven motioned for me to sit in a chair in front of her desk. I obeyed, and she dug through a drawer and thrust a notepad and crayon-like writing utensil at me. She took a notepad of her own and drew two stick figures on it: one obviously a woman, and the other obviously a man, judging from the crude anatomy she added.

"Ishtik," she said, pointing to the woman. Then, "Washtik." I scribbled both words down on my notepad, spelling them phonetically, and added their meaning next to them.

"Ishtik," I said, pointing at her. I then pointed at myself. "Washtik."

She placed her right hand on top of her head and smiled. It occurred to me that she was "nodding" in her people's own way, so I'd gotten it right.

Over the next hour, she taught me the words for desk, chair, wall, door, floor, ceiling, arm, leg, and head. To pluralize, you had to add the prefix "la" to the word, so "women" was "laishtik" and "men" was "lawashtik," and I was pretty proud of myself that I was picking it up so easily. When I sensed that our session was drawing to its conclusion, Veeven smiled at me and said something that sounded kind. I decided then that this was the best friend I'd ever had: she'd accidentally abducted me, and now was trying to be nice by helping me assimilate to her world.

She took me home that night. Not to bed, mind you, but to stay there, as I had nowhere else to go. I met her husband and daughter, whom I'd seen in the photograph on the ship, and they looked at me with pity after Veeven explained to them what had happened.

Jibna, her husband, lent me some clothing and indicated through gestures that I must shower as often as I could, and for ages I spent the eerie twilit nights on their sofa, wondering about you, Stacy, and my parents and brothers. I know you all think I'm dead. I try not to think about that much now, but it still creeps in during the quieter moments of life, and I hope you've all been able to handle it okay.

Night on Glomsuet is not like night on Earth. Not usually, at least. Glomsuet orbits one member of a binary star, so part of the year the other star appears like a brilliant full moon during the "night," and as Glomsuet's orbit brings it around the other side, two suns appear together in the daytime sky, and the nights are much darker.

Time moves along differently here. Since I can't follow Earth time on my dead phone, I can only guess at how long the intervals of time are. They divide their days up into twenty smaller units like hours, and the days feel a bit shorter than I remember them on Earth. Their years consist of fifteen months of thirty-nine days each, and in the region where we landed, most of those months are extremely hot.

About three months into my stay at Veeven's house, I'd picked up enough of their language to have the most basic conversations. I learned that Veeven and Jibna had been together for twelve of their years, that they liked me but wished I smelled better than I did, and that the place they all went off to on the seventh day of every thirteen-day week was a temple where they worshipped a god called Jo. Jo, I learned, created the heavens and the Glomsuet, and rested on the seventh day before continuing his divine work for the rest of the thirteen-day week.

I wonder what Earth would have been like if God had kept on working after the seventh day there, but I digress.

Now, you've got to be wondering why I wasn't being hounded by reporters wanting to know about Earth life, and all that jazz. I wondered it, too—if some poor alien got stranded in Indiana, you can bet it would make some headline if the government didn't hush it up first. If not mainstream headlines, then at least the tabloids, which thrived on that kind of stuff. While Veeven's family did own a large, TV-like screen on which they occasionally watched fictional shows I couldn't make much sense of, I'd never seen anything on it resembling CNN, or even TMZ.

I did my best to express this to Veeven one day after she'd gotten off work.

"I have a question," I said as she rummaged through kitchen cabinets for dinner ingredients.

She paused in her task and smiled in her kind way. "You have many, Emilio."

I strained to think of how to phrase it with my limited vocabulary. "Here, on your planet, do people share important things that are happening?"

"That is what conversation is, is it not?"

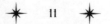

"Yes, but I mean…on your screen, there. You have programs that you watch. Do any of them show true things, like what your leaders are doing?"

Her face lit up, and she hurried over to the screen and switched it on, then dialed it to a different channel. "Yes, yes, of course we do. Here, see? This is our president, right now."

Their word for "live" appeared in a corner of the screen. A dark-skinned man about Veeven's age sat in a plush chair weaving something with yarn, seeming to explain to the viewer how it was done, like something you'd see on PBS.

I felt there must have been some communication error between me and Veeven. "No, I mean a leader of your people. Someone who's boss."

She pointed at the screen. "Elarra is our president. He enjoys making things and loves to share his craft with the people."

Bewildered, I said, "This is important?"

"It is very important."

"But what about…" I broke off, not yet knowing the words for "war," or "crime," or "government." "Never mind."

I decided that if the president making doilies was important, I probably wasn't. A good thing, too, because I never did like being in the spotlight. I'm just a low-key kind of guy.

I started to feel confident enough to put my newly-found language skills to the test, so I went out into the marketplace with some *opkik* Veeven had given me for helping her and Jibna mow their lawn and trim the hedges while they were at work. I did my best to look people in the eye as I greeted them with the proper Glomsuet words, and as I drew near a stall selling fresh vegetables, I spotted the most gorgeous woman I'd ever seen on that world. Her skin was a rosy shade I hadn't seen on anyone else in that city, and long, snowy white hair fell past her shoulders. She wore silky robes that seemed out of place compared to the cotton outfits that everyone else wore, and when she caught me staring, I awkwardly said, "Hello."

Her cheeks flushed an even rosier color, and she jabbered something at me I couldn't understand.

"Could you repeat that, please?" I asked. "I'm not from around here—I'm still learning your language."

The woman said something else to me and hurried away. Confused, I glanced to the bluish man operating the vegetable stall. "Did I say something wrong?" I asked.

The man laughed. "She was speaking Rinishin. You haven't heard it before? They come down from the other side of the mountains."

I stared at him blankly. For the first time, I realized I'd never asked Veeven the name of the tongue she'd been teaching me. "What language am I speaking, then?" I asked, feeling stupid.

The man's pale blue forehead crinkled. "Jikkinik, of course. Are you from Aloroop? You have an unusual accent."

I placed my left hand on top of my head, which meant "no." "Is Aloroop another planet?"

The vendor shifted on his stool and leaned closer to me. "Didn't they teach you anything in school? It's another country."

"What country is this that we're in?" For some reason I'd assumed Glomsuet was one united place, though I'm not entirely sure why, since Earth certainly wasn't.

"Jikkin," he said. "You're really not from around here, are you?"

"Not exactly." I paused. "How many countries are there on this planet?"

The vendor blinked as if unsure as to whether or not I was having him on. "At least a hundred. I'd have to look up the exact number. Jikkin, Aloroop, Rinish, and Vo are the four countries on this continent, but West Horon has sixty-something little countries all squashed together. You need to brush up on your geography, I think."

I walked back to Veeven's house in a daze. Here I thought I was finally understanding this place, when it turned out I didn't understand it at all.

Nobody else was home, so I logged into the family computer to see about researching more about this planet. I was still learning to read their alphabet, which has seventy-two different letters, twelve number shapes, and forty punctuation marks, so it took me a while, but at last I figured out that Glomsuet is home to 108 countries. The largest, Lamma, is an entire continent to itself, and is home to half a billion people who speak a language called Kyule. Sixty-five percent of everyone who lives on Glomsuet are fluent in Kyule, and it's taught in most of the schools here in Jikkin.

Only two hundred thousand people in the whole world can speak Jikkinik, the language I'd been working so hard to learn. I was like an alien stranded on Earth, trying to learn Welsh.

In spite of my sadness that I was only learning about the tiniest fraction of Glomsuet life, I threw myself into the work Veeven provided me with. When she deemed my speaking skills sufficient enough, she helped me apply for real jobs, the first of which was a custodial position at the biology laboratory where she works. While I mopped floors, I thought of my grandparents, who'd left everything they'd known behind to come to a new country. They'd been forced to learn new words and new customs, and slowly went from performing menial jobs to managing their own businesses.

The stories they'd told me as a child gave me heart. If they could adapt to a new life, then so could I. Their indomitable spirits would live on in me!

I still thought of you a lot, Stacy, especially at night when the stars came out and I'd sit on Veeven's patio and watch thousands of glimmering pinpricks waltz across the heavens. I harassed you so much about how foolish you were to think our Earth was a sphere, and felt so guilty for having put you through that. You deserved better. I hope you know I'm sorry.

When I'd been on Glomsuet for an entire Glomsuet year, I sat alone in their backyard as the primary sun set, and I remembered a silly argument you and I had not long before my accidental abduction. We'd been driving to dinner one evening, and sunlight had burst through holes in the cloud cover in a spray of angled rays, and I'd said something like, "You know the sun has to be close by for the sunbeams to slant like that."

You'd rolled your eyes like you always did and said, "Sunbeams are parallel to each other. We've gone over this a thousand times. They only look angled because they're so long, our perspective makes it look like they're angling together in the distance."

"I don't get it," I said.

You gestured at the road in front of us. "Look at the white lines on each shoulder. They look like they angle together to meet at a point in the distance, but they don't. It's an illusion. The sun is big, Emilio, and millions of miles from here. You need to stop reading internet conspiracy theories."

I'd laughed. Like I'd give up my hobbies for anyone, even you! Sure,

I'd started reading those theories as a skeptic, but over time I realized *they made sense.* I could just see the government faking lunar landings and pictures of Earth from space to feed people with a happy fantasy to distract them from all the crap happening down on the ground. Someone with his gaze fixed on the heavens dreaming about leaving the Earth isn't going to pay as much attention to poverty and suffering, because their focus is elsewhere. Space programs were a soothing balm for the masses. It gave them hope that humanity could be something more than it was.

I'd considered myself enlightened. I knew that life sucked, and that faked photographs of a spherical Earth from space might make people think different. So I ate, I drank, I attended flat-Earth conventions, I was merry.

My life on Glomsuet went on. As my language skills improved, I got a new job as the biology lab's property manager, because the current manager was about to retire and move to Kshinni, an island nation not far from here that seems to be the Glomsuet equivalent of Florida, due to its large population of lizards and senior citizens.

I'd periodically ask Veeven if she and her team were planning any more botanical missions to Earth, but she'd shake her head and tell me they tended to only visit a place once, and that it wasn't up to her, it was up to the program head, who never seemed to be available when I tried to contact him.

For a space-faring civilization, these people sure stay on the ground a lot. Mining operations head out to different planets to collect ore, as I stated earlier, and one organization is discussing the possibility of terraforming another planet in their system so people can live there, too, but the vast majority of people get up in the morning, go to work, and come home without hardly glancing at the sky over their heads, even though they know that scientists and miners are constantly visiting other worlds. I guess when a society is used to something that noteworthy, it loses some of its luster.

Now Stacy, there's something important I need to tell you, and I hope you take this okay. I've been gone a long time. I used to dream of seeing you again, of running into your arms and sweeping you off your feet with a kiss to tell you *I'm home, Stacy, and I'll never leave you again.*

But time has passed. I'm a realist. I figure you moved on a long time ago. In fact, I hope you have.

About a year ago, I started noticing this woman down at the bar where I spend some evenings hanging out with Jibna and his friends. She's one of the blue-tinged people and has long, white hair, which is just a normal hair color here and doesn't necessarily mean someone's a geezer. She works as a barmaid, and though I have been and always will be refining my knowledge of Glomsuet gestures, I had the feeling she was flirting with me every time I ordered a drink.

I nudged Jibna on one of the occasions this happened. "Hey," I said in a low voice. "Do you think she likes me?"

Jibna threw his dark head back and laughed. "Are there six moons in the sky? Of course she likes you! Why don't you find out her name?"

I decided that might be a good idea. I hadn't been with anyone since you, Stacy, and it had been years already at that point, and I didn't see too much harm in it.

I sidled back up to the counter. "Hi," I said to the bluish barmaid. "What's your name?"

Her cheeks turned a shade of purple as she blushed. "Reena. And you?"

"I'm Emilio."

She tilted her head with curiosity. "That's a different sort of name, isn't it? Are you from Aloroop?"

"Nope, not from Aloroop." I grinned at her. "Sorry if this seems bold, but do you want to go to dinner with me sometime?"

She flashed me a smile that showed off her porcelain-white teeth. "That would be great!"

To make a long story much shorter, Reena and I went to dinner the next evening, and again a few days after that. On our days off from work, we would walk along the beach or the riverbanks or go on hikes up into the mountains. She never seemed to mind my human smell.

I avoided talking too much about my pre-Glomsuet life since I didn't see any other extraterrestrials like me out and about and I didn't want to exhibit myself as a freak, so I mostly talked about what I did at work and which *slurbik* teams I thought were going to win the next championship, and everyday Glomsuet things like that.

Reena talked about writing music and poetry, and how she was working at the bar while she tried to get her creative career off the ground. She laughed a lot and shared her most ambitious dreams with me, and before I realized it, I'd fallen in love with her.

Don't get me wrong, Stacy. I appreciate the time you and I had together. We may have argued, but you were fun, and I hope you can appreciate those times, too. So, yeah—I didn't want to hitch a ride with the miners to go back to Earth for good. I was merely hoping for a visit and to let you and my folks know I'm still out there, far, far away.

But Stacy, I have this funny feeling that you *knew* I would find someone else, and that you sensed the moment it happened from far across the stars and found a way to curse me.

I love Reena. I love her so much that we plan on getting married on the thirty-eighth of Zenk.

But.

About two weeks ago, Reena and I spent a long evening discussing wedding plans, and afterward we left her house and went for a walk up the hill in the dark. It's the time of year with darker nights now, when two suns appear during the day, instead of one bright sun during the day and a somewhat dimmer one at night—you would not believe how much better I sleep when it's this way.

Anyway, we laid a sheet down on the grass and flopped on our backs to stargaze—something she and I had never done before, because we've always been so busy with work and building our relationship, but now we felt it was time to slow down for a moment and just relax.

"It's beautiful, isn't it?" I said.

I could sense her smiling in the dark. "Yes."

"Do you ever wonder how many worlds might be out there, waiting to be discovered?"

She laughed. "The only world is this one, Emilio."

I turned to her, still lying on the sheet. "What?"

Reena remained on her back. "I'm not stupid. I know what the government has been trying to do for centuries. They want us to think something else is out there so we work together to get there instead of killing each other. It works, too, since there hasn't been a war for centuries."

I gaped at her, though in the dark she couldn't see it. "What about the scientific expeditions? Where do you think they get all the ore, and all those alien plants they have on display at the botanical gardens?"

"The ore comes from the ground, and the plants are engineered in the lab."

Bewildered, I gestured at the sky. "But what do you think all that is? Party lights? Do you think Glomsuet is flat, too?"

Now I could feel her glaring at me in the darkness. "Dad always told me to make my own assumptions rather than take someone else's word for it. Look at the horizon, Emilio. Glomsuet isn't round. It's as flat as a sheet of paper, and our suns aren't giant hydrogen balls in space, they're small and close to us. If they were far away, we wouldn't even be able to feel their heat, would we?"

I would have thought Reena was joking, but she's one of the sincerest people I've ever known. "You do realize I'm not from Glomsuet," I said. "I'm from a planet called Earth. I accidentally boarded Veeven's ship right before it lifted off, and since it was on autopilot, she couldn't bring me back."

Reena's silhouette shook its head. "You may act like an alien sometimes, but you're just like everyone else."

"Who else do you know whose skin is like mine? Where do you think I get this ridiculous accent?"

"The people of Fregg have light brown skin just like yours, and I've always known your accent is from Aloroop. I don't know why you always deny it. I guess I've always assumed your childhood was so traumatic, you just didn't want to talk about it, and I respect that. I figured you would tell me about it whenever you were ready."

"I am telling you, and you're not listening!" I shouted, more in exasperation than anger. "I'm from Earth. I saw it from space, and it's a sphere, and when we were landing on Glomsuet, I saw it's a sphere, too."

"*Urth* is the Kyule word for 'toothpick.' I studied it in school."

"Reena, I'm not lying to you! I would never lie to you!"

And then she was caressing me, and cooing in my ear as if we hadn't just been arguing. "Emilio, I know you've had a hard life. The mind does strange things when it's under trauma. I know you wouldn't lie to me, but the fact is, even though your mind believes all that is true, it's just a fantasy. Maybe we can go to a psychologist and have them help you remember your true history so you can move past whatever trauma made you invent this thing."

Before I could say anything else, she was giving me the deepest, most passionate kiss she's ever given me, and I knew she'd always love me despite the fact she thinks I'm bonkers.

And yet, I can't help but think…

Did I really imagine a place called Earth, with oceans and a sky just as blue as Glomsuet's? Did Veeven play along with that fantasy to protect me from a darker truth? Are you even real, Stacy, or are you some figment of a fractured psyche?

No! It has to be real. I would know—wouldn't I?

Stacy, I hate you.

Sincerely,
Emilio

THE MAN OF HER
DREAMS

IT WAS A SAD DAY when Tom Suarez passed on to his final reward, but perhaps no one was sadder than Chloe Glasgow and Heather Soni, who had both purchased tickets to meet him at the upcoming CinemaCon.

His appearance had been summarily canceled. They were still waiting for their refund.

To mourn, both Chloe and Heather had drunk themselves into a near-stupor while rewatching some of Tom's best films.

"I just can't believe he's gone," Heather murmured as the credits rolled at the end of *Mission Impossible 27*.

"I know." Chloe sniffled and dabbed at her eyes with a wrinkly tissue. The alcohol had made her arms feel detached somehow, as if they belonged to someone else. "And to think we could have met him in two weeks if he'd just…he'd just…held out a little longer." Her vision blurred, and she blinked to correct it. "I'd already made a spot on my wall for our photo."

"You could fake a photo," Heather suggested, and hiccupped.

"It wouldn't be the same." Chloe took another swig of margarita.

She wasn't sure how many glasses she'd had anymore. Didn't care. Tom was dead, and Tom had meant everything to her.

"I mean, he *was* a hundred and seven years old," Heather went on. "This thing was to be expected, sooner or later."

More tears cascaded down Chloe's cheeks, and margarita sloshed over the side of her glass when she plunked it back onto the coffee table. "It was a good, long life, I guess."

Heather barked a laugh. "He may have—*hic*—been the best damned actor to ever walk this Earth, but he was anything but good."

Chloe looked over at one of Heather's posters of Tom posing on the red carpet some decades before. He wore a blue suit and a red tie, and his dark hair had been slicked back and shone with mousse. "They just don't make them like Tom anymore. When I first saw him in that third remake of *It's a Wonderful Life*, I cried."

"Oh, me too." Wistfulness glinted in Heather's reddened eyes. "The first movie I saw him in was *Casablanca*. The remake, of course. Damn good film. Not as good as the original, but Tom made it work. And he was so handsome back then! It's—*hic*—weird to think neither of us were born yet."

Chloe sighed, not for the first time and not for the last. "I just wish we'd gotten to meet him."

"I heard he could be mean to fans if he thought they were bothering him. Remember how he was arrested for punching a fan in the face for asking him for an autograph in the—*hic*—waiting room at his proctologist?"

"Can you blame him?" Chloe lifted an eyebrow, which felt like it was about five miles away from the rest of her face. She would have to call it quits on the alcohol after she finished this glass. Her future self would thank her.

Heather hit the power button on the remote control after a few unsuccessful tries and folded her arms somewhat lopsidedly. "Not for that, no. *Hic.* But maybe we shouldn't idolize someone who could be such an ass."

"You have sixteen Tom Suarez posters on your walls."

"And what are they all for, now?"

"To remember him by," Chloe said. "And dream." She lifted her glass off the table and raised it toward the nearest poster, on which a black-haired Tom Suarez rode shirtless on the back of a horse. "In memory of Tom!" she said, and slurped down more margarita.

"In memory of Tom," Heather repeated softly, then straightened. "I read an interview where he bragged about having exactly five hundred and seventeen one-night stands."

"It's a shame I wasn't one of them." Chloe giggled and set her empty glass so crookedly on the table that it fell over and rolled off onto the floor. She pictured herself waltzing out of a hotel bathroom in nothing but a sheer, black nightie while a very young, very robust Tom Suarez awaited her in all his majestic glory on the bed.

If only she'd been born decades sooner!

"Maybe not meeting him was for the best," Heather said. "If we'd met him, we might have hated him."

"But you've always loved Tom Suarez!"

"As an actor, yes. As a—*hic*—beautiful man, yes. But as a person, he was trash. Don't you remember how he refused to donate money to a charity for the homeless because the woman who asked him for a donation wasn't pretty enough for him?"

"So, he was a man of particular tastes." Chloe stared at her empty glass on the floor, wishing it could refill itself. "I don't know; I just have this feeling that if I'd been around when he was younger, he and I could have made it work. You know I like me a bad boy."

Heather rolled her eyes and groped once more for the remote. "Whatever you say. Now which of his movies do you want to watch next?"

Chloe dragged her feet through the door into work the next day, head pounding in spite of the four extra-strength pain pills she'd taken before leaving her apartment. She crossed the wide lab floor, nodding to some of the researchers, who nodded back at her as coworkers did.

It felt like someone was jabbing a set of screwdrivers into Chloe's eye sockets by the time she shut herself into her private office. She logged into her computer, dialed the screen brightness down to a more manageable level, and continued proofreading the report she hadn't been able to finish during her previous shift.

After a few minutes, she had to shut her eyes and pinch the bridge of her nose. Maybe caffeine would help?

She rose and busied herself at the coffee maker she rarely used, filling it with water from her personal tap. The moment she switched the machine on, there came a sharp rapping at the office door.

Chloe grimaced. "Come in."

Her immediate supervisor, Ellis Thielmann, let himself inside. Ten years older than she was, the man's dark hair and chocolate eyes had always captivated her, but he wasn't nearly as handsome as the young Tom Suarez she dreamed about day and night.

"Morning, Glasgow," Ellis said. "Have you gotten through the report yet on the pod?"

Chloe gave her head a shake. It made her temples throb and the room tilt. "I think that's the next one in my queue."

"Then you'll need to drop what you're doing and work on that one. We want the final, error-free report turned in by one o'clock." He clasped his hands together excitedly in front of him. "This is groundbreaking stuff, Glasgow. Once the report is published, we're going to make history—and we need to do it fast, because rumor has it that one of our competitors is working on a similar project right now."

"I'll get right on it, sir." Chloe tried to sound enthusiastic; a difficult feat when her skull felt like it was trying to crack itself open in about seventeen places at the same time.

Ellis smiled. "If you run into anything you're not sure about, let me know. I'll be in my office."

"Will do, sir."

He left, and Chloe plopped back down into her swivel chair. While her coffee brewed, she closed out of the current report and opened the one pertaining to the pod.

The document contained 152 pages. She'd expected longer.

The coffee maker dinged. Chloe filled her color-changing Tom Suarez mug and got to work.

During her college years, she never once guessed that her English degree might get her a job proofreading page after page of scientific technobabble, yet that's precisely what had happened. The work could be dull, but the pay wasn't bad, and it helped fund her Tom Suarez-related hobbies, such as finding his autographs at auction and collecting every edition of every film he'd ever been in.

She sipped at her coffee as the hours passed. She changed a "them" to a "then," and deleted an extra R from "temporal."

One paragraph of the report stuck out at her like a flashing sign:

It is important to note that any alterations to the timeline that the traveler will cause either intentionally or by mistake will not, in fact, 'change' time, as is seen in popular culture. What will happen instead is that a new universe will be born in place of the old, containing the new set of events. It is unknown whether or not the original universe will be destroyed, or if it will exist parallel to the new one.

Well, that was depressing. Those scientists had better be careful before they erased Chloe and her hobby from existence.

She popped two more painkillers and washed them down with a second cup of coffee.

·· ✦ ✳ ✦ ✳ ✦ ··

Chloe turned in the proofread report three minutes shy of the one o'clock deadline, then took the rest of the day off so she might properly nurse her pounding head.

As soon as she arrived home, she fixed herself a heaping plate of nachos and put on one of the many remakes of *Gone With the Wind*, starring—who else?—a young Tom Suarez.

Falling asleep in the middle of the movie hadn't been on Chloe's list of afternoon plans, but before she knew it, she'd entered a dream version of her house where the furniture was all a garish shade of

✦ 27 ✦

purple and the carpet was covered in soft flower petals.

A knock on her dream home's door brought Chloe gliding across the room. Belatedly, she realized she was wearing a sheer, black nightie and nothing else. Yanking open the door anyway, Chloe gasped to see Tom Suarez waiting for her wearing the finest of suits and smelling of expensive cologne. His dark hair had been slicked back like on Heather's poster, and his brown eyes twinkled when he said, "I have a present for you, Miss Glasgow."

He withdrew an immense bouquet of lilies from behind his back and held it out for her to take. "They're almost as beautiful as you are," he said with a wink that turned her insides into a balmy mush.

"They're perfect!" Chloe exclaimed, throwing herself into his arms like a swooning damsel in one of those ancient movies that had been popular even long before Tom Suarez came into the world. "But how did you get here? You're dead!"

"I got my hands on a little time machine, baby." Tom's eyes actually twinkled for real. "And I did it all for you."

Chloe's eyes snapped open. She was back in her house in the real world, the man of her dreams painfully absent save for the myriad posters of him throughout his career tacked to the living room walls like mismatched wallpaper. A cardboard cutout of him in swim trunks lurked in one corner, the throw blanket on the couch bore a repeating pattern of his face making various expressions, and her bookshelf contained five different biographies and memoirs chronicling his life. She even owned action figures of his character from an adventure series for kids—those, she'd posed on the dresser in her bedroom.

Her brother had taken to calling her apartment The Suarez Shrine. He wasn't wrong.

"Tom, you don't know how much I wish I could have been around when you were younger," she said, gazing at the cardboard cutout. "Maybe then my life would have actually been interesting."

Too bad she couldn't get her hands on that nifty pod she'd read so much about at work today. One click of a button, and BAM! She could go back to Tom Suarez's days of glory and work her way into that bad boy's heart.

Of course, it was a little more complicated than simply slipping a relay band around her wrist, stepping into a time pod, and zapping herself numerous decades into the past. She'd need an exact set of coordinates and an accomplice to operate the controls meant to drag her back to the present. She was smart, though. She could determine space-time coordinates through her own research, or trick a scientist into calculating them for her.

Chloe was only half-present as she glided through work like an automaton over the next few days. Virtually all of her thoughts became consumed with visions of her and Tom Suarez going for walks on the beach, dining by candlelight in five-star restaurants, watching plays from expensive box seats, returning to quiet hotel rooms...

Her fantasies soon crowded out all else, and she found herself yearning more than anything that she could go back in time and spend the rest of her life with the one man who had brightened it on so many dark days. Who else, besides Heather, had kept her "company" after her parents had died? Who else was there when Chloe needed someone to lean on?

She pondered how much money she'd saved up and decided it might be just enough for a little bribery. But who here would help her? Not one of the higher-ups; they were too law-abiding for that sort of thing. Someone lower on the ladder, then, but someone who'd still have clearance to access the pod.

·· ✳ ✴ ✴ ✴ ✳ ··

One month later, Chloe met up with Dirk Miller, one of the junior researchers, in the back of a local dive called The Spittoon. Ancient country music twanged through the overhead speakers, effectively preventing their voices from traveling beyond their booth.

Dirk was a few years younger than she was, scrawny, with eyes that seemed to see more than other people's. Chloe had dug into his background and learned that he'd served time for theft before turning his life around and becoming a scientist.

"Nice to see you, Miss Glasgow," Dirk said when she arrived. "You look different without your uniform."

Chloe wasn't sure if he was flirting or not, so she simply said, "Let's just get down to business. I need to know if I can trust you."

Dirk shrugged. "Yeah, sure. Trustworthy's my middle name. Now what's this all about?"

Chloe cleared her throat. "I'd like to use a piece of equipment I'm not authorized to access. It's for a personal matter; nothing dangerous."

Dirk leaned forward; interest evident in his all-knowing eyes. "And you want me to get it for you."

"It's too big for anyone to just 'get.' I need you to be there to help me use it."

"All right, I'll bite. What is it?"

Here it was, then. "The pod."

His eyebrows shot up. "*The* pod."

"It isn't like there's more than one to choose from."

Enlightenment dawned on the man's face. "Ah. You want to stop something from happening, or cause something to happen that hadn't before. You do realize that's extremely dangerous."

"I've read the report. I had to correct twenty-two typos in it."

"You could destroy the whole universe; even wipe yourself out of existence depending on how far back you go."

"Or," Chloe said with a smile, "I could simply create a parallel universe running alongside this one. Nothing here could change at all."

"That remains to be seen."

"I know." She grinned to mask a sudden spike of anxiety, and hoped she was doing the right thing.

"So," Dirk said, "can I ask what you'll be needing it for?"

Chloe made a point of looking sheepish. "I want to meet my favorite actor. He passed away recently, and I never got the chance to see him in person."

"Who was it? Egbert Walliams? I loved all his movies."

"No, Tom Suarez. He's been my favorite since I was a teenager."

Dirk gave an appreciative nod. "I've seen some of his films. So, that's all you want to do? Meet him and chat a few minutes, get his autograph?"

Chloe nodded, and a genuine tear trickled from one eye. "It would mean the world to me."

Dirk bit his lip, and his brow furrowed. "It doesn't sound too cataclysmic, does it? But it'll cost you."

"How much?"

He told her a number that made her wince.

"It's a deal," she said. "When can we get this done?"

It occurred to Chloe that night after leaving The Spittoon that her journey back in time would have to be a one-way trip, meaning she would never see Heather or her coworkers or her relatives again. Would it really be that bad, though? Her parents were both gone, and she rarely saw her brother anymore since he lived in a different state with his wife and kids.

She could leave a note for everyone: *Gone back in time. Don't expect me.* Yes, it would probably be better that way. If going back in time deleted this universe, she'd be deleted right along with it, but if it made a new universe *without* deleting this one, then everything would be all right. It was a fifty-fifty shot. She'd play the lottery with those odds.

When she arrived home, she went straight into her bedroom and stared at the mousy person in her dresser mirror. She was just Chloe Glasgow, a nobody proofreader who got to copyedit reports written by people whose IQs were several tens of points ahead of her own. Her life was going nowhere—she hadn't been on a date in three years, or was it four? So leaving it all behind shouldn't be so bad.

"You're crazy for even thinking like this," she told her reflection. "They ought to lock you away somewhere safe."

She and Dirk had settled on a date three days from now to use the pod. She hadn't told him she had no plans of ever coming back from the past. He wouldn't have agreed to help her otherwise.

"All ready for tonight?" Dirk asked Chloe when they spotted each other in the hallway close to the end of Chloe's shift.

"I'm as ready as I'll ever be," she said, though her insides had twisted themselves into intricate knots. "Did you find an appropriate set of coordinates?"

"You bet I did." Dirk lowered his voice. "I can get you to the day that old Tom was signing autographs for fans in front of the town hall in a little village near Pittsburgh—he was filming a movie there that week. You'll materialize in an alleyway a few blocks away. I can give you a full hour there in case the line is too long."

"How long ago was this day?"

"Seventy-one years and a handful of months. Old Tom would have been about thirty-six. I hope you're okay with that."

Chloe's lips twisted into a grin. "A thirty-six-year-old Tom would be perfect."

Instead of going home after work, Chloe slipped into a nearby café and sat by herself, brooding. What if Tom didn't like her, or give her the time of day? What if she missed her brother and Heather so badly it made her sick? What if she didn't like living seventy-one years ago, when most of her favorite movies hadn't even been filmed yet?

She wished she could take a bag with her containing her most personal mementos, but that would make Dirk start to suspect, if he

didn't already. No, she would have to start over completely fresh back then. She had the guts and the determination; she could do it.

At last, Chloe walked back to the lab, taking note of the wide, ancient trees lining the thoroughfare, the charming row houses, the manicured lawns.

It stung a bit, knowing she would never see any of this again.

The lab parking lot was nearly empty, yet still too full for her liking. She used her access code to gain entry into the building. A researcher whose name she could never remember met her just as she was passing through the otherwise vacant lobby.

"You're here late tonight," he said.

"Forgot something in my office." Chloe bared her teeth in the world's fakest grin. "Silly old me."

The researcher gave her an expression of curiosity but went about his business, exiting through the door Chloe had just entered. She let out a pent-up breath and continued to her office to await the signal from Dirk.

Five minutes later, a sharp rapping on her door made her jump even though she'd been expecting it. She crossed the small room and let Dirk inside.

"Well?" she asked, feeling already breathless.

"I've put the security cameras on a loop." Dirk panted as if he'd been running. "We should be safe, for now."

"But the other people here…"

"There's a custodian vacuuming up on the third floor and Dr. Huang is living out of her office as usual, but there isn't anything I can do about that. Now let's get this over with before she gets bored and takes a stroll through the corridors."

"Okay." Chloe tried to swallow, but her mouth was too dry.

Dirk led her into part of the facility she'd never seen before, given that she had no clearance to access it. Lots of spotless chrome and white tiles, as if to give the appearance of sterility. It made her think of an old sci-fi film.

One restricted door led into a chamber containing the pod Chloe had read about in the report. Dirk opened the door and swept his arm to the side. "After you!"

Chloe stepped inside, studying the room with wonder. The space was sparsely furnished and bore limited equipment save for the pod, which reminded her of a smaller transporter mechanism from those old *Star Trek* shows. A door in the back of the room led to a decontamination shower—not that Chloe had any plans of coming back and using it.

"Here."

Chloe jumped and turned. Dirk held the relay band out for her, and she stuck out her left arm so he could fasten it around her wrist.

"Once I've set the coordinates, all you have to do is step into the pod and push that button," Dirk said. "Like I said, I'll give you an hour. If you can't get the autograph then, we'll have to pick different coordinates and try again a different day."

"I understand," Chloe croaked.

Dirk clicked the relay band into place. It felt loose on her slender wrist. She hoped it wouldn't slide off mid-transit and strand her in the void for all of eternity.

She went and stood inside the pod, feeling beads of nervous sweat well up on her skin. Dirk went to a computer monitor and input what Chloe hoped was the correct data. "You're all set," he said, lifting his gaze to hers with a smile that spoke of secrets shared. "Are you ready?"

Chloe felt her head nod. "Yes."

She thought about telling him thank you and goodbye and what a pleasure it had been working with him in that final nanosecond before her departure, but before she could speak, there came a brief instant of darkness followed by the appearance of brick walls on either side of her.

It took her a moment to acknowledge the obvious facts that she had changed both location and time of day. A sliver of sunlight spilled into the alley from above, and the air smelled faintly of car exhaust and pollen.

Chloe tentatively emerged from the alley. She blinked to adjust her eyes to the midday light, eyed a crowd of people heading down the sidewalk, and followed them.

"Excuse me!" Chloe called to a teenage girl, one of the stragglers. "Where is everybody going?"

The girl stopped and gave her a dull stare. She had pink and blue hair done in pigtails. "You don't know?"

"I'm just passing through."

The teenager seemed to accept this as an answer. "Tom Suarez has been filming here for the past week, and he's signing autographs in front of the town hall today."

Chloe feigned surprise. "*The* Tom Suarez? The one who starred in the best adaptation of *The Birds* since the original?"

The teenager's eyes narrowed. "That's the movie he's filming. They're not done making it yet."

"Oh, yes, that's right!" Chloe's laugh came out too high-pitched. "Sorry, I don't know what I was thinking. Just nerves, I suppose. It isn't every day I might get to meet a movie star."

They continued onward toward the two-story brick town hall, where a crowd of three hundred had already gathered on its lawn. Eyeing a wastebasket outside a hair salon directly across the street from the building, Chloe removed the relay band and placed it gently inside, then covered it up with some loose papers.

It felt a bit like being in a ship out at sea and sawing off the anchor.

The crowd was so thick that Chloe had no way of seeing Tom Suarez from her current position. How could she get herself to stand out among so many? She wasn't particularly gorgeous, or tall, or buxom, which probably meant she was too plain for the man's tastes. Tom would *have* to take notice of her somehow without Chloe throwing herself at him like a woman in the throes of desperation, which she was.

"Last in line," she murmured to herself. "I have to be last in line."

Half an hour passed, then an hour. People kept on coming, and Chloe let everyone ahead of her. Surely Tom would have a cramp in his hand after signing his name so many times!

After a while, the massive crowd did seem to be dying down by a few marginal degrees. Chloe drew in a shaky breath and meandered over to what looked like the tail end of the line.

Two people joined the line behind Chloe. She let them both move in front of her.

As the sun lowered in the western sky, the crowd dwindled to the point where she could actually see Tom Suarez laughing and smiling as he signed photographs and had his picture taken with fan after adoring fan. Her breath stuck in her throat as if the air had become too thick to inhale. It was him—in real life!

Chloe's entire body turned into rubber as Tom signed a piece of stationery for the person two spots up from her. Then he signed a poster for the man right in front of her, and the next thing she knew, she was face to face with Tom Suarez himself, in the flesh.

Chloe didn't know how long she stood there without saying anything. Tom Suarez was no longer a mere idea. He'd become a human being standing right in front of her as if he were Heather or her brother or anyone else.

"Hi," she said, and felt crimson fill her cheeks.

"Hello there," Tom said in his golden baritone voice. His brown eyes glittered. "And what am I signing for you today?"

"I—I didn't bring anything. I just wanted to see you." Chloe glanced over her shoulder. She was still the last in line, and the remnants of the larger crowd had dispersed into clumps to compare the pictures they'd had taken. "I've loved your movies since I was a kid."

"You've got to be older than that!" Tom laughed, and it was a musical sound Chloe would never forget. "I mean, no offense. You just don't seem that much younger than me."

"Well, it feels like I've loved your movies forever," Chloe amended, realizing she would have to be very careful about what she said. "They just don't make them like you."

"I certainly hope not! Do you know how hard it would be for a guy to compete with that?" He winked. "What's your name, by the way?"

"Chloe," she replied. "Chloe Glasgow. I'm not from around here but heard you'd be in town, and..." She shrugged.

"That makes two of us, then. It's been nice meeting you, Carrie."

Chloe's cheeks burned. "Chloe."

"Oh, that's right." Tom turned to the yawning man standing beside him. "Crowd's gone. We can call it a day."

Panic surged through Chloe's veins. Tom couldn't just dismiss her like this! She was stranded here without money and without a way of getting back to her own time unless Dirk had gone back in after her when the relay band returned to the pod without her.

Since she hadn't seen an anachronistic Dirk frantically searching the crowd, she guessed he hadn't wanted to further risk his own career by asking another scientist to work the controls while he went to go find her.

"Um, Tom?" Chloe asked as the man of her dreams started to step away from her.

He glanced back at her, half-distracted. "Yeah, what is it?"

Fighting to keep her voice from squeaking, Chloe said, "I know you're probably very busy, but if you have any time tonight, do you want to go out for a drink?"

Tom's eyes lit up, and his mouth quirked into the same smile that had been immortalized on so many posters in Chloe's apartment. "You're asking me on a date?"

Heat crawled up Chloe's face. "I think I am."

Laughing, he said, "Do you know how many women have asked me out on dates?"

"Judging from the size of the crowd, I'd say you probably had a few offers just this afternoon."

He shook his head, and his dark hair glinted in the waning sunlight. "No! These women always want *me* to make the first move, like I'll think they're needy if they ask me. You're the first to ask I haven't had to call security on. Meet me at seven tonight at The Colonnade—it's a little place just a few blocks from here. Their filet mignon is to die for."

He turned away from her again to say something to his assistant.

Chloe's chest was so tight she could scarcely draw in a breath. Seven? Tonight? He was really accepting her request? Just like that? Had she died and gone on to her own personal heaven?

"Um—see you then!" Chloe managed to stammer, and she hurried off in no particular direction so she could compose herself. If only Heather could see her now! But she couldn't think about Heather, because she would never see her friend again. Their many long nights of drinking themselves into comas while Tom Suarez fought and laughed and wept on the screen were all a part of the past now—or a part of the future, depending on how she looked at it.

Since Chloe had taken nothing with her on this one-way trip, she couldn't go and freshen up with a new outfit anywhere. She couldn't even buy a drink or food to pass the time, or stay in a motel to relax until seven o'clock.

She really should have thought this through a little better.

She idly strolled through the streets of the unfamiliar Pennsylvania town, taking in the quaint sights and trying not to laugh at some of the clothing people sported. The cuts of her crisp white uniform shirt and plain black slacks probably looked just as outlandish to these people, but at least they were clean.

Fatigue had begun to eat at her by the time seven o'clock rolled around, as it had been late in the evening in her own time when she transported herself here, and she had gotten no rest since. Fighting to stay awake, she spotted the sign for The Colonnade about two blocks from the town hall. Chloe peered nervously up at the Art Deco-styled building with wide, glass windows in the front, crossed the busy parking area, and pushed her way inside before she got cold feet.

It was a nice enough restaurant for a small town, with a gray and indigo color scheme decorating the space and small, crystal chandeliers dangling above the tables. Soft music played from the speakers overhead, and a hostess in a formal-looking navy pantsuit greeted her upon entering.

"How many?" the woman asked in a faint Appalachian accent.

"Two," Chloe said, craning her neck to see if Tom occupied any of the tables nearest to her. "I'm meeting someone here, but I don't see him yet."

"What's his name?" the hostess asked, peering down at her list.

Chloe blushed even before she spoke. "Tom Suarez."

The hostess's words were tinged with a veneer of professionalism when she said, "We don't have his name listed yet, but feel free to wait until he arrives. We'll go ahead and get a table ready for the two of you."

Chloe nodded and moved closer to the door so she could see out into the parking lot filled with vintage vehicles that of course were mostly brand new to these people. A weight settled into her stomach as she imagined Tom standing her up. He had no obligation to be here, after all. She was no one to him. Probably most people on Earth were no one to Tom Suarez. He was a mighty Adonis; a god towering above mere mortals. He'd probably forgotten all about her by now and was having room service bring caviar to him and some other bimbo he'd picked up in the past couple of hours.

A car pulled into the lot, and its lights winked out. It took Chloe too many seconds to realize that the aforementioned Adonis had emerged from the vehicle and was striding right toward the door, unaccompanied.

Chloe staggered back a step and must have had some gaping look on her face, for when Tom swept into the restaurant lobby, he grinned at her and said, "You don't have to act so surprised. I don't have that bad of a reputation, do I?"

"I—I've heard things," Chloe said. "People talk."

"People are full of shit. Table for two, please!"

"So," Tom said, browsing the menu laid out in front of him. "What brings you to Pikesburg?"

Nerves were making it difficult for Chloe to form thoughts into coherent sentences. "Um, Hugh did. I mean, *you* did. I don't know anyone named Hugh. You know what I mean. Sorry, I'm not used to this kind of thing." Lord, he must think she was a head case. "I've been wanting to meet you for a long time. Is that weird?"

Tom shrugged. His shoulders looked wide and firm beneath his suit jacket, and she imagined herself giving him a massage to buff out all of the stresses of the day.

"Why would it be weird?" he asked. "I'm a household name. People make it their life mission to meet me all the time. More power to them."

"But it must feel strange, having perfect strangers want to see you."

"I'm used to it. I got my big break when I was twenty, you know. That remake of *The Sound of Music* changed my life."

"Do you miss being a normal person? Not that I mean you're not normal, but you know." She silently swore at herself for sounding like a journalist interviewing him for a piece about the effects of fame on his life. Why couldn't she just relax and enjoy his company, when that's why she'd come here in the first place?

Then Tom did something she'd seen him do a thousand times in interviews: he folded his arms and leaned his weight upon them, then tilted his head ever so slightly to the left as he regarded her. The gesture was ordinary, but he handled it in such a Tom Suarez-like manner that it served only as a reminder that yes, this really was him, and yes, she really was speaking to him in person.

"No," he said. "And yes."

A server came and took their order (Chloe ordered a tuna salad wrap, one of the cheapest items on the menu), and when she'd gone, Chloe said, "It must be hard having to deal with people hounding you everywhere you go." Since they'd been sitting there together, she'd spotted at least three other diners discreetly snapping pictures of her and Tom on their smartphones. Social media had been a popular commodity in this age, and Chloe was sure her face had been plastered on more than a few sites already, probably complete with disparaging comments over what she was wearing.

"The only reason the paparazzi haven't kicked down the door here," Tom said, "is because I have a few buddies hanging out in the parking lot to deter them."

"Deter them, how?"

A wicked glint appeared in his dark eyes. "In any way necessary. I hate photographers and journalists. The whole bunch of them can go die, for all I care. All I've ever wanted to do is pretend to be other people, and when it turned out I'm kind of good at it, the whole world lost their minds. 'Tom, what's your favorite kind of deodorant?' people ask. 'Will you endorse my new gizmo in a commercial?' 'What do you think about this year's presidential candidates?' 'Will you help pay for my dog's cancer treatments?' It doesn't stop."

"I'm sorry," Chloe murmured. "That must be annoying."

"I miss taking a shit and not having the whole world know about it," Tom said as a twentysomething woman timidly approached their table with a scrap of paper and a pen. He offered the woman a gracious smile, scrawled his name on the paper, and passed it back to her, saying, "It was nice meeting you. Have a good day."

The woman let out a half-squeak in reply and hurried back to her table.

When he refocused his attention on Chloe, he said, "You don't know what I'd give to go to the grocery store by myself and pick out my own food, or go for a neighborhood jog like any other guy. Some days it's like being in a cage with eight billion people watching me."

There was a note of resignation in his voice that made it seem as though he'd given up the hope of ever having an anonymous moment again. Unexpected tears welled in Chloe's eyes, and she said, "If you could go back in time and do things different, would you?"

Tom chewed on his lip. "Hell no."

Their food arrived, and neither of them said much while they ate. Two more people approached the table wanting pictures or autographs, and Chloe felt a shred of pity for them that they felt such a need to be acknowledged by a famous stranger.

"Do you ever watch the movies you've been in?" she asked him between bites.

"Sometimes." Tom paused to sample the champagne he'd ordered. Chloe, who wanted to keep a clear head for once, had declined any alcohol. "It's just not that interesting to me, you know? I enjoy the work itself, not the finished product. Watching my movies is for other people to do."

"They *are* very good movies," Chloe said. "They've meant a lot to so many people."

Tom shrugged again. "Good for them." He appeared briefly contemplative, then said, "That's enough about me. I want to know more about you. It isn't every day I talk to someone who doesn't go completely giddy on me."

Chloe cleared her throat and tried to look him directly in the eye. "Well, I told you my name is Chloe Glasgow. I proofread scientific reports for a living. Scientists aren't always the greatest at spelling and grammar. You wouldn't believe how badly some of them mess up their sentences."

"A high IQ doesn't necessarily make a good writer," Tom agreed with a nod. "That sounds like an interesting occupation."

"Oh, it is, sometimes, depending on which report I'm proofing. Some are so dull, they could cure insomnia."

Tom chuckled. "And what else do you do? Do you have any hobbies?"

"I'm a collector," Chloe said, thinking of The Suarez Shrine, which now lay seventy-one years in the future. "I collect movie memorabilia—posters, action figures, things like that."

"Would this 'memorabilia' have anything to do with me?"

"Oh, a bit of it." Chloe blushed, and she was sure he saw see the truth on her face. "That must be a weird feeling for you, too."

"The weirdest thing I've seen so far is a throw blanket with a repeating pattern of my face on it," he said. "Someone brought one up to me at a convention and asked if I'd sign it for them. Can you imagine how hard it is to sign a blanket? I ended up having to use fabric paint and a little brush."

Chloe let out a giggle-snort that set Tom to laughing, too, and for a moment it was the most blissful feeling in the world, laughing with the man of her dreams who'd been dead but was alive again. Any doubts she'd had about making a mistake evaporated like droplets of water in the sun.

She'd done the right thing.

She was sure of it.

They did not go to bed together that night.

In fact, they didn't do anything together, to Chloe's extraordinary disappointment. After Tom had paid their bill, he rose from the table and said, "Miss Glasgow, it has certainly been a pleasure meeting you today, but I've got to go get some sleep before I'm a dead man. I've been up since four." He gave her a tired smile that made him seem more human than godlike. "They had me filming scenes for six hours before the autograph session in the middle of town."

"Oh, wow," Chloe said, trying not to panic. It felt like Tom was a receding tide she attempted to grasp in her hands. "It sounds like you do need some sleep."

"I have to be up and at 'em again bright and early, too," Tom said. "We're filming over by the old sawmill just south of town. They're going to have to add in so many CGI birds, it won't even be funny."

He grinned, but Chloe didn't smile back at him. She had traveled so far to see him, and it broke her heart knowing that they couldn't be together every moment.

Another thing she should have thought of before she left her own time behind forever.

Since Chloe had few options for lodging, she rapped on the door of a plain, brick Methodist church at the western end of town. The sky had grown completely dark, and the evening chill was making her clammy. Though Chloe had never been particularly religious (in a way, Tom Suarez had been her religion), she'd heard that churches could be accommodating for those in need.

Few people needed more things than Chloe did that evening; a shower, clean clothes, and a place to sleep being the most prominent on her list at the moment.

Nobody came to the door. She tried the knob and found it unlocked, so she went inside.

The space was shrouded in shadow, and two candles that had been left burning on the altar cast a faint but warm glow over the pews toward the front of the room. Luckily, the pews were cushioned, and Chloe lay on her side on one of them a few rows back from the altar.

She closed her eyes and tried to relax, but the more she willed her limbs into jelly, the more she thought about how she herself wouldn't be born for another forty years, and that she'd never go on another shopping expedition with Heather, and never give her brother surprise phone calls again.

"I hope you like your present," Heather had said to her on her most recent birthday, blushing as she passed her a lime-colored giftbag. "It's not something you'd normally use, but I thought of you immediately when I saw it."

With some trepidation, Chloe had lifted out a velvet box and pried

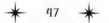

the lid open to see a sterling silver necklace in the shape of a curving branch sprouting evenly-spaced leaves along its length. A printed card lay beneath the necklace in the box, and Chloe pulled it out and read aloud, "To my dearest friend—you complete me, and I will always be grateful for the years we've spent together. May this branch symbolize our growing friendship, which may never fade!"

"I have a matching one," Heather said, pulling her own pendant out of her shirt for Chloe to see. It was the exact same necklace, and Chloe had felt tears in her eyes at how thoughtful Heather had been when choosing the gift.

Chloe wore the necklace now. She'd slipped it on that morning before work without even thinking about it. She touched a hand absently to the pendant and felt her heart ache.

Had she made a mistake by coming here? Was meeting Tom worth the sacrifice?

It would have to be, because it was too late for alternatives.

"Why, hello there!"

Chloe startled awake at the sound of the voice. A fiftyish woman with short, platinum-blonde hair stood over her wearing an expression of benign curiosity. Sheepishly, Chloe sat up and said, "I'm not in trouble for sneaking in here, am I?"

The light of dawn slanted in through the rose and green stained glass. Both candles on the altar had been blown out, and wisps of smoke drifted through the air.

"Not at all," the woman said. "I'm the Reverend Margaret Hewitt.

We leave the doors unlocked at night for a reason."

Chloe got to her feet and couldn't help but stretch. She wondered if Tom had already begun filming, or if he was still at breakfast. "Well, I appreciate it. I didn't have anywhere else to go."

The reverend appeared chagrined. "I'm sorry to hear that. Is there anything I can do for you?"

Chloe started to say no, that she would handle things just fine on her own, but then she remembered that she was seventy-one years farther back in time than she'd been one day ago, and severely lacking in any kind of resources. "Could I use your shower?" she asked. "And I don't have any money—long story. I'd like to find a change of clothes."

"I live in the house next door," Margaret said. "You are more than welcome to use my shower, and I'll see if we have any clothes in your size. We try to keep a variety of things on hand for cases like this," she added.

It felt strange to be relying on strangers for basic necessities, and Chloe couldn't help but say, "I feel so bad using you like this. I'm sorry to be a burden."

Margaret waved a dismissing hand. "No need to apologize. Christ called each of us to serve one another, and if I ever turned down anyone in need, I wouldn't be able to live with myself. I can even fix you some breakfast, if you'd like."

Chloe thanked her profusely. Ten minutes later, she was blasting herself clean beneath a scalding shower, and after that, she squeezed into a pair of blue jeans and a form-fitting t-shirt that smelled like something from a thrift store.

She couldn't complain.

"So, what brings you to Pikesburg?" Margaret asked when Chloe emerged into her kitchen, coincidentally repeating what Tom had said to her at dinner the evening before.

"How do you know I'm not from here?" Chloe asked.

"Your accent's a bit different. You don't need to tell me where you're from; it isn't any of my business."

"I'm from an awfully long way away," Chloe said, taking a seat at the table. A bowl of fruit sat in the center of it. Margaret caught her looking at it and nodded, and Chloe gingerly took a banana for herself and peeled it with care. "And I came here because I wanted to meet Tom Suarez."

Margaret sat down across from her. "Who?"

"He's an actor. They're filming a movie here this week."

"Ah, I thought I saw a camera crew down near the ballfields the other day. Tom must mean a lot to you, if you came all the way out here to meet him."

"He's my favorite actor." Heat blossomed across Chloe's cheeks. "He took me to dinner last night."

"Did he, now?" Margaret's eyes narrowed, as if she didn't quite believe her. "That must have been exciting."

Chloe swallowed a chunk of banana. "It was. He didn't know I'm... I'm broke. I, um, lost my job recently." Which wasn't entirely a lie.

"I'm sorry to hear it. Is there anything I can do to help?"

Chloe desperately wished she could decline any additional charity from the woman, but she wasn't in a position where she could refuse. "Could I maybe have a little bit of money to take with me? Just enough to get me through the next few days. I'll pay you back as soon as I can."

"There's no need to worry about that. You don't even need to promise me that you'll spend it wisely. Hold on just a minute."

Margaret rose and went to a plain black purse sitting on the kitchen counter. She withdrew a wallet and counted out several bills, which Chloe accepted without complaint.

"I—I appreciate it," Chloe said. Seventy-one years of inflation made the amount in her hands seem abysmally small, but she knew that the value they held now would be enough to help her.

Margaret smiled. "Anytime, sweetie. Anytime."

After breakfast, Chloe set out toward the sawmill Tom had mentioned during dinner (she'd gotten the directions from Margaret, who had to have been the nicest person Chloe had ever met). She soon spotted a clump of vehicles parked off the road, and a small group of onlookers had gathered at the edge of a sagging split-rail fence to observe the action in front of them.

Chloe drifted up to them and peered in the direction they were looking. Tom and a brown-skinned woman stood in front of the sawmill with a couple of cameras pointed at them.

She immediately recognized the scene, as she'd watched it many times both with Heather and by herself.

"We've got to get out of this town before we end up like the rest of them!" the woman shrieked, looking mad with desperation.

Tom, who wore a ripped t-shirt that showed off his muscles, ran a hand through his already-tousled hair and said, "And leave everyone else to die? Could you really live with that, Melanie? I thought you were better than that."

"It's us or them, Mitch! Now give me the damned car keys, or I'll—

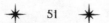

oh, *shit*."

"Cut!" a woman cried so loudly that Chloe jumped.

"Isn't this awesome?" asked a young man standing beside her. "It's like watching TV in person." He held up his smartphone and snapped a few pictures, which he then immediately uploaded to three different social media sites.

A twentysomething woman standing next to the young man kept popping potato chips into her mouth. "TV is better than watching this. They've already shot this scene six times since I've been here. Carla keeps flubbing her lines."

"Tom is *so* hot," murmured another woman. "Do you ever wonder how big his—"

The woman with the chips crunched into them so loudly that it drowned out the rest of the other woman's words, but Chloe felt a flare of jealousy regardless. Tom was *hers*! That woman had no right to fantasize about him!

The director said something to Tom and the other actor, and they changed where they were standing before filming continued. They redid the scene ten more times before a break was finally called, and Tom drifted away from the sawmill to accept a bottle of water from an assistant.

Chloe wanted to jump the fence and join him but knew she couldn't. She would just have to stay here and wait until filming concluded for the day before continuing to woo Tom.

As the hours progressed, she wondered how precisely their relationship would evolve. She imagined going to party after wild party with him, squealing off down the street in a sportscar to evade the ever-preying paparazzi, getting wasted together in a hotel room, and spending the rest of the night in the frenzied bliss of each other's arms.

Filming didn't stop for good until midafternoon. The crew and actors dispersed, and Tom swaggered up to the fence to greet Chloe and the other onlookers.

"Nice of you all to stop by," Tom said, scribbling his name onto a proffered photograph. "There's *nothing* I love more than my fans." He appeared surprised when he caught sight of Chloe. "Oh, hi. Carrie, is it?"

"It's Chloe." She tried not to scowl. Had the man not paid the slightest attention to her last night?

Tom barely batted an eye when she corrected him. "Oh, that's right. So, what did you think, watching us today?"

"I think it's going to be a great movie," Chloe said, because it had been, and would be. It would even go on to win an Academy Award for Best Soundtrack, not that Tom had anything to do with that.

"We're trying to go for a different vibe than the Hitchcock version," he went on. "It'll be more character-focused than slice-and-dice. Or claw-and-peck, since they're birds." He grinned. "Anyway, it was nice seeing you again, Carr—*Chloe*. But I've got to go clean up before I start attracting flies."

One of the women who had yet to leave threw Chloe an irritated glance. Chloe gave the woman a sardonic grin and felt a swell of pride.

All was going according to plan.

The next few days continued in much the same manner, with Chloe scouting out the filming location of the day and hanging around watching until Tom got a break. It was hard to hold in her laughter while she watched Tom and his costars trying to fend off demented birds that wouldn't exist until an animator had drawn them on a computer. She even felt a little thrill inside her when Tom cussed out an overzealous fan who'd bolted onto set in the middle of a scene.

He was just the swaggery sort of bad boy she'd always dreamed him to be, and he was even remembering her name now without any trouble.

Chloe had decided to help earn her keep at Margaret's house by mowing her lawn and weeding her flowerbeds in exchange for a place to lay her head at night. On the fourth evening of her stay, Margaret came outside, sat down beside Chloe on the stoop, and said, "When are they going to be done filming here?"

Chloe, who had been staring vacantly off toward the homes in the distance, said, "Tomorrow is the last day. Then they're flying back to Los Angeles to finish up there."

"Are you going to stay here, or follow him out there?"

"I have to follow him. I don't have any other place to go."

"Do you have any family?"

"Not anymore." Chloe's own parents hadn't even been born yet, and she wasn't about to go disrupting her own timeline by dropping by her grandparents' house to see if they'd be accommodating for a penniless, unborn descendant.

"How will you afford to travel all the way out there?" Margaret asked, giving her a motherly look that made Chloe's eyes grow misty.

Chloe glanced away from her. "I'll find a way, even if I have to walk."

Margaret sighed. "Chloe, I don't want you to take this the wrong way, but are you sure it's wise throwing yourself at Mr. Suarez like this? I've looked him up online, and it seems like he isn't always the nicest person."

"Bad boys happen to be my type."

"He was arrested for initiating a barroom brawl last winter. He threw a beer bottle at someone's head and caused them to get five stitches."

"I'm sure he didn't mean to." Chloe tried hard not to crack a grin as she remembered reading about that incident. The man who'd received the stitches had been exceedingly drunk and made an attempt to kiss Tom on the cheek. Everything had gone downhill from there, and poor Tom had gotten into trouble even though he'd been trying to defend himself against unwanted advances.

"Just be careful, sweetie," Margaret said. "I wouldn't want you to throw your life away over one man who might not even be worth it."

"You dedicated your life to one man," Chloe said, nodding toward the church next door. "What's the big difference?"

"I'll let you figure that one out for yourself." Margaret rose and went back into the house, the door shutting behind her with a soft click.

Chloe let out a long sigh once she was alone, and she continued to daydream about the countless wonderful and exciting things she and Tom would do once she, too, arrived in Los Angeles.

Hitchhiking across America forty years before her own birth had never been on a list of expectations Chloe had held about her life, which had, thus far, included getting old, retiring, and wasting away in front of a screen watching Tom Suarez movies with Heather until her bones turned into dust.

Hitchhiking across America without being murdered, abducted, or worse was such a miracle in itself that Chloe suspected Margaret had put a decent word in with her Boss to keep Chloe safe.

Needless to say, she arrived in Los Angeles without incident.

She applied for a minimum-wage restaurant job just outside Hollywood and roomed with three wannabe actors in a drafty loft apartment reeking of cigarette smoke, cannabis, and booze. The hours she served tables were long and grueling, and some days she grew so consumed with the mundanity of work that she forgot she had lived any other life but this one.

At night she dreamed of Heather, and of the many times they'd enjoyed Tom Suarez's movies together, and when Chloe would wake, she'd find her cheeks damp with fleeting regret.

Two months later, when Chloe had developed a paltry savings, she took a cab to the studio where Tom was filming his newest movie, *Alien vs. Godzilla*. She wasn't allowed inside, but she had the patience of a cavern intent on growing new stalactites, so she waited on a nearby bench for the man of her dreams to emerge.

And emerge, he did; with an olive-skinned woman hanging onto his arm like a schoolgirl swept up in the throes of puppy love. Chloe leapt to her feet and blurted, "Tom!"

He whipped his head toward her, and his mouth fell open in surprise. "Carr—Chloe?"

"You remembered," she said lamely. He'd probably taken a dozen or more women to bed already since Pennsylvania. He was a bad boy, after all.

"Who's this?" the olive-skinned woman asked, letting go of Tom's arm as her lip curled.

A faint bewilderment remained evident in Tom's eyes. "She's a friend I met in Pennsylvania when I was filming *The Birds*. Do you live out here, Chloe?"

"I do now." Chloe gave the woman what she hoped was a smug look. "I got a job, and here I am."

"And here you are," he said. His mouth remained open ever so slightly, and he looked vaguely troubled, as if suddenly unsure of why he was standing in that precise spot at that moment. "Vanessa, could you excuse us a minute?"

"Sure," Vanessa said with a sneer, and folded her arms tightly across her bosom.

Tom motioned for Chloe to step off to one side. "What are you doing here?" he asked in a low tone. "Are you following me?"

"You're an intriguing man. Why shouldn't I?"

He gave her a long stare. "Look, if you're wanting to be some kind of groupie, I have a few fan clubs you could join up with instead."

"I don't want to be a groupie."

Understanding must have clicked into place, for his lips twisted into a sly smile. "You don't, huh?"

"Being a groupie is for other girls. I'd rather…well, you'd think I'm too bold." She winked at him. Actually winked. Goodness, what kind of brazen person was she turning into? If only Heather could see her now!

"I don't see anything wrong with a bold woman," Tom said, sizing her up as if truly regarding her for the first time. "The question is, are you bold, or are you someone I'll have to take out a restraining order on in a few weeks when I find you peering in my windows in the middle of the night?"

She laughed. "I'm not that extreme, am I?"

"You traveled two thousand miles just to see me again."

He had a point, and she blushed. "I have no plans of ever peering in your windows," she said.

"Well, then, that settles it." Tom's dark eyes flashed, and Chloe struggled not to swoon.

"Settles what?" she asked, almost afraid to find out.

He tilted his head to one side. "You're someone with a story, and I happen to like stories just as much as the next person. How about we go to Los Ranchos tonight for dinner, and you can tell me yours?"

Chloe's heart skipped about seven beats. "But what about your friend over there?"

"Vanessa?" Tom sounded surprised. "She's nothing to me. I only just met her this morning."

Vanessa, who had still been lurking nearby, let out an enraged huff and stormed off down the sidewalk in the opposite direction. Chloe wasn't sad to see her go. The poor girl was just a groupie, after all.

"In that case," Chloe said, "I accept your invitation."

Looking back, even years later, Chloe still couldn't believe the ease at which everything had taken place. Dinner at Los Ranchos that night had turned into something of a spectacle when a giddy woman had slid into their booth to take a "selfie" with Tom, who'd then called her an ugly cow before shoving her away from him.

It was a mean thing for him to say, but the woman deserved it for being so rude. Chloe admired Tom for standing up for himself. So

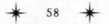

many people wouldn't.

Part of Chloe had feared that Tom would cast her away, too, as he'd done with so many other women, but she'd decided to tell him the truth about herself, even though he'd never believe it. He listened to her story of time travel with rapt attention, and when he asked her to dinner again a week later, she knew she'd done the right thing by being open with him about it. Relationships built upon webs of lies were doomed to fail from the start.

It wasn't long before rumors about her and Tom began to circulate in the tabloids. "Is Hollywood's biggest playboy finally going steady?" one headline read above an image the paparazzi had snapped of her and Tom dining together at a Korean restaurant that Chloe could never remember the name of. She herself hadn't looked too flattering in the picture, which had been snapped at the same moment she'd been forking a glob of kimchi into her mouth, but she was okay with that. Nobody was perfect, except for Tom, who'd appeared characteristically suave in the picture.

And yes, he'd taken her to bed. Chloe blushed whenever she thought about it, which was frequently.

About six months after she and Tom began seeing each other, Chloe lounged on the couch in Tom's Bel-Air mansion reading the latest gossip rag when the air shimmered in front of her, and Heather Soni and Dirk Miller materialized six feet from the couch, wearing matching relay bands and deep scowls.

Chloe scrambled to sit upright, all too aware of the thin, silken kimono she'd slipped on over the lingerie that Tom had bought her.

"What are you doing here?" she asked, voice rising even though she was secretly glad to see them.

"We ought to be the ones asking you that," Heather snapped, making surreptitious glances around the lavish room. "Do you realize how hard it's been to find you? We've been popping in and out of this era for two years trying to pinpoint where you are."

"I take it the original universe wasn't destroyed, then, since you're both here," Chloe commented, closing her magazine and rising.

"You don't say." Heather glared at her. She wore a v-neck shirt that displayed her own friendship necklace. The curving, silver branch pendant seemed to mock Chloe. "Dirk contacted me right after that relay band came back without you. He thought you might have been hurt or killed, but I knew better because of that little note you left for me to find."

"You created a brand-new universe by coming back here and staying," Dirk said. "Do you have any idea how hard it was to calculate the coordinates to jump back not only in time, but into a different universe from ours?"

"I...imagine there's easier things you've done," Chloe hedged. "Since you two came here together, should I assume you've found a helper on the other end?"

"Jamie Patel is working the controls," Dirk said. "She's smart enough to keep quiet about this whole thing. Everyone else thinks you're dead. Except your relatives, of course, because you wrote them a letter about how stupid you decided to be. But officially, you're a missing person. Now come back home with us and give everyone some peace of mind."

Chloe folded her arms. "I'm perfectly happy here."

"How can you *say* that?" Heather blurted, her eyes red. "I was so mad at you, I gathered up all my Tom Suarez merchandise and burned it."

Chloe felt her jaw drop open. "You didn't!"

"I did. Tom took you away from me. It was the only way I could get even with him."

"Who's getting even with who?" Tom asked, striding into the room from the entryway. He wore a plain white t-shirt and black denim pants, and his dark hair had been styled with mousse just the way Chloe liked it.

Heather gaped like a fish washed up on the beach, but she quickly recovered and planted her hands on her hips.

"Tom," Chloe said delicately, moving closer to his side, "these are my friends Heather Soni and Dirk Miller. They come from my time period."

Tom blinked. "I see."

"You *told* him about that?" Dirk asked, incredulous.

Chloe bit her lip. "I'm not very good at lying."

"But you believed her," Dirk said, eyeing Tom with suspicion. "Who does that?"

Tom shrugged. "I didn't at first, but then Chloe wrote down a list of everything she remembered happening to me. She knew I'd be starring in *Hamlet* before I even did. Either she has psychic powers, or she's from the future."

"To travel in time, or not to travel in time," Dirk murmured bitterly. "You must think it's awfully cute; her taking advantage of my trust and using highly-restricted equipment to create her very own universe just for her."

"I don't see a problem with it." Tom stuck out his lip thoughtfully. "I'll never know the difference about anything that's changed, so why should it bother me?"

"Because this isn't how things were supposed to be!" Heather's glare turned sharper than knives. "Tom, right now you were supposed to be bar-hopping in Malibu, getting into a fight with one of the Carruthers brothers. You had the most amazing black eye."

"Why would I fight with a Carruthers?"

"Because they said you were a hack, and you said that at least you were born with an ounce of talent. Someone recorded the fight. I must have watched it a hundred times, and now it will never, ever happen." Heather's jaw tightened.

"It doesn't seem too bad, avoiding a fight," Tom said. "The makeup department hates it when I come in with a black eye."

"It's not the fight that matters. It's the fact that things that were meant to happen aren't happening now that Chloe has come along and bungled things up."

"You're just jealous that I thought of doing this before you did." Chloe held her head up high, refusing to be deterred by her friend's anger. She didn't have to do everything the way Heather wanted. Chloe was her own person, free to make her own choices.

Heather sniffed. "Like *I* knew you had access to a time travel pod at work."

Okay, so Heather did have a point there.

"I think you two should just go," Chloe said, glancing to Tom, who seemed mildly amused at the whole exchange. "It's been lovely seeing you, but this is where I stay."

She moved close to Tom's side, and he put a protective arm around her waist that sent chills up Chloe's spine. Heather looked on the verge of being ill when she said, "Fine. Dirk and I are scheduled to jump back in about an hour. You two go have fun doing whatever it is you do. But don't think this is over."

"I don't like the way she said that," Tom said that night as they sat out on the veranda imagining they could see stars in the light-polluted sky. "What do you think she meant?"

Chloe snuggled closer to him, enjoying the scent of the cologne he'd spritzed all over himself after stepping out of the shower. "It means she's planning on coming back at the first available opportunity."

"That's what I was afraid of." He sighed. "I really got in a fight with a Carruthers?"

"You did. And not just that one time. You and Jonny Carruthers developed a sort of feud after that, and you two got into it every time you crossed paths."

"I don't think I've ever even met Jonny Carruthers."

"And maybe you won't, now. Does it matter?"

"I guess not. That's a different universe now, like you said. It doesn't affect us, here and now." Tom fell into a contemplative silence, and Chloe took the moment to appreciate the tranquil evening colored by the scents of the flowers growing in beds in the tiny, landscaped lawn wedged between his mansion and the one behind it. She had come such a long way to be here, and everything so far had been more than perfect—it had been bliss.

"What else am I like, in that other universe?" Tom asked.

Chloe cleared her throat and sat up a little straighter. "You died at the age of a hundred and seven. Heather and I bought tickets to see you at

CinemaCon, but you died a few weeks before the event."

"That's awfully sobering. A hundred and seven...I think I can handle a lifespan like that. What else?"

"You admitted to having five hundred and seventeen one-night stands before you were too old to do it anymore."

Tom actually laughed out loud. "I kept track?"

"So you said." Chloe paused, then gave him a sidelong glance. "You don't keep track?"

"I'm a busy man, Chloe. I don't have time to make tally marks every time I...oh, hell. That other me probably made it up to sound impressive. It seems like something I'd do to keep up appearances in my old age."

Chloe folded her arms. "How many do you think you *have* had?"

"It doesn't matter, Chloe. You're a nice girl, and you've made my life infinitely more interesting. The past doesn't matter to me anymore."

"I want to know. We need to be honest with each other, right?"

He let out a long sigh. "Fine...let me think. I didn't really start dating until I was eighteen—you might not believe it now, but I was something of a drama geek in school, and the girls in my class just weren't interested in that kind of thing. I had to turn myself into someone else to get anyone to notice me." He lapsed into silence, and Chloe could hear the faint sounds of evening traffic over on the 405. "I dated a girl for a couple weeks the summer I left high school. We slept together a few times. I picked up a girl maybe once a month on average after that, and once I got some full-time acting gigs, it ended up being maybe once every six weeks. I flirted with plenty of women at bars, but honestly, I'm just too dead tired some days to even think about that kind of thing. I'm sure you've noticed."

Chloe had, but hadn't said anything about it. "So, let's say you averaged 10 women per year. You're thirty-seven now. If you started at eighteen, that means you've had somewhere around 190 one-night stands."

Tom blinked. "Wow. That is a lot, now that I think about it. What about you?"

"I had three boyfriends before you. I'm a good girl."

He let out a soft chuckle. "Good girls don't hijack scientific equipment to create their own universe, Chloe. But anyway, what else am I like in the future?"

Life continued for Chloe at a thrilling pace. Tom flew out to Utah to film some scenes for another movie—he was so constantly bombarded with roles that he rarely had a break. Chloe patiently spoke with the press every time they wanted to write a piece about The Woman Who'd Stolen Tom Suarez's Heart, and she suffered through a couple of tortuous television interviews that mostly involved the interviewer asking intimate details about Chloe and Tom's love life.

Chloe would lament her woes to Tom via videochat, and he'd laugh in reply. "You got yourself into this life, Chloe," he'd say. "Now you've got to own everything that comes with it."

After Utah, where Tom had gotten into a fistfight with a photographer who'd attempted to snap pictures of him using the john, Tom flew home and stayed for a couple weeks before deploying to distant Vancouver to film yet another movie.

Chloe would have gone with him, except she hadn't been feeling too well, and preferred to sit on the bathroom floor with bottles of ginger ale while sleeves of saltines were stacked on the kitchen counter, at the ready.

She wasn't an entirely stupid person; she knew what was going on, and could have slapped herself for it.

"I have something to tell you," Chloe said to Tom the evening he returned from Vancouver.

His expression clouded as he set aside the glass of scotch on which he'd been sipping. "What?"

She scrunched her eyes shut. "I'm pregnant."

Then she cracked open one lid to await his response.

Chloe had thought that the famous playboy would grow enraged. She'd thought he might yell and throw things as he did whenever the press irritated him beyond reason.

Instead, his face broke into the most excited, buoyant grin she'd ever seen on him, and she knew he wasn't acting.

"Chloe, that's great!" he exclaimed. "Have you been to the doctor?"

"Not yet. I wanted to wait and see what you thought."

"What I thought…?" Tom's expression hardened. "Did you really think I wouldn't want a baby? I love kids. You've met my nieces."

"But Tom Suarez never had any children," Chloe croaked. "None that he ever knew about, anyway. This wasn't supposed to happen."

"We weren't supposed to happen, either, but here we are." Tom's eyes glistened with joyous, unshed tears. "Oh, this is going to be *great!*"

·· ✦ ✳ ✦ ✳ ✦ ··

Seven months of morning sickness and swollen ankles later, Thomas Eduardo Suarez II was born, weighing six pounds, eleven ounces.

Tom's parents and siblings crowded the hospital room to pass the squalling infant around to each other, cooing over him like he was the most adorable being to ever grace the Earth with his presence.

Chloe, entirely spent from twelve hours of labor, smiled weakly as Tom bent over her and gave her a gentle kiss on the lips. "You did it, baby," he said, and squeezed her hand.

·· ✦ ✳ ✦ ✳ ✦ ··

Heather and Dirk appeared again a few weeks later while Chloe was doing her best to calm a fussy Tommy by walking back and forth across the vast living room while rocking him in her arms.

"Hush little baby, don't say a word," Chloe cooed at him, yet still he kept on wailing even though he'd been fed and wore a fresh diaper, having soiled the previous one so badly that Chloe wanted to gag. "Mama's gonna buy you a mockingbird…"

"Aww, how sweet," said a voice behind her, dripping sarcasm.

Chloe had to give herself some credit for not dropping the baby in surprise. She whirled and glared at Heather, who wore the same outfit she had on the other occasion she'd popped on over here. Heck, maybe for Heather, it was the very same day.

"I'm not going with you," Chloe said, shifting Tommy to her other shoulder as she flicked her gaze to Dirk, whose mouth had dropped open at the sight of the baby.

"Your brother's sick," Heather said. "He wants to see you."

"You're just making that up to get me to leave."

Heather rolled her eyes. "So, what's his name?" She nodded at the baby.

"It's Tommy, not that it's any of your business." Chloe's temper, which was not the best it could have been since she'd been trying to calm a baby for the past half an hour, rose like the mercury in a sunbaked thermometer. "Why can't you just leave me alone? I'm a little busy here, if you haven't noticed."

"Tom Suarez wasn't supposed to have kids."

"As if I didn't know that!" Chloe snapped, which made Tommy scream even louder. "This isn't your universe, Heather; it's mine. Now *go*."

Heather's jaw quivered. "Did our friendship ever mean anything to you at all?"

In response, Chloe tugged her friendship necklace out of her shirt for Heather to see.

"I see." Tears glistened in Heather's eyes briefly before she blinked them away. Heather's gaze went out of focus as she pondered unspoken thoughts, and then she withdrew a black object from her pocket and said, "We brought a relay band for you to keep. It won't come back with me and Dirk."

"Jamie Patel programmed it so it'll jump you over into our universe about five minutes after Heather and I get back today," Dirk said. "You'll have it ready for whenever you need it, okay? All you have to do is wake the screen and tap the Return icon. It never even needs to be charged."

Heather stepped forward and slapped the relay band into Chloe's free hand. She stared dumbly at it, then looked back up to Heather. "You really think I'm going to leave my fiancé and baby behind?"

"Fiancé!"

"He proposed last week." Chloe pursed her lips. "Dropped down on one knee and everything." She set the relay band down on the coffee table and held up her left hand so Heather could see the immense rock glittering on her ring finger. Tom hadn't told her how much it cost, and she wasn't sure she wanted to know.

Heather looked as though she wanted to wish her congratulations but couldn't bring herself to do it. "Well. You have a whole lifetime to think about it, don't you?"

She and Dirk exchanged a glance, checked the time, and dematerialized.

Chloe lay Tommy down on the couch so he could cry out all his problems on his own, and she picked up the relay band and turned it around so she could see it from all sides. It was exactly like the one that had brought her here, and maybe it was, with added bonus features.

She considered tossing it into the waste can, then decided she didn't want anyone else to accidentally get their hands on it and zap themselves into her old universe. Instead, she took it upstairs into the master bedroom and tucked it into her sock drawer, where nobody but she would ever find it.

·· ✦ ❋ ✦ ❋ ✦ ··

"I'm not so sure I should take this role, Chloe." Tom peered up from the audition script laid out in front of him on the table. Tommy sat in his high chair, smearing applesauce all over his face. He had dark hair and dark eyes just like his father, and would probably grow up to break more than a few hearts.

"But you have to," Chloe insisted. "You won Best Actor for it."

"That was a different me. That me didn't have a baby to take care of."

"I can take care of Tommy just fine on my own. I'm not completely incompetent."

"Chloe, you haven't had a good night's rest in months." His eyes were kind and loving as he regarded her, yet for some reason it only made her angry. "I don't want to be one of these guys who misses his kids growing up because he's too busy smirking at cameras. You and Tommy mean the world to me. What kind of father would I be if I never spent time with my boy?"

"You would be the kind of father who has an Academy Award to show off for the rest of his life."

"It's just an award. There are more important things to me now."

Chloe's mouth dropped open. "I can't believe I'm hearing this."

Tom's jaw stiffened. "What, you *want* me to be an absent father? Is that all I am to you—some kind of status symbol? Our son deserves better."

"That's not fair."

"It's the truth, Chloe. You were so obsessed with me that you traveled across time just to see me, which of course thrilled me at first, and I admit it boosted my ego by a few decent notches, but then I saw you for who I thought you were: a kind, loving woman who loved me for the man I was, not the characters I played. I guess I was wrong."

He rose, crumpled the first page of the script, and tossed it across the room, where it landed with a rustle next to a potted ficus tree.

"I'm not accepting this role, Chloe. *It's a Wonderful Life* can have a different lead. It's not like I would have held a candle to James Stewart, anyway."

He stormed from the room. Hot tears stung the corners of Chloe's eyes as devastation coursed through her. *It's a Wonderful Life* had been the first Tom Suarez film she'd ever seen, and his performance as the tormented George Bailey had made her weep in such a good way that she'd immediately watched it again.

And now it would never happen. Not like it had before.

She turned her tear-streaked gaze to her son, who was now gleefully slapping his hands in the applesauce on his tray, oblivious to his mother's sorrow.

Dear God, what had she done?

"Who's a big boy? Tommy's a big boy!"

Chloe could hardly focus on the gossip magazine she'd tried to immerse herself in because Tom was having far too good a time lifting Tommy into the air and making him giggle. He'd been home so much the past few months, it was driving her mad. He had to snap pictures every time Tommy so much as moved, and he hovered over the boy like a protective guard, unable to stand it if Tommy was ever out of sight.

I've ruined him, she thought. *I've ruined Tom Suarez, and there's no way I can ever put things right again.*

Tom no longer hung out in bars flirting with women and punching out journalists. He'd even lost the arrogant swagger he'd adopted when he rose to fame, and despite his barrels of wealth and infamy, he was turning out to be a perfectly normal guy.

No, not a normal guy. A nice guy. Maybe even *the* nicest guy, because he'd told her he wanted Tommy to grow up and be a respectable person who would never harm a fly, and Tom had to lead by example. He rarely even swore anymore. What kind of person aside from a preacher didn't swear?

Tom kept pestering her about setting a wedding date. She couldn't bring herself to pick one. How would marriage improve their relationship, which had been built on pure adoration and devolved into mind-numbing normalcy?

She rose from the couch in frustration and stormed from the room, ascending the curving staircase and arriving in the master bedroom.

"Urgh!" she cried as she flopped onto the bed, glaring up at the molded ceiling that could have belonged in a palace. Her hands balled into fists so tight that her nails dug into her palms. She welcomed the pain. It was the only way to fight back against a world that had turned itself so readily against her.

Soft footsteps in the corridor made her wince.

"Chloe?" Tom asked. "Is everything okay?"

"Nothing is okay."

She felt his weight settle onto the opposite edge of the bed, and heard Tommy burble out a line of baby talk. "Do you want to talk about it?"

Her eyes snapped open, and she glared at him. "What's talking going to do? This isn't you, Tom. You were the world's biggest asshole, and I loved you for it. I never should have let you knock me up; at least then you'd be normal."

His nostrils flared. "You're being extremely selfish."

"Why? Because I want things to be back to how they were supposed to be?"

"This is how they're supposed to be! Right here, right now! I've grown up, Chloe. Little boys pick fights and use women. Meeting you and having Tommy lifted blinders from my eyes. How in the *heck* could anyone ever find a problem with that?"

Heck. He'd said *heck.* Chloe wanted to laugh and cry and scream, but instead she said, "What if I was the one who'd changed? How would you like it then?"

He leveled his gaze at her. "Right now, depending on which way you changed, I might not mind the improvement. Get over yourself and grow up. Our son deserves it."

Chloe walked down the street with her hands jammed into the pockets of her slacks, glaring as if the whole world had done her wrong. Pedestrians of all ages surged past her as she walked, unaware of the turmoil that broiled within her.

Tom and Tommy had stayed home to play with blocks. She welcomed the reprieve.

"Why so glum, honey?" asked a fortyish woman who stopped suddenly beside her. "If I were banging Tom Suarez, I'd have a happier look on my face."

Chloe scowled and made no reply, opting instead to keep moving. Oh, the woes of second-hand fame—when you couldn't even sulk properly because everyone in L.A. knew who you were!

She walked until she passed a shopfront that bore a blinking neon sign proclaiming "Psychic Readings!" and backtracked a few steps.

A poster taped to the inside of the bay window read, "Tarot, palmistry, seances, and more. Walk-ins welcome. Out-of-state checks not accepted."

Oh, what the hell. It wasn't like she had anything better to do today other than listen to Tom baby-talking at their son like a babbling idiot.

She pushed her way into the shop, which smelled of incense and a cloying potpourri that itched her sinuses. A thin man wearing gold bangle earrings stood behind a narrow counter. "Good afternoon, miss," he said in what was probably supposed to sound like an ethereal voice. "What can I do for you today?"

"You can keep me entertained before I lose the final remnants of my sanity at home," she said. "I don't even care what we do, as long as you make it interesting."

The man's eyes seemed to flash. "Of course, of course. My name is Monsieur Garry, and I would love to help you today."

"I'm glad to hear it." Chloe hid a smirk. "Monsieur" Garry didn't even have a foreign accent, meaning he'd crafted a new persona for himself just like everyone else in this godforsaken city.

"Come this way, please," Garry said, gliding out from behind the counter as if floating on a pocket of air. Completing his ensemble were a sky-blue silken shirt, black slacks, and some gaudy bracelets clinking together around his wrists. What a getup—put him in jeans and a t-shirt, and he'd be as unnoticeable as anybody else.

He led her through a doorway into a tiny room crammed full of violet beanbag chairs and tapestries covered in constellations. Candles flickered on the low table in the center of the space, and Chloe tried not to roll her eyes at the crystal ball perched on a shelf off to one side.

"Take a seat, take a seat," Garry said, gesturing at one of the beanbag chairs. "Get comfortable and stay awhile, and Monsieur Garry will tell you everything you need to know."

Chloe dragged the "chair" closer to the short-legged table and plopped into it, and Garry did the same across from her. He reached a hand under the table and must have pushed a button, for soft, exotic music started playing from a hidden speaker.

"You say that you come here for entertainment," Garry continued in his ethereal tones, "but Monsieur Garry knows you really came here for guidance."

"Oh, for goodness' sake, would you stop referring to yourself in the third person?" Chloe blurted. "It's nauseating. Just be yourself, and I'll be me."

Garry's eyes widened, and then he smirked. "Suit yourself, Miss Glasgow," he said, his speech morphing into typical Southern Californian.

She wasn't surprised he knew her name. Most people did, these days.

"So, what's first?" she asked. "You tell me my future and which lottery numbers to pick?"

He raised a sculpted eyebrow. "Why in the world would *you* need to play the lottery?"

"It would give me something to do."

Garry's smirk deepened. "I sense some unrest within you, Miss Glasgow."

"Please, just call me Chloe. And you don't have to be psychic to figure that one out, *Monsieur*."

"You're going to be a fun one, I see. If you think you can manage it, close your eyes and hold out your hands toward me, palm-side up."

Chloe let out a terse breath and complied, and she felt Garry take each of her hands in his. "Interesting," he murmured. "*Very* interesting."

She respectfully held her tongue instead of pestering him with questions. The man was only trying to make a living, after all.

"There's much regret in you," Garry said. "Not uncommon, given which city we're in. People have certain expectations about a place, and when they're let down by reality, they start to drown in it all."

Chloe, her eyes still shut, nodded. "That makes sense."

"Why did you come to Los Angeles, Miss Glasgow?"

"To be with Tom Suarez."

"Are you sure you weren't running away from something else?"

She opened her eyes. "You're supposed to be a psychic, not a shrink."

"I'm a psychic with morals. I tell people what they need to hear, not what they want to hear. Which might be why I don't get many clients," he added, thoughtfully, and smiled. "Are you going to answer the question?"

"Was I running away from something?" She laughed. "Sure. My life was boring, and I ran away from it to be with Tom."

"And now that you're with him, you want to run away again."

"I just want things to be how they used to be. Is that too much to ask for?"

Garry, though he was of an age with Chloe, regarded her as if he were a wise, old mentor and she a naïve student. "Things always change, Miss Glasgow. If they didn't, we'd all be stuck in ruts, and then where would we be? The important thing to do is embrace the change while smiling back on the way things were. That's the only way you'll be able to find true peace within yourself."

Chloe pulled her hands away from his and folded her arms. She'd come here for entertainment, not life lessons. "I can see this isn't going to work out," she said, and slapped a hundred-dollar bill on the table. "Thank you for your time, but I could have spent it better elsewhere."

Garry was too astonished to speak as Chloe scooped up her handbag and strode back out of the shop without another word. Honestly, why had she wasted her time stopping by a psychic shop, of all places? She knew they were all charlatans. She ought to stop by the nearest liquor store instead and drink her way through its inventory. That would give her plenty of entertainment!

A woman heading toward Chloe on the sidewalk stumbled a bit and bumped into her so suddenly that she dropped her handbag, sending bottles of sleeping pills and Advil skittering across the concrete.

"I am *so* sorry!" the woman exclaimed at the same moment Chloe screamed, "Why the hell don't you watch where you're going?"

In a huff, Chloe gathered up the bottles and crammed them back where they belonged, and when she looked up, a thirtyish guy was snapping photos of her on his phone in mild amusement.

It was as if the entire world morphed into shades of red. A raging heat bathed Chloe's skin from her head down to the soles of her feet, and she charged at the man with a feral cry, slapped the phone out of his hands, and slugged him right in the eye before he could so much as cry out in surprise.

He instinctively swung out a hand in defense and hit her in the left temple. The blow was so unexpected that Chloe staggered backward and knocked into yet another pedestrian, and the next thing she knew, she'd been engulfed in a maelstrom of flying fists and four-letter words.

"Do you mind explaining this?"

Tom held up the gossip magazine, on the front of which was a photograph of a deranged-looking Chloe socking Photo Guy in the eye just a few yards past the psychic shop.

"I didn't get arrested," Chloe said. Tommy was sleeping contentedly in his crib, and she envied him for it.

Tom sighed and laid the magazine down on the bedside table. "That's beside the point."

"I dropped my purse. He was taking pictures. I got angry."

"You can't just beat people up every time they irritate you."

"You're one to talk."

Tom looked as though he wanted to say more, but thought better of it. "Just be careful, okay?" he said, pulling her closer to his side. He smelled of aftershave and shampoo. "I don't want you to get into any trouble."

I'll get into as much trouble as I want to, she thought as she closed her eyes and willed herself to sleep.

The next day, Chloe woke late and tried to pinpoint the mysterious noises coming from the floor below her.

"Vroom vroom vroom!"

A baby's giggle carried up the stairs and through the open bedroom doorway.

"Vroom vroom vroom vroom vroom!"

Chloe slipped on her favorite bathrobe and padded from the room, scowling at the morning sunlight slanting through the windows. Her head was pounding, and if that godawful sound didn't stop this minute, she was going to scream.

In the living room, Tom was on his hands and knees pushing Tommy around the floor in a cardboard box. Tommy squealed with delight as his father swung him into a hairpin curve, to the accompaniment of Tom's incessant *vrooming*.

Tom, noticing Chloe standing halfway up the curving staircase, paused a moment and locked gazes with her. Though she knew it was all in her mind, time seemed to draw to a standstill, and she saw the unadulterated joy on Tom's face and the pure and unconditional love he felt for their child.

This was not the heartthrob who'd wooed millions with his heartbreaking performances.

This was a changeling—an imposter who'd taken her heartthrob away from her.

She made an about-face on the stairs and stormed back up to her room.

Without thinking, she slipped out of her robe and put on slacks, shoes, and a sweater, then yanked open the dresser drawer where she'd stashed the relay band Heather and Dirk had left for her so many months ago now.

She fastened it around her wrist and slapped the screen to wake it. A glowing blue icon reading "RETURN" glowed in the center of it, and before she could convince herself otherwise, she prodded it with a finger.

The time travel pod materialized around her as her bedroom vanished. Dirk stood off to one side munching on a donut, and Heather rose from a folding chair wearing a smirk that said, *I told you so.*

"Wow, you were right when you said she'd be predictable," said Jamie Patel, the dark-haired woman sitting at a computer monitor nearby.

Chloe stepped out of the pod but didn't remove the band from her wrist. Though it had been more than half a year since she'd seen Heather and Dirk, she knew it had only been a few minutes for them.

"How's married life been treating you?" Heather asked slyly, rising from her seat.

Chloe gave her a long stare. "I'm not married yet."

"Ah. And what about motherhood?"

"Tommy's a sweet kid. But Tom acts so ridiculous around him, it makes me want to puke."

Jamie let out a soft snicker. Chloe ignored her.

"Well, what do you plan on doing now that you're back here?" Heather asked. "Want to watch some movies for old times' sake?" She winked.

"I don't know what I want to do." Chloe sighed. "Can I stay with you for a while, though? I don't have anywhere else to go while I think some things over."

"*Mi casa es tu casa*," Heather said in the worst Mexican accent Chloe had ever heard.

They caught a shuttle that dumped them off a block from Heather's apartment. Dusk had already fallen, despite Chloe just having risen from bed in her own time.

That thought gave her pause. Her own time? What was this, then? Didn't she belong here, and not there?

Heather unlocked her apartment door and pushed it open so Chloe could go ahead of her. The interior seemed alien now with all the posters gone. The walls had been repainted a soft yellow, and a few artistic prints hung on them in the places where Tom Suarez had once stared out at the room.

"It's different, isn't it?" Heather asked, watching Chloe with her hands on her hips.

"You really did have a bonfire." Chloe felt a knot in her throat, and couldn't have said exactly why.

"Oh, I was kidding about that. I sold most of the Tom stuff I'd had and kept a few of my favorites in a box. I can't really be mad at *him*, you know. Here, in this universe, he's still dead, still childless, and still the best damned actor who ever lived. What can you say about your Tom?"

"He's pushing a baby around in a cardboard box making engine noises."

Heather burst into a peal of merry laughter that made Chloe crack a smile. "I know I can't keep you here forever since you have a kid to take care of, but boy, am I glad to have you back again. Jamie says she'll let you use the pod whenever you want to; you just have to give her a heads-up so she can make sure nobody else finds out about what you're doing. She and Dirk would be in enough trouble as it is if anyone knew they let me use their equipment."

"I can imagine." Chloe glanced down at her feet, then back up to Heather. She wanted to talk about the last couple of years, how she'd melded right into L.A. life like any other newcomer, and decided that maybe it just didn't matter. "How have you been?" she asked instead, sinking onto her old, usual end of Heather's couch.

"Fine," Heather said. "I got promoted to manager at work, and I started dating your old buddy Dirk once we realized we had something in common."

Chloe let out a snort. "Buddy? I barely knew him."

"Oh, but he knows you. Once you pulled your little vanishing act, he started digging into your personal information, and that's how he came across me. He's a nice guy, so I guess I have you to thank for that."

"You're welcome?"

An awkward silence settled over the two of them, and a tendril of sorrow passed through Chloe. This was the world she'd left behind, but then again, it really wasn't. The world had changed—as it always did—and life had gone on.

"You're sure Jamie will let me use that pod whenever I want to," she said.

"As long as it's available. She won't keep you away from your baby. She has kids of her own, you know."

Chloe didn't know. She'd barely known Jamie, either.

"Well," Heather said at last. "I know it's late, but I can put in a pizza."

"Pizza sounds good. I haven't had breakfast yet."

"Breakfast? Oh, right—I forgot we're not exactly on the same time zone right now." Heather bustled into her kitchen, and Chloe's shoulders slumped.

She wasn't sure what she was thinking.

She wasn't sure of anything, anymore.

"Sure, I can do that," Jamie Patel said to Chloe over Heather's private video messaging channel the next day while Heather was at work and Chloe languished on the couch with nothing better to do. "But I'm not entirely sure why you want me to."

"Please," Chloe said. "I won't foul anything up. I just want to see her—me."

Jamie blew a strand of black hair out of her face. "Okay, okay. It's

going to take me a few days to map out the coordinates, and it'll probably take you a few times to get to the right place at the right time."

"I have all the time in the world," Chloe said. "Take as long as you need to."

"If you say so. Just pray none of us gets busted before then, or you're stuck here forever."

The screen went dark on the data pad, and Chloe tossed it onto the table, where it landed with a clatter.

Now all she could do was wait.

$$\cdot \cdot + \ast \to \ast \leftarrow \ast + \cdot \cdot$$

Jamie had been right; it did take Chloe a few tries to find the precise spot.

She finally materialized in the back room of the coffee shop down the street from her old apartment, only this time, she was back in the universe where she and Tom had loved each other and given birth to Tommy.

Many decades later, of course.

Chloe straightened her blouse and smoothed out a wrinkle from her slacks, then pushed her way into the alley behind the row of shops and headed toward the street.

The air smelled fresh, and the sun beat down upon her, lifting her spirits. Chloe turned in the direction of the apartment complex, keeping her eyes peeled.

Her heart nearly stopped when she saw her up ahead—and not just her, but them.

Striding toward her on the sidewalk were Heather Soni and Chloe

Glasgow, both in their mid-twenties. They were laughing about something but drew up short when they spotted Chloe blocking their way.

"Holy smokes," the other Chloe said, looking Chloe up and down in astonishment. "You're like my older twin!"

"That's what I was thinking, too," Chloe said, smiling weakly. This was not the younger woman she'd been, but a copy of the younger woman she'd been; spawned when Chloe created this universe. "What's your name?"

"I'm Chloe," said her lookalike. "And this is my friend, Heather. Do you have a friend who looks like her?"

"Yes, but she's not with me today," Chloe said, which of course brought on a few giggles from the younger women. "This is really something, you know? It isn't every day I run into someone who looks just like me. It's like in that old Tom Suarez movie where he plays his own doppelganger."

The other Chloe's eyes narrowed. "Who's Tom Suarez?"

"Oh, he's that actor who died a couple years ago," the other Heather said. "He was ninety-nine years old, or something. His kid was Tommy Turtledove—that was his stage name, of course."

"Tommy Turtledove!" the other Chloe exclaimed, her face brightening. "I had such a big crush on him when I was younger! His movies were the best."

Chloe blinked. "Tommy Turtledove?"

"Oh, yeah, he's in his sixties now, but he was so cute back in the day. He still thanks his parents for everything every time he wins an acting award. It's really sweet—they always sat in the front row, cheering him on. His mom's name is Chloe—best name in the world, if you ask me!"

"His sister made it pretty big, too," Heather added. "I think she's won something like four Oscars, *and* she started that big charity to help end world hunger."

"Sister?" Chloe asked, hearing a tremor in her voice.

"Yeah, her name is Heather, too." The other Chloe grinned. "Heather Suarez—she kept her real name when she started acting. She's just a little younger than Tommy. I'm surprised you haven't heard of her."

"I don't keep up with movie stars quite like I used to," Chloe said. It became an effort to keep a straight face. "Anyway, I should probably leave you two alone. Have a nice day, Younger Twin."

"You too!"

Sister, Chloe thought dazedly as she walked away from them. Tommy had a sister.

She put a hand on her stomach and smiled; a weight she hadn't realized had been pressing down on her finally lifting away.

Chloe materialized in the bedroom in the mansion she shared with Tom and Tommy. She could still hear her fiancé making engine noises as he hauled the baby back and forth across the living room in his box.

"I've been an idiot," she said under her breath. "A complete, utter idiot."

Framed photos hung on her bedroom wall: she and Tom at an award ceremony, baby Tommy grinning toothlessly at the camera, the three of them on a sunny beach. Knowing that another child would soon be added to the mix made her feel balmy inside.

Every day was different from the one before it. The world kept on changing, and the people living there changed right with it. Tom couldn't be the same man even if he wanted to be.

And if she put in the effort, Chloe could change, too.

In fact, she'd start right now.

She tossed the relay band onto the bed, activated the tiny screen, and hit RETURN.

The device vanished from atop the covers as if it had never been there.

Chloe took a few moments to compose herself, then strode down the staircase. Tom looked up at her expectantly, his dark eyes glimmering with a fatherly joy that couldn't be faked by the most skilled actor on Earth.

"Everything okay?" he asked.

"Everything's fine," Chloe said. She sat cross-legged on the floor beside the cardboard box and scooped little Tommy out of it. He cracked a gummy smile and let out a jubilant burble that could have melted glaciers. "I've got everything I ever wanted right here."

JAY

HE SHOWED UP AT ASSEMBLY Church out of the blue one day, just in time for the spring potluck.

"See that guy?" Morgan Anderson's friend Angie Willis whispered to her.

Morgan, who'd been too preoccupied with the imminent consumption of food to notice much of anything else, looked up from the buffet line in the direction Angie had indicated and wrinkled her nose. Standing near the door to the church's spacious multipurpose room was a thirtysomething man with dark, scruffy hair and a patchy beard. He wore a gray t-shirt with a tear on the sleeve and dingy blue jeans.

"What about him?" Morgan asked, spooning a dollop of scalloped potatoes onto her plate.

"He's hot." Angie giggled. Morgan rolled her eyes. Angie was always crushing on guys twice her age, and they invariably looked like something that had crawled out of a dumpster.

"Come on," Angie said, noting Morgan's annoyance. "Don't you think so?"

"I don't like beards," Morgan said, adding a small mound of cheesy broccoli next to the potatoes.

"I wasn't looking at his beard. I was looking at his eyes. See them?"

The man in question looked unsure of where to go, as if he had never been to Assembly Church before. Morgan certainly didn't recognize him.

Then he looked right at Morgan, who could feel her insides freeze. The man's eyes were a rich blue-green ringed in brown, and they were staring right into Morgan's soul.

"I kissed your brother behind your garden shed last night," Morgan blurted suddenly to Angie.

Angie wheeled on her, her eyes both unbelieving and livid. "You *what*?"

"We—we've been going out for a few weeks. I just thought you should know."

"Morgan, he's eighteen!" Angie hissed. "Your parents will kill you!"

"Will you two stop holding up the line?" asked an irritated voice behind them.

"Sorry," Morgan muttered as she hurried off to the long table where her parents had already taken seats. While she nibbled at her meal, she kept sneaking surreptitious glances at the stranger, who had opted to join the line for the buffet. Old Mrs. Watson passed him holding her plate and gave him a wide berth. Morgan felt bad for him. With the way he was dressed, he might have been homeless, and probably slipped into today's potluck just to get a decent bite to eat.

Angie had sat down across from Morgan at the table and was chowing down on green bean casserole when she lifted an eyebrow. "What are you looking at?"

"Nothing." Even as she said it, Morgan could feel herself blush.

Angie grinned. "You *do* think that guy is hot!"

"Shh! I don't think he's hot. There's just something strange about him."

"I told you it was his eyes."

Shrugging, Morgan watched the stranger sit down at a far table, right next to Clyde Phillips, the town drunk. Clyde's face lit up at the idea of someone giving him a bit of company, and he said something to the stranger unheard amid the dozens of babbling voices.

Yes, the stranger was strange, but it wasn't because of his eyes.

Morgan and her family arrived at church late the next morning because her baby brother Joey, a first-grader, had thrown a tantrum when their mother told him to put on his tiny dress shirt and slacks. The four of them slid into the very back pew on the right-hand side of the church while Pastor Chris was giving his sermon, and to Morgan's surprise, the stranger from yesterday's potluck sat in the back pew on the left, looking just as grungy as before.

In fact, Morgan was fairly sure he was even wearing the same clothes—a stark contrast to everyone else's "Sunday best."

"Morgan, pay attention!" Her mother nudged her in the side.

Not desiring to be witness to another argument today, Morgan turned her attention toward Pastor Chris, but his words about peace and forgiveness had less substance to her than air. All she could think about was the dirty stranger with the captivating eyes, and how lonely he must feel being new to the church.

Why was she even thinking like that, anyway? She'd never cared

about sad, lonely people before. Although, she *was* turning fifteen in two weeks. Maybe this was what it meant to grow up.

When the service let out at noon, Morgan's parents drifted off to chat with some of their friends with little Joey in tow. While she waited for them to finish their conversation, Morgan found herself listening in—a bad habit she just couldn't break.

"You heard the news last night?" Morgan's mother asked, her voice grim.

"No, what?" asked Mrs. Tucker, one of her mother's friends who always wore flowery dresses and too much perfume.

Morgan took a discreet step closer to them, making a point to not look like she was eavesdropping.

"They found the Brauns' boy. I heard it from June at the potluck."

"And?" Mrs. Tucker's voice was hesitant.

"Apparently he was just like the others."

"Lord have mercy," Mrs. Tucker breathed.

Morgan stepped away from them before she could hear any more. She'd reached the age where she could read between some of the lines, and what she saw there didn't look so good. There had been whispers around town for months in regard to some children younger than Morgan disappearing without explanation. The adults had tried so hard to hide most of the grisly facts from the town's younger citizens, but that hadn't stopped Morgan from going online and learning that the two children who'd disappeared first had been found down in Hunter's Creek, their throats slashed from one ear to the other.

And now Noah Braun was just like them. Dear God. She'd *known* him!

"Hello."

Morgan whirled, her heart flying into her throat. Instead of a psycho with a knife, it was the stranger who stood beside her.

She blinked at him. "Hello," she said, uncertain of what else to say.

He smiled. "I saw you at the potluck yesterday. I'm Jay, by the way. I just moved here."

"I'm Morgan Anderson." She blushed yet again, and felt silly for it. "I didn't want to go to the potluck, but my parents made me. I just think they're so boring, except for the food. I don't even like most of the people who go to those things."

There she was again, admitting secrets in the man's presence.

"What's not to like about them?" Jay asked. "They seem okay to me."

Jay must not have been paying much attention to all the stares he'd received yesterday and today. Morgan was about to mention something in regard to that when Clyde, the town drunk, bustled up to them and said, "Morning, Jay! I brought that book I was telling you about yesterday. I've got it out in the car."

Jay turned back to Morgan, still wearing that smile. "It was nice talking to you. I'm sure I'll see you next Sunday."

Then he was off with Clyde as they walked toward the parking lot. Morgan felt sad to see him go, and wondered why.

"Did you *see* him?"

"See who?"

"That dirty man in the back of church on Sunday."

Elaine looked up from her quilting to regard her friend. "Willa, you know I don't see half as well as I used to. It's a miracle I can see my

stitches."

Willa, who had paused in her crocheting, had cross lines etched into her face. "Well, he was a mess. Torn clothes, hadn't shaved… Marie Higgins said she saw him at Saturday's potluck, too, wearing the exact same thing." She returned her attention to the doily she was constructing and made a few furious stitches. "Some people have no respect."

"Mm," Elaine said, because that was all she *could* say whenever Willa got into one of her moods. Best to let her friend blow some steam for a bit before she found something else to get outraged about, like gas prices or whatever the President had said last week.

"My daddy always used to say, 'In the Lord's house, dress as you would for a king.' These younger people, they just don't care anymore. It's disgraceful."

"Mm," Elaine said.

Willa set her half-finished doily in her lap again. "And I just remembered. I ran into Liz Watson down at the IGA yesterday, and she saw the man, too. Said he was talking to Clyde Phillips and the Andersons' little whore."

Elaine scrunched up her forehead. "Morgan?"

"That's her name. Rumor has it Morgan's been sneaking off with Max Willis. Someone ought to call the police on those two. Morgan's underage." Willa snorted. "If this dirty man thinks it's right to talk with Clyde, it's no wonder he'd talk to Morgan, too. It's just a disgrace."

After school on Wednesday, Morgan sat on one of the swings on Joey's swing set, licking an ice cream cone she'd snuck from the freezer.

Her parents were both at work (as usual), and Joey hadn't gotten off the bus yet, so she was supposed to meet Max Willis here. Her almost-fifteen-year-old heart fluttered at the thought of seeing his gorgeous hazel eyes and swooshy hair. So what if he was eighteen? He had to be the one for her. She just knew it.

He'd told her he would stop by at two-thirty. At two forty-five, she checked her phone.

No messages.

If Max was any younger, Morgan would have feared that whoever had killed Noah Braun and the others had gotten him, too, but Max was a grown man; someone the killer didn't seem to be interested in. She rose from the swing and marched across the yard in a huff, crumpling the sticky ice cream cone wrapper in her fist. She'd been stood up! That *so* wasn't cool. She would have to walk down to Max's house right now and demand an explanation.

Morgan yanked open the back door and stormed through the mudroom and into the kitchen so she could throw her wrapper away, then yanked open the front door and took a startled step in reverse when she saw Jay, the dirty stranger, standing on the porch with his hand raised to knock.

"Hello!" Jay said brightly. "I didn't know this was your house."

"What are you doing here?" Morgan asked, recovering from her surprise, though her heart still raced with adrenaline.

Jay's smile reached all the way into his pretty eyes, unlike the mouth-only smiles that Morgan's mother used when chatting with busybody neighbors and salesmen. "I wondered if your parents would pay me to mow their lawn. I've been going up and down the street hoping to ask everyone, but no one seems to be home."

Morgan shrugged. "My parents are at work. Actually, pretty much everyone on our street's at work. Dad calls it a 'bedroom community' because people are only ever home to sleep." Then, almost irrationally, she said, "Do you have a house?"

Jay laughed, and it was a musical sound that made Morgan relax. "If you want to call it that."

Morgan immediately had the mental image of Jay huddled in a half-crushed box in an alley somewhere while rain drummed on the cardboard over his head. Whether or not Jay truly lived in such circumstances didn't matter—he was still wearing the same outfit in which she'd seen him twice previously, and she didn't think he'd showered.

Her parents wouldn't be home until six that night, and Joey's bus wasn't due for another hour and a half.

"I'll pay you $20 to mow our yard," Morgan said. "And when you're done, you can come in and shower."

The grin that stretched across Jay's face made him look a decade younger. "Are you sure your parents will be okay with that?"

"Oh, they help people all the time. They won't mind at all."

·· ✦ ✳ ✦ ✳ ✦ ··

Morgan's heart felt light again as she showed Jay where the lawn mower was in the garden shed, and once he'd gotten it started and was pushing it up and down the yard, Morgan skipped inside and mixed up a pitcher of lemonade so Jay could have something refreshing to drink once he'd finished.

It wasn't until she'd put the pitcher in the refrigerator that she remembered Max had stood her up.

She froze with her hand on the fridge door handle, trying to reevaluate her emotions. She was supposed to be furious right now, right? And she had been until she'd come face to face with Jay on her doorstep.

There was something really, *really* weird about that guy.

Morgan chewed on her lip, trying to rebuild the rage she'd felt when she realized Max had found something better to do than hang out with her that afternoon.

She felt nothing but disappointment—at Max for lying to her, and at herself for falling for it.

There was only one thing she could do, and it was something she'd never done in all her almost-fifteen years: she slid her phone out of her pocket and called—yes, *called*—Max's number.

He sounded surprised when he answered. "Babe? What is it? Why did you call?"

Morgan chose to get straight to the point. "You stood me up, and I don't want to see you anymore," she said, devoid of both anger and tears.

"Stood you up…? Oh, crap. That was today?"

Morgan wasn't about to fall for any excuses. He'd probably met some sixteen-year-old blonde who wasn't a kid like her. "Goodbye, Max. Have a nice life."

She ended the call wearing a satisfied grin, then pocketed her phone and went to the back window to observe Jay's progress. He was halfway finished with the backyard, and his clothes had become soaked with sweat. It would be awful for him to put on those same nasty clothes when he got out of the shower, so Morgan went up to her parents' room and dragged a pair of her father's jeans and a t-shirt from the closet. She would have gotten Jay some clean underwear, too, but that would have just been too creepy. Even she had her limits.

$$\cdot\cdot + \divideontimes + \divideontimes + \divideontimes + \cdot\cdot$$

Jay emerged from the bathroom just past four o'clock, freshly shaved and smelling like the lavender shampoo Morgan's mother bought in bulk at the local Costco.

"Thanks again," he said, running a hand over his damp hair. "Are you sure your parents won't mind about this?"

"Even if they do, it's too late now, isn't it?" Morgan held out the $20 bill she'd been saving for a trip to the mall. "Go buy yourself something nice."

Jay took the twenty with care, folded it precisely in half, and put it in his pocket. Morgan didn't think she'd ever seen anyone look more grateful, and she was glad she was able to make his day.

$$\cdot\cdot + \divideontimes + \divideontimes + \divideontimes + \cdot\cdot$$

Willa peered through the slats toward the Anderson house across the street. She'd been peeking out for over an hour, ever since she'd noticed that dirty man show up on her neighbors' doorstep.

"He's leaving now," Willa said to Elaine, who responded with one of her typical grunts. "And he's wearing different clothes!"

Elaine actually looked up at her, alarmed. "Are you sure?"

"When he got there, he was wearing a gray shirt and dirty jeans. Now he's wearing a blue shirt and clean jeans. He's shaved, too."

Elaine abandoned the quilt she'd been working on all month and joined Willa at the window. Together they watched the stranger stroll down the sidewalk, looking like he'd just won a million dollars. He held a plastic store bag in one hand that probably contained his first set of clothes.

"You said he was out there mowing the lawn," Elaine said, uncertain. "He could have showered to get all the gunk off of him."

Just then, a school bus pulled up in front of the Anderson residence and deposited their young son Joey at the end of the walk. The child skipped up to the door with his lunchbox and backpack and let himself inside.

Willa wrinkled her nose. If that boy had gotten home just a little bit sooner…

"Would you let *your* hired help use *your* shower?" Willa asked, turning from the window in disgust. "I'd say that little whore sank her talons into him."

Elaine cocked a gray eyebrow. "Are you going to tell her parents?"

"Of course not. They're smart people. They can figure it out on their own."

Morgan could hardly sleep that night, so nervous was she about her parents finding out about Jay. When her father asked who had cut the grass, she'd told him she'd done it herself, and the lie made her feel sick to her stomach. She had the feeling Jay wouldn't be happy to know she'd lied, and the thought of disappointing him made her feel all the guiltier.

She rolled over and checked her phone. A green dot next to Angie's profile picture indicated that her friend was online, so she sent her a short message: **Can we talk?**

Angie: Is this about Max? He's been ranting about you this evening.

Morgan: Not about Max. Remember the guy from the potluck?

Angie: What about him?

Morgan: I paid him to cut our grass. Don't tell!

Angie: What? How did you find him?

Morgan: He found me. Long story.

Angie: Be careful, girl. That guy is way too old for you.

Morgan rolled her eyes and set her phone back on her bedside table. Did Angie really think she was trying to get involved with Jay? That was so gross. He was probably like thirty-five, which was almost as old as her dad.

Seriously. *So. Gross.*

·· ✦ ✳ ✦ ✳ ✦ ··

In the darkness, Trevor Ramirez stepped over tree roots appearing one by one in the weak beam of his flashlight. He'd almost reached the Safe Place in the woods down near the gully running between the back of the church property and the wooded acreage belonging to his parents. He and his older brother Eric had built the Safe Place out of fallen tree branches and bound them together with vines, creating a sort of teepee shape. It was big enough inside to lay out two sleeping bags, but didn't fit much else.

Trevor liked to go there when his parents fought. Eric had liked to go there, too, but he was in jail now because his boss at the grocery store had caught him snorting coke during his lunch break.

He finally caught sight of the deer trail that led the rest of the way to his destination. Three paces later Trevor thought he heard a noise behind him. He stopped, cocked his head to listen—silence.

He'd taken only two more steps when footsteps came up behind him and a hand grabbed a fistful of his hair. He tried to struggle, but before he could worm himself away from the person and run for help, something sharp sliced across his throat with a vivid, jerking motion, and he collapsed to the forest floor.

In his final moments he had the dim awareness that someone was standing beside him, watching, smiling.

Clyde Phillips blundered along the sidewalk, straining to focus on putting one foot in front of the other so he could get home before Jane tore him a new one for being out so late again. He'd tried to limit himself to just three drinks tonight, but as usual, he'd gotten carried away and lost count. Might have been six. Might have been seven. It didn't really matter. Jane would kill him anyway.

He was about to round the corner onto his own street when his toe caught on an uneven slab of pavement and sent him sprawling.

He simply lay there on his side for a few minutes or an hour, too wasted to haul himself back onto his sorry feet. The sidewalk didn't feel too uncomfortable—not much harder than his own bed at home, come to think of it.

"Here, let me help you up."

Clyde forced his eyes open. Jay from church stood over him, hand extended.

"Jay?" he spluttered, reaching out and latching onto Jay's callused hand. "What are you doing here?"

"I was just going for a nighttime stroll. Lucky I came this way." With a heave and a tug, Jay got Clyde back onto his feet. Clyde wiped a hand across his shirt to brush the dust off, then squinted hard at his new friend.

"Not many folks 'round here would have helped me up, you know," Clyde said. "I hear them talking sometimes. They think I'm some big, stupid oaf who can't do anything but drink."

"Are you?" Jay asked, his tone curious. Strangely, Clyde didn't think he was making fun of him.

"Yes!" Clyde blurted, humiliating tears springing into his eyes. "It started when I hurt my back at the steel mill back in…whenever that was." Clyde wasn't sure why he was telling Jay any of this, but he went on. "I couldn't work anymore. Got on disability, but it's not the same, you know? And I just…I started on the bottle, and I haven't stopped."

Jay nodded in understanding. "I'm sorry that happened. If you want, I can walk you home in case you fall again."

"Sure, thanks." Clyde blinked to bring his wavering vision into focus. "Our apartment's in the brick building just around the corner here." He hiccuped and staggered off toward home again, with Jay acting as a spotter.

Jay probably thought he was a terrible person for getting so drunk. It was beyond him why the man even bothered to help. Starting tomorrow, Clyde would start to get his act together. He had to put himself right so he wouldn't lose his new friend.

And maybe Jane would finally stop yelling at him. That would be nice, too.

Thursday morning, Pastor Chris Egred sat in his office at the church, poring over financial statements when there came a timid knock at the door. With a sigh, he set the stack of papers aside and said, "What is it?"

Judith, the office manager, poked her head around the corner. Her square glasses were perched so close to the tip of her nose they were about to fall off. "There's a man here to see you, sir. He wants to know if you have any work for him."

Chris narrowed his eyes. "What kind of work?"

"You'll have to ask him. He's right here."

"Let him in, then."

Judith ducked out of sight, and a vaguely familiar man slipped into the room.

"Hello," the man said. "I'm Jay."

It took Chris a moment to speak. Ordinarily he took little notice of the appearance of others since looks were petty things in the grand scheme of everything, but this man's eyes were staring right into him so deeply, he wanted to cry. Steeling himself against the inexplicable emotion, he said, "Nice to meet you, Jay. I'm Chris Egred, the pastor here. What can I do for you?"

"I'm just a tad bit down on my luck," Jay admitted, "so I was hoping I might find some work around here. I can mow the lawn, make repairs…"

Chris hardly heard what the man was saying. Thoughts of that one time with Judith down at the park one night rose from his swamp of undesirable memories under Jay's stare as if the man were conjuring it with his very presence.

He'd never told anyone about him and Judith—certainly not his wife, Billie. It was one foolish night he had no intention of repeating. Though sometimes, like today, when it was just him and Judith in the office, he could feel her magnetism drawing him in as if he were caught in some dark tide. Perhaps it was the curve of her hips, or her bright lipstick of the sort that Billie never wore...

"Are you okay?" Jay asked, startling Chris back to the present.

"What? Yes, of course. We have a lawn care service that comes once a week to take care of the grounds, but you're more than welcome to vacuum out the church. I can pay you...twenty dollars." He hoped the amount wasn't too low for the man. Assembly Church operated on a tiny budget, and they never had much to spare.

Jay's face lit up like the sunrise. "That would be great! When can I start?"

"Right now, if you'd like. Judith can show you where the vacuum is. In the meantime, I've got to get back to this." He gestured at his stack of papers. "I hope you have a nice day."

"You as well—and thanks."

Jay left the office, and Chris heaved a sigh of relief. He knew he was being irrational—people could not stare into each other's souls like they were looking through windows. Yet something about the man's presence had triggered that one damnable memory he'd worked so hard to bury, and he'd very nearly blurted the truth aloud like some nincompoop just asking for more trouble.

Oh, well. Jay was out of his sight now.

Hopefully he wouldn't come back after he'd been paid.

Willa bustled into the church office with the chocolate chip cookie recipe she'd promised to bring to Judith last week. Judith, who at forty was twenty years Willa's junior, looked up from her desk with a tired smile.

"You remembered it," Judith said. There was something odd about her tone that Willa couldn't place. "Thanks."

"Yes, I'm sorry I forgot to bring it Sunday. If my head wasn't attached to me, I'd forget it, too. Is everything all right?"

Judith opened her mouth. "I...it's this man, Jay. He's inside the church vacuuming right now."

"What about him? Did he do something to you?" Willa folded her arms together. *Nobody* messed with her younger friend.

Judith gave her a sheepish smile. "No, it's nothing like that. I... just looking at him made me remember some things I would have preferred to forget. I don't know what it is. Something about his eyes."

Willa shook her head. Judith was normally more level-headed than this. How could someone's eyes do anything to a person?

"You don't believe me," Judith said. "Why don't you go into the church and see if they do it to you, too?"

Figuring there would be no harm in it, Willa said, "I'll go do that." She left the office and strode down the hallway that connected it to the main part of the church. The whine of a vacuum cleaner issued from beyond the door, and when Willa pushed it open, she had to do a quadruple-take.

The man vacuuming the floor was the dirty stranger, not looking quite so dirty since his shower at the Anderson place.

"You!" she gasped.

He turned to her with a smile and switched off the vacuum. "Hello there!"

As soon as his gaze met hers, her breath caught in her throat. His eyes—they were a sort of bright bluish-green shade with a brownish ring around the edges. And Judith was right about them.

They were the most unnerving things she had ever seen.

"You shouldn't be here," Willa said, fighting a sea of unbidden thoughts. Through her head flitted images of her slipping items into her purse down at the supermarket owned by that stingy Charles Wardle, who deserved to have a few things slip out of the store without meeting a cashier. Willa had more than paid for them with the absurdly high prices Wardle stuck on everything.

Why she was thinking of that *now* was beyond her.

Jay, as Judith had called him, frowned and tilted his head to the side as if studying her. "I have permission to be here. The pastor says it's okay."

"That's because the pastor doesn't know what you've been up to!" Willa snapped.

"And you do?"

Willa took one menacing step closer to the man. "I saw you talking with Morgan Anderson, and I know you went to her house. You realize she's only fourteen?"

Jay nodded. "Morgan was kind enough to give me work and the use of her shower. What have you been kind enough to do?"

Willa felt the heat rising in her face. "How *dare* you insinuate that I…that I…" She clamped her mouth shut when the words wouldn't come.

"It seems to me, Willa, that the only person you've been kind to is yourself—but it doesn't have to be that way."

"How do you know my name?" Willa demanded.

Jay responded with a shrug and switched the vacuum cleaner back on. Disgusted and more than a little anxious, she stormed from the church back to her car.

She started the engine and squealed backward out of the parking spot.

There were a few phone calls she needed to make.

That night during dinner, the Andersons' telephone rang. With a sigh, Morgan's mother rose from the table and plucked it off the kitchen counter. "Hello?"

Morgan picked over her food, still guilty about lying to her parents. She'd considered telling them what really happened but hadn't worked up the courage to do it.

She sensed a change in her mother's demeanor, and when she looked up from her plate, her mother was glaring through the archway into the dining room, right at Morgan.

That didn't seem to bode too well for her.

"I'll talk to her about it," her mother said in the coldest tone Morgan had ever heard her use. "Thanks for letting me know."

"What's the matter?" Morgan's father asked once her mother ended the call. "Did they find that Ramirez boy yet?"

"I don't know about the boy. That was Willa from across the street on the phone." She leveled her gaze at her daughter, who suddenly felt very small. "She says you let a man in here yesterday. An *older* man."

Morgan's mouth went dry. She looked to her father and said, "It's not what you think."

Her father's face was darkening to an unnatural shade of red. "You don't deny this?"

"He needed help! He was going up the street asking for mowing jobs, and I felt bad for him and paid him $20 to cut the grass."

"Willa said he left wearing different clothes."

Tears welled in Morgan's eyes. "I let him use the shower and borrow some of your clothes because his were so dirty. I—I shouldn't have lied to you. I'm so sorry."

"How *stupid* could you possibly be?" Her father rose from his seat. Beside him, Joey let out a whimper, his meal all but forgotten. "How could you ever have thought it would be a good idea to let a man in here in the first place? For all we know, he could be the one killing those kids!"

Morgan's face burned with shame. "But he's a nice person."

"Morgan, you don't even know him."

"I talked to him at church on Sunday."

"About *what*?" her mother asked, her face clouded with a dark expression Morgan couldn't quite identify.

"Just the potluck. He was there, too. That's when I first saw him."

"So he's been stalking you," her father said. "I should call the police."

"He hasn't been stalking me! He's just poor and needs help. Isn't that what Pastor Chris says we should do for people?"

"This is different. You never should have let a stranger into this house. As of now, you're grounded."

"Meaning what?"

"Meaning no going outside when we aren't here, and no phone. Hand it over."

Knowing it would be pointless to argue when her father had made a decision, Morgan grudgingly pulled her phone from her pocket and handed it to him. "When do I get it back?" she croaked, dreading the answer.

"When I feel like you've learned your lesson. And if I find out you've let anyone else into this house, you'll never get it back again. Is that clear?"

Morgan just nodded because there was no point in trying to speak.

The very next day, Morgan's father arrived home from work several hours early so he could install new locks on all the doors—something he waited to do until after Morgan got off the bus, presumably so he could make some kind of point.

While her father set about replacing the front doorknob, Morgan worked up the courage to ask, "Why are you doing that?"

"Because you could have given your little friend a key so he can show up here whenever he wants."

"I didn't give him a key."

"He could have taken a spare from the hook in the kitchen."

"Then wouldn't one be missing?"

Her father didn't answer, and Morgan slunk up the steps to her room and flopped onto her bed with her backpack. Gazing out the window that overlooked the backyard, she sighed.

It just wasn't fair. None of it was. Her parents hadn't met Jay, and it was wrong for them to act like he was a terrible person just because he needed some help. And that Willa woman across the street—how was any of this her business? Didn't she have anything better to do than spy on their house?

She chewed on her lip, itching to message Angie about the injustice of it all, but she didn't dare ask her father if she could have her phone back less than twenty-four hours after it had been removed from her possession.

Oh, well. If people in the olden days had lived without smartphones, she could, too.

She slid out her math textbook and turned to page 100, then started working on the equations she'd been assigned for homework that weekend.

If only life's problems could be solved as easily as these.

When Morgan got halfway through the first page of her homework, footsteps ascended the stairs, and her father rapped on her bedroom door. "You've got a phone call," he said.

With a smirk, Morgan hopped off the bed and opened the door to see her father holding out the landline telephone for her to take. "Thanks," she said as he relinquished it to her.

Once she was certain he'd retreated to the ground floor, Morgan held the phone to her ear. "Hello?"

"What's going on?" asked Angie. "Why won't you reply to any of my messages?"

"Dad took my phone away. I'm grounded."

"*You?*" Angie laughed. "No way."

"I already told you some of it," Morgan said, then proceeded to tell her friend how she had let Jay use the shower and borrow some clothes after using the lawn mower.

"Wow," Angie said when Morgan finished. "That really was dumb. What if he's the psycho killer?"

"If he were the psycho killer, I'd be dead, and I'm not. Besides, you saw him the other day, and you thought he was hot."

"Psycho killers can be hot, too. You be careful, girl. If he shows up at your house again, don't let him in."

Pastor Chris was back in his office Monday morning, trying but failing to rub the sleep from his eyes. He'd seen Jay sitting in the back row of pews on Sunday, and the moment he'd laid eyes on him, he'd faltered in his sermon, and it took him far too many seconds to regain his train of thought.

When he and his wife got home after the service was over, he told her everything that had happened between him and Judith.

Understandably, Billie had stormed from the house amid a deluge of tears and drove to her parents' house thirty miles away.

She hadn't come back.

Judith rapped on his office door. "Jay's here to see you again, sir."

Chris cringed, and not just because of her use of the word "sir." Jay again? That figured. He was probably looking for another job to do.

Bracing himself against Jay's unnerving eyes, Chris said, "Send him in."

His door opened, and in came Jay, looking as peaceful and serene as a child untouched by the world.

Despite Chris's mental preparation, he blurted, "How do you do that?"

"Do what?" Jay asked, taking a seat in the chair across from him even though Chris hadn't invited him to. He folded his hands in his lap and regarded Chris expectantly.

Chris swallowed, and beads of sweat crept down the back of his scalp onto his neck. "When I look at you, I see inside myself."

Instead of decrying Chris's admission as insanity like a normal person would, Jay cocked an eyebrow and said, "Do you not like what you see?"

"No!" Chris blushed, and it felt even more humiliating than when he'd admitted his brief affair to Billie the day before, and *that* had been pure torture.

"Then perhaps you should make an effort to better yourself," Jay said, his tone calm.

Chris's chest tightened. "What do you even want with me?"

"I'm just looking for work, that's all."

Chris raced to think of something that could preoccupy the man so he could get him out of his hair. "I bought a bookshelf last week," he said, saying the first thing that came to mind. "It's still in the box. I'll pay you twenty bucks to put it together."

Jay glanced to his left, then his right. "Where is it?"

"Out in the main office by Judith's desk. You can't miss it."

"Thanks again. I appreciate it." Jay dipped his head and walked out, leaving the door open just a crack.

Chris mopped his forehead with the handkerchief he kept in his pocket. He could hear Judith say something to Jay, and then Jay walked past the gap toward the large box and started tearing it open.

Oh, Judith. Why hadn't he fired her after The Incident? She was the one who'd seduced him, after all.

He should have stayed far, far away from her.

Why had he gotten involved with her in the first place?

Because she's put a spell on you, whispered a tiny voice, and Chris shivered.

Jay didn't mind assembling the bookcase, for he always loved having useful work to do. Sitting on the floor, he slid all of the components out of the box and started reading the assembly instructions when he realized that Judith, the office manager, was staring at him as if he were a worm.

"Can I help you?" he asked, looking up from his work.

He didn't cower under her scrutiny, for he feared nothing, especially not her. Her lip curled, and in a voice barely concealing her rage, she said, "You're ruining me."

"What makes you say that?"

A visible tremor passed through her body. "When I look at you," she hissed, "it makes me think of things I don't want to."

Jay folded his hands together in a calm manner and said nothing.

"Don't look at me like that!" she shrieked, and she launched herself over the desk at him wielding a pair of scissors.

Pastor Chris burst from his own office as Jay scrambled to his feet to get out of the way—the scissors had taken him by surprise.

All color drained from the pastor's face. "What in the name of—"

"It was me!" Judith screeched as she attempted to stab Jay, who was deft enough to dodge each swipe, though he didn't trust his luck to hold out too long. "I did it! I did it!"

Chris rushed up to try to subdue her. "Judith, it's…it's not necessary to tell him *that*."

She wheeled on her boss, giving Jay a momentary reprieve.

"This has nothing to do with you! *I'm* the one who took the children and killed them! It was all me!"

Suddenly she sank to the floor, sobbing, letting the scissors fall from her hands. She gripped her ankles and rocked violently back and forth. "I had to do it," she choked through her tears. "The first kids…they saw us, Chris. I didn't want them to tell, so I made sure they wouldn't."

Chris's mouth fell open. "Oh my God."

"And the others…" Judith swallowed. "The first time I did it, it was fun. I needed to try it again. And again. And it was wonderful."

It's about time, Jay thought.

He stepped past her, picked up the phone on her desk, and called the police.

A knock sounded at the front door Tuesday afternoon not long after Morgan got off the bus. Heaving herself off her bed and dragging her feet down the stairs, she let out a sigh. What could it be now?

She pulled the door open and staggered back a step when she saw it was Jay. He'd put on his old clothes again and was holding out her father's folded clothes for her to take. Strangely, they smelled of detergent.

"You shouldn't be here," Morgan said, taking the clothes from him. "That lady across the street is going to call my parents again, and this time I'll be grounded for eternity."

"You mean Willa?" Jay's lips formed a wry smile. "Don't worry about her; I'm pretty sure she's not home. A little bird told me she's turned herself in for shoplifting a few things from the IGA."

Morgan didn't bother asking how he knew Willa.

Jay went on. "You heard that Judith McIntosh at the church confessed to murdering four children?"

Morgan shivered. "Everyone was talking about it at school. Why?"

"Well, let's just say my work in this town is finished for now."

Ah. Morgan was fairly certain she understood what that meant. "So you're leaving?"

"That's right. I wanted to thank you again for your kindness—it means a lot. Please, never change that about yourself."

A pang of sadness filled Morgan's heart as Jay turned around and walked away down the sidewalk. She would miss him, but if she guessed right, there were probably other towns that needed him, too.

She watched him until he disappeared around the corner, then went back inside to finish her homework.

DAILY LOG FROM OUTPOST #602

Day 1

GREETINGS, DAILY LOG! WOW, IT'S fun talking into this thing—I don't even have to type! Good thing, because I'm all butterfingers on a keyboard. Right, right…okay. My name is Kwame Pattison, not that *I'm* important. Porter and I arrived at Outpost #602 on Kuiper Belt Object Perez 9276b this morning at 0800 hours Eastern Daylight Time. Morris and Jeong were so glad we came to replace them, they burst into actual tears. It's a funny thing to watch in ultra-low gravity. They said they'd nearly died of boredom out here. I'm smart; I brought some old shows with me, a stack of books, and a few two-player games. Porter brought knitting needles and a basket of yarn. Some people are just full of surprises.

Day 2

This place is the shape of a potato, and isn't much bigger than one. While Porter stayed inside the compound, I suited up and went for a walk around the surface of Perez 9276b. There's no air, of course, and the ground is the color of old concrete. Before he and Morris left, Jeong warned me not to attempt running outside; the gravity is so low I could send myself into orbit if I go too fast.

I'm tempted to try, but I'm not entirely stupid. I won't die in space.

Day 3

When I was assigned this job, I was told that Outpost #602 had been listening for signals from interstellar space for nine and a half years. Nobody's ever heard an abnormal peep out of the scanners in that entire length of time, but it's still a good-paying gig. By the time they send me back to Earth in four months, I'll have enough money to put a down payment on a house. Kimmy and I were thinking of looking at places near Denver. I can practically smell the mountain air!

Day 4

I guess I should be talking more about actual work in this log. Well, guess what: I haven't heard anything, and I have a fairly decent ear for anomalies. My elbow hurts from leaning on it half the day while I listen to the equipment. Once I thought I heard an eerie warbling coming through, but it was just Porter singing in the shower.

Day 5

It's getting a little dreary out here. The sun is so far away, it's just a

bright dot a little bigger than the other stars. This rock's orbit isn't much farther out than the orbit of Neptune, but Neptune is way around the other side of the sun right now, so we can't even look at that.

I wish there were sunshine, or weather, or something. Even a little earthquake would be nice for some excitement, but you can't have an earthquake if you're not on Earth.

Day 6

Still no alien signals. I started watching reruns of *I Love Lucy*. Porter tried to make some cakes in the kitchen but made a sloppy mess everywhere that I had to help clean up. Spilling flour in ultra-low gravity should be a punishable offense.

I've sent Kimmy a few messages letting her know I'm safe. I hope my messages don't interfere with anything the aliens might be sending us. If there even are aliens. It's not like anyone's actually heard one, or seen one. I'm starting to think they're as real as Bigfoot.

Day 7

Porter and I have been discussing what the aliens might look like, if we ever do meet them. We agree they would probably be humanoid, with opposable thumbs that would help them build their spaceships. But what color would they be? Would they have hair and wear clothes, like us?

Yes, Porter, I'm talking to myself. Where have you been the past week when I record the day's thoughts? And you say you have a degree in physics. I guess nobody can major in The Obvious.

Day 8

Porter is pouting now. I didn't mean to hurt his feelings, but come on.

Yes, Porter, I'm talking about you again. It's called "venting." Who the hell else am I going to talk to out here? The ghost of Neil Armstrong?

Sorry, getting back on track now. I spent part of the day suited up outside, getting my exercise in. It only takes an hour and a half to completely circumnavigate this rock. Magellan would be green with envy! Did I mention how glorious the stars all look out here, with no atmospheric haze to dim them? It's a backyard astronomer's wet dream.

But still no alien signals.

Day 9

Today was boring. Porter still isn't talking to me. I might hold a séance later to conjure up old Neil. I bet he didn't have to deal with this crap on the moon.

Day 10, Part 1

Nothing new to report. I—

What the hell was that? Porter, get in here!

Day 10, Part 2

Something's shown up in our sector, heading straight toward us from the direction of interstellar space. It's like it just materialized there, but now it's moving fast. Our scanners can't identify it as any previously-known object in this region. We've already alerted the other Kuiper Belt bases, as well as the ones on Titan and Ceres, even though they're farther in. It'll take a little longer for the alert to reach Earth.

This thing isn't moving like an ordinary space rock. What if it hits us? There shouldn't have been anything like this out here at all, dammit!

Day 11

The object moved sharply off course early this morning, saving us from certain disaster.

We can't just shrug it off, though. Four more objects like it popped up out of nowhere on the scanners today. My teeth won't stop chattering. Porter's used the lavatory about seventeen times. We received the confirmation that Earth and all outlying bases have been placed on Red Alert. The first object is already closing in on Jupiter's orbit. Scanning probes near the Jupiter system indicate the object is metal. I'd bet my salary all the new ones are, too.

Oh, God. One of the new objects is coming right toward us.

Day 12, Part 1

We've requested evacuation. It sounds nice, but it won't be fast enough. This thing will be here in three hours if it doesn't change course. A ship from the Titan base will be here next week. If there is a next week for us. We don't have any weapons.

Day 12, Part 2

I can see the damned thing. The object is a bright light moving toward us. This is utter insanity. Can I please wake up now? They must have picked up our signals and homed in on us. Porter picked up a frequency coming from the object and dialed the volume all the way up. It sounded like a pure cacophony that had to be biological in origin. We think it was the aliens talking to some of their other ships. No humanoids would make sounds like that.

I don't think I want to know what the aliens look like. God, get me off this rock!

Day 12, Part 3

The object has just landed on Kuiper Belt Object Perez 9276b, about one kilometer from the compound. We can see it through the viewports—it's shaped kind of like a big, metal chicken egg with some running lights around it. I keep praying these people are friendly. I can't stop shaking. We're about to make history here...

Shit, figures just started emerging from the object. Three—no, four, of them. They're suited up, so they clearly need air like us. But what kind of air? Oxygen? Methane? Oh, who the hell cares! They're moving right toward the airlock!

I can see them better now. They're tall, at least two meters, with round, plump bodies. And they're walking on two slender legs.

Porter just vomited on the floor—of course I'm telling that to the machine; I just saw it happen! Don't worry about cleaning it up. Maybe they won't mind the mess? Oh, boy. They're at the airlock now. I'm going to go arm myself...there's a knife in the kitchen... okay. I've got the knife now.

Use your knitting needles, Porter! Stab only if provoked!

They're inside the airlock. The knob is turning...

They're stepping into the room. Oh, Jesus...okay. Their suits are blue, and their helmets have tinted face plates. Their necks are a meter long—about half the height of their entire bodies. Their legs are *so* skinny, it just reminds me of something...

One seems to be scanning the air in here with an alien piece of equipment...it just said something in its own language. Now they're taking off their helmets!

Jesus Christ, they look exactly like...

Porter, watch out! They're firing at us! They're—

Day 12, Part 4

Quack. Quack. Quack-quack quack. Quack quack? Quack.

NO GOOD
REASON

THE MAN STUMBLED INTO THE café amid a gust of rain and wind that sent loose cups and papers scattering. He was thin, with patchy brown stubble and a fraying fedora jammed over his head, and his khaki pants and sweater were more ragged than thrift shop rejects.

He repositioned his sodden hat while he eyed the menu on the wall, and as he stepped up to the counter, Clarissa noticed that one of his eyes had been blackened, as if from a forceful blow.

"What can I get for you today?" she asked in her best customer service voice.

The man's eyes, blackened and not, lingered on the menu a moment longer. "I'll just have plain coffee, black." A bone-deep weariness was evident in his voice, along with the subtle twang of Kentucky hills. "Make it a large one, please."

Clarissa keyed the price into the register. "Is that all for you today, sir?"

He sighed. "It should be. My name's Bill, by the way, if you need it." He handed her the exact change with a frown that spoke less of what he thought of Clarissa's service, and more of some inner, unvoiced turmoil.

Poor guy must have been through the ringer a few times, Clarissa thought as she dutifully plucked a large paper cup off the neat stack and scrawled the man's name upon it with a permanent marker even though he was the only customer in the shop at that moment other than Theo, who sat at a table tapping away at his laptop every afternoon from one to four. Theo had told Clarissa he was working on a novel—it must have been something epic since he'd been sitting there typing every single day for the past 460 days and still wasn't finished.

Clarissa and her employees had been keeping track. They'd thought about taking bets on when he finally completed the thing.

She filled Bill's cup, smacked a plastic lid onto it, and handed it to him. "Careful, it's hot. You have a great day, sir."

Bill took a sip anyway despite her warning and made no move to leave. Clarissa couldn't blame him. The storm outside raged so hard that she was starting to have some serious misgivings about it. Tornadoes didn't hit too often here in these parts, but that didn't mean one wouldn't defy the odds by popping up here today and sucking Clarissa and her shop into the sky.

"I think I'll stay here awhile, if that's okay," Bill said. "The rain…"

"Hey, don't you feel bad about taking a seat. We've got plenty of room here with just you and Theo."

Theo flicked his gaze up from his computer, ran a hand through his already-ruffled hair, and returned his attention to his manuscript.

Bill sat down at the nearest table to the counter and took another sip of coffee.

"You need some ice for that eye?" Clarissa asked.

Bill jumped. "Oh, sure, that would be great, thanks. Had a little accident earlier. I appreciate it."

Clarissa scooped ice out of the freezer and into a plastic baggie, which she wrapped with a towel. "You look like you just lost a boxing match," she said as she handed him the makeshift icepack.

"Lady, you don't even *know*." Bill pressed the icepack against his eye and seemed to relax a bit. "Things like this? They're practically the story of my life."

"What do you mean? What happened to you?"

Bill barked a humorless laugh. "You wouldn't believe me if I told you."

Clarissa thought that sounded entirely too cliché, but she said, "I'm always up for a good story, whether I believe it or not."

Bill took a moment to drink more of his too-hot coffee. "I wouldn't call it a good story, but it sure is a crazy one."

"Okay. So what happened to your eye?"

"It's simple, really. I was attacked."

Clarissa glanced in alarm toward the plate glass window in case his attacker might have followed him here. "Attacked? Why?"

Bill chuckled. "For no good reason."

And he began his tale.

I think life began normal enough for me. I come from down past Lexington, if you couldn't tell. My family's always lived there—Dad was a cop, Mama taught school, and we were the most typical people you could ever meet. My brother was the smart one; he went off to California and became an attorney. I went into sales, but that was all later.

The first time I remember it happening, I must have been seven or so. I was playing in the sandbox out in our backyard when our neighbor Bryan Wilson came at me out of nowhere with a lead pipe and knocked out six of my teeth. If my daddy hadn't come running out of the house in time, Bryan would have turned me into a pulp.

I know it's crazy a grown man would go after a boy like that. His excuse in court was he just got annoyed by the sight of me being a kid doing kid stuff, and he just flipped his lid. He got a few years in prison for assault. I don't think it was enough.

I thought life would be good after that, but I was wrong.

It was a few years later the next time it happened. I was ten at that point, and me and a good friend were walking down our road to go get ice creams from the shop on the corner. Halfway there, we ran into a group of older boys, maybe fifteen or sixteen years old, and I'll be darned if they didn't lay into me with their fists like I was some kind of human punching bag. Jimmy, my friend, ran to get help. Those boys didn't even try to lay a finger on him.

By the time Jimmy came back with his dad, the boys had gone and left me a bruised, bloodied heap on the sidewalk. We never did figure out who those boys were, and neither me nor Jimmy ever saw them again.

Then, about a month later, I was standing in line at the supermarket picking up a loaf of bread for Mama, when all of a sudden the lady in front of me turned and slapped me hard across the face. Said I'd been giving her funny looks she didn't like, but there was no way she could have seen my face even if I *was* doing that, seeing as she was facing the other direction up until she turned and nailed me.

My dad whipped me when he found out about that one. He said I must have been ogling that woman at the checkout and that I deserved getting slapped. But I hadn't done anything other than mind my own business. I was only ten years old. I hadn't even *noticed* women yet.

The fourth time it happened, I started to get a little suspicious. *Why me?* I asked myself, and still do. I haven't ever done anything to nobody, and all I get in return is pain.

Let's see…that fourth time happened not long after the third. Some kids beat me up on the monkey bars at school. I hadn't even been talking to them. That's how it always goes. I mind my own business, and people—strangers, most of them—end up beating the absolute stuffing out of me. But that's how it is. It's happened hundreds of times now, and I've never instigated any of it.

I went to a priest once; asked him if he thought I might be hexed, or possessed, or something. He threw a hymnal at my face and told me to get the hell out of his church before he called the police.

I tried to get help other places, too, but never did learn much of anything useful. The shrink I wanted to talk to pulled a gun on me during my first and only visit, and the Baptist pastor I visited a week later bashed me in the head with a Bible the size of a coffee table and had his office manager escort me out to my car.

The only thing I can figure is there's something about me that people just don't like. I'm an easy mark, and I have to live with that. I've been beaten up on the bus, in department stores, by police during traffic stops, by sales clerks at gas stations. Once I had a plumber over to fix my sink, and he beamed me with his wrench when I asked him if he'd figured out why it kept plugging up. Oddly enough, I've mostly been safe working in sales—only ever had two potential customers take swings at me. Kind of ironic, if you think about it. You'd think lots of people would want to beat up a salesman.

As for this black eye I've got right now? It's nothing too complicated.

I was just at the post office picking up stamps, and the man behind me in line punched me in the eye. He said he thought I was the guy his wife had had an affair with. Didn't even apologize. It's pretty boring if you think about it.

So, that's my story. I'm Bill, and people hurt me—not all of them, but enough to give me hell. The coffee's great, by the way.

·· ✦ ✳ ✦ ✳ ✦ ··

"Oh, thank you," Clarissa said, shaken by Bill's tale. The tiniest part of her wondered if he might be lying, but surely it was too extraordinary to be fiction.

"I'm sorry you've had to go through all of that," she went on. "It must be very—"

Clarissa jumped as she detected movement off to her left. Theo had risen from his table, his face contorted with rage. Before Clarissa could ask what in the world had gotten into the aspiring novelist, he'd picked up the wooden chair in which he'd been seated and charged at Bill with the chair raised like a bludgeon.

Bill scrambled out of his own chair like a fire had ignited beneath him and was out the door and into the downpour in roughly three nanoseconds, quickly disappearing from sight.

Theo stopped at the door and lowered the chair, panting from the sudden exertion.

"What in the world did you do *that* for?" Clarissa screeched.

Theo crossed his arms, a scowl still etched on his face. "Do you have any idea how hard it is to write when someone's yakking like that just a few feet away from you? I didn't think he was ever going to shut up."

✦ 127 ✦

HOW TO MAKE
MONEY FAST

"PSST! HEY YOU!"

Kyle Burton twitched in surprise and groaned inwardly when he saw that the speaker stood beneath a white tent set up on the campus plaza close to the Fine Arts building. He hadn't noticed it before, as he typically traveled with his head down, desiring little to no human interaction.

Seeing tents and booths out here wasn't uncommon. Various groups and individuals were often out and about on the plaza promoting something or another, usually stuff involving religion, politics, or social justice issues. Most students found it all a minor annoyance, Kyle included.

The single tent set up today had three sides and a long table across the front buried in pamphlets. The man and woman standing behind it looked to be in their mid to late twenties, and they beckoned for him to come on over.

"He *does* hear us!" the woman said to her companion. "Hey you, come here a minute."

Kyle let out a resigned sigh and dragged himself over to the tent, wondering what sorts of ideas the couple planned on peddling to him. He didn't see any signage, political or otherwise, and he supposed that might have been their way of piquing students' curiosity.

"Hi," Kyle said meekly as he approached their table. "What have you got here?"

The woman, dressed all in black with multiple facial piercings and a neon pink streak in her hair, flashed him a toothy grin. "You're a student, yes?"

"Right." Kyle shifted the weight of his bulging backpack, stuffed full of notebooks and various tomes he studied for hours each night so he wouldn't lose his scholarship. "I'm a sophomore."

"And what's your name, Sophomore?"

"Kyle Burton. I'm majoring in history. I want to be a professor."

The woman's male friend nodded enthusiastically, as if somehow the prospect of Kyle's future career excited him—not a common reaction he got when people learned his aspirations.

"I have heard how it is being in college," the woman said. "You work a part time job to help yourself through, and you're still too broke to go do whatever you want in your free time. You probably spend the whole weekend either at work or holed up in your room because it costs too much to do anything else. Am I right?"

"Right," Kyle said, marveling that she had read him so well. He made minimum wage working twelve hours a week at the county library, and that was about enough to pay for his groceries.

"Since that's the case," the woman said, "Flea and I might have just the solution for you." She plucked a pamphlet off the nearest stack and held it out for Kyle to take—it was printed on solid black paper with a green dollar sign on the front. "Be sure to read this when you get the chance. I think it will help." She flashed him another smile. "Have a great day."

Kyle didn't get a chance to open the pamphlet until he made it back to his dorm room that evening, starving and bone-tired. His mind overflowing from the day's lessons about the Tudor family, what a Gross Domestic Product was, and the like, he plopped his backpack down on the table in the tiny dorm kitchen and pulled out the pamphlet, which had become quite crinkled over the past several hours.

The dollar sign on the front seemed to beckon to him. Shrugging to himself, he unfolded the paper and read:

ARE YOU IN NEED OF CASH?
FEAR NOT–YOU'VE COME TO THE RIGHT PLACE!
BRING THIS FLYER TO
798 EAST WALNUT STREET
AT 9PM ON FRIDAY, OCTOBER 8
TO RECEIVE INSTRUCTIONS ON HOW TO MAKE MONEY FASST!

Kyle read it over twice. The misspelling of the final word disturbed him. Hadn't they thought to proofread before sending these to print?

He jumped when the door to the dorm room opened. His roommate Paulo came through carrying a box heaped high with papers.

"What's that?" Kyle asked, stepping aside so Paulo could put his box on the table.

"Barnes was cleaning out his office and said I could have a bunch of physics articles he'd saved over the years."

"Geek."

"Speak for yourself, history man. What's that?" Paulo nodded toward the pamphlet.

"The people in the tent on the plaza were handing these out today."

"I don't remember seeing a tent."

"They must have left before you came through. Here, read this and tell me what you think."

Paulo took the folded black paper from him and read it. "I think they don't know how to spell, and English isn't even my first language." He threw it back on the table.

"But do you think I should go there and see what the job is? It's tomorrow night."

"I don't care what you do. I've got a date."

"With Cheyenne again?"

Paulo grinned. "Yep, and you're not going to bother us when we come back here, amigo."

He walked past Kyle and shut himself in his bedroom. Kyle picked the pamphlet off the table and read it a third time.

He wondered what the job was and how much it paid.

The next evening, Kyle zipped up his brown hoodie and set out on foot toward 798 East Walnut Street, which, according to his research, sat eight blocks away from campus in a neighborhood that had seen better days.

Maybe these people wanted him to smuggle drugs onto campus. He knew people who'd done worse.

The sun had gone down before Kyle left his dorm, and as he drew closer to his mysterious destination, a cool breeze kicked up fallen leaves and sent them skittering down the sidewalk in front of him like a retreating army.

He turned a corner onto East Walnut Street. Most of the streetlamps had burnt out, and the few that didn't need replacing illuminated somber rows of faded brick buildings dating from the century before last, if Kyle was to judge from pictures he'd seen in his history books. If this wasn't about drugs, maybe someone needed a strapping young man to help with repairs.

Kyle, who was not the least bit strapping, could only hope he'd be fit enough for whatever needed done.

798 East Walnut Street, Kyle soon saw, was perhaps one of the oldest and most dilapidated buildings on the block. Five brick stories rose into the air, and most of the windows had been boarded over, possibly before Kyle himself had been born.

So, this was probably about drugs. But hey, he needed cash, so who was he to complain?

Kyle glanced both ways before stepping up to the peeling front door of 798. Not a soul in sight. What a depressing neighborhood, when even bums and panhandlers didn't hang around.

He rapped on the door. Flakes of red paint fell free and drifted to the ground. While he waited to be granted entry, he wondered what type of building this had been. Maybe an old tenement, or something.

The door creaked open. The woman with the pink streak in her hair appeared in the gap. Her face brightened when she saw him. "Come in!"

she said. "We were starting to wonder if anyone was going to show."

She opened the door wide and motioned for him to enter. Feeling suddenly bewildered, Kyle stepped over the threshold into a dusty corridor. Light glowed from beneath a door on the right.

Kyle twisted his hands together as the woman placed a hand on the knob of that second door. Had no one else responded to the pamphlets the woman and her friend had been passing out?

The woman paused to regard him. "Is everything all right?"

"Look," Kyle said, "this might seem a little awkward, but I'm really not sure who you people are."

The woman's laugh came out sounding higher-pitched than it should have. "That's because we didn't tell you! I thought that was obvious." She pronounced the latter word as if it ended in a Z. "My name is Tam. My friend Flea and I need some help."

"Okay," Kyle said, because there was nothing else to say.

Tam opened the second door. Kyle hesitated, then stepped through into a surprisingly cozy living room where a fire glowed in the hearth and the man called Flea sat at a table tinkering around with some electronic equipment Kyle didn't recognize.

Flea looked up and smiled when Kyle and Tam entered. "Ah, some help has arrived. Good."

Tam closed the door behind them. Kyle jumped and silently cursed himself for it.

"So, what's the job?" Kyle asked.

Flea rose and solemnly clasped his hands together. "We lost something, and we need someone to go find it."

Kyle could feel his heart sinking like a doomed ship. "I'm not very good at finding things. I could never even find Waldo."

"Well, you're in luck," Tam said. "We know who has it. We just need someone to get it for us."

"So it's not lost?"

The couple stared at him a moment. Kyle noticed that one of Flea's eyes was dilated slightly more than the other, as if he'd recently suffered a concussion.

"It's lost to us," Tam said.

Puzzle pieces were slowly snapping into place inside Kyle's head, and he didn't much like the picture he saw emerging from them. "Let me get this straight," he said. "Someone stole something from you, and you want me to steal it back from them."

Tam and Flea were smiling and nodding. "You understand, then," Flea said.

Kyle sighed and ran a hand over his face. "Will this involve breaking and entering?"

"Yes. Possibly. There's no guarantee."

"And you want me to do it because you'd rather I got caught than you."

"Getting caught would be most disastrous for us," Flea said. "You wouldn't understand."

"How much are you offering me to do this?"

"If you're successful in retrieving the item," Tam said, "we will pay you ten thousand dollars."

Kyle's stomach turned a cartwheel. "You live in this dump but have ten thousand dollars?"

"Oh, we don't *live* here. We're merely using this as our, hmm, base of operations."

"I want to see the money."

"Of course." Flea hurried toward a far corner of the room, slid open a filing cabinet that looked like it belonged in a museum, and withdrew a metal box fastened shut with a latch. He unhooked the latch and flipped the lid open.

Kyle craned his neck to see better and forced himself not to gasp. Stacks and stacks of twenty-dollar bills nestled inside in orderly ranks.

"Why pay a student?" Kyle blurted. "Why not hire a professional?"

The man and woman blinked at him.

"The individual who has what we want is connected to your institution," Tam said. "Is ten thousand not enough?"

Kyle put his finger on his chin and pretended to think. "I don't know. Who am I taking the thing from?"

"A mister Wolfgang Collins. Our sources tell us he is the head of the Archaeology Department."

"Ten thousand is definitely not enough," Kyle said. "Now what did he take from you?"

"It's hard to explain," Flea said, his face full of genuine chagrin. "Here, let me show you a picture." He pulled a device out of his pocket. It looked like a smartphone, only slightly larger and squarer. He must have hit a button, for a revolving holographic image appeared midair.

Kyle squinted, trying not to look too impressed by the fancy tech. The image floating above the squarish device looked like a clump of flesh-colored rubber bands about the size of a softball.

"That's how big it is?" Kyle asked.

"Yes."

"What does it do?"

The couple said nothing.

"Look," Kyle went on. "I can't help you if I don't know what I'm dealing with."

They exchanged a glance, and some unspoken communication seemed to pass between them. "It's extremely precious to us," Tam said. "We had gone for a walk late one night pushing a pram full of them. We didn't know one had rolled out until we got back to the... our vehicle and realized one was missing. We quickly retraced our route, and we watched as Wolfgang Collins found the missing one laying in the grass and put it into his pocket."

"Why didn't you just take it from him then?"

"Because we weren't," Tam began. "We couldn't..."

"It would not have been proper for Wolfgang Collins to see us," Flea said. "Preparations had to be made before we could hope to get it back."

Genuinely intrigued, Kyle said, "Like what?"

"Well, we had to learn the language, for one, and work jobs to earn us a living here. And before that, we had to synthesize organic exoskeletons so we could...oh, never mind. Will you take the job, or not?"

"Just one more thing," Kyle said. "I'll only take the job if you answer one question. What is the thing they took? What's it called?"

Tam swallowed and looked him right in the eye. "It's an egg. Please tell us you'll take the job. We've waited so long to try to get it back."

Wondering what in the world might be born of an egg looking like that, Kyle said, "What if it's hatched already?"

She laughed. "Oh, it won't have done that yet. It was newly-laid when we lost it, and it takes forty-two Earth years for that to happen."

"When did Wolfgang take the egg?"

"Let's see...it was when the Hunter Stars lined up with your Neptune, and the Great Nebula sang...which makes twenty-seven.

That's right! Wolfgang Collins took our egg twenty-seven years ago, and we're finally ready to get it back."

Kyle didn't know what to think, or what to say. He stared at Tam and Flea, who stared right back at him in eager anticipation, like bright-eyed children waiting for their parents to tell them it was okay to go eat their ice cream.

"You don't even look twenty-seven," he finally managed to say. He flicked his gaze discreetly to the upper corners of the room in search of cameras but saw none.

"Of course we don't look twenty-seven!" Tam let out that high-pitched laugh again. "Using your time scale, Flea and I are over eight thousand—"

"Never mind about that," Flea butted in. "Kyle Burton, will you help us?"

Oh, boy. If Kyle said yes, he'd look like a complete dunce on whatever half-assed reality show he'd apparently walked into. If he said no, he'd be out thousands of dollars.

"I'll do it," Kyle said. "If you pay me twenty thousand, not ten."

Two brows furrowed in deep thought. "Excuse us one moment," Flea said, and stepped off to one side with Tam. They put their heads together and started murmuring amongst themselves. Kyle strained to hear, but the only syllables he could make out belonged to a language unknown to him.

The couple turned back to him. "We agree to your terms," Tam said, straightening her shoulders. "Bring our egg back unharmed, and the money will be yours."

"That's it? I don't have to sign a contract, or anything?"

"Your word is contract enough for us. Now go, so our egg may be reunited with its siblings. We have been waiting too long for this."

"Okay, yeah, sure. I'll get on it. Wish me luck, I guess."

"Good luck."

The couple smiled.

Kyle rolled his eyes at himself when he made it back to the campus dormitories. He hoped he hadn't looked too stupid on whatever cameras the couple had concealed from him. This one could go down in the history books—Kyle Burton, reality TV star! Professor Collins was probably in on it too, since his name had been brought up.

He would have to play things super cool when he went to talk to the man.

"Thanks for letting me come see you, sir," Kyle said on Monday afternoon. Professor Collins's office was haphazardly arranged; books jammed onto shelves every which way and replica artifacts from myriad cultures hung from the ceiling and walls like exhibits in a museum.

None of the artifacts looked like a ball of rubber bands.

"Anytime," Professor Collins said, his grin evident behind his short, salt-and-pepper beard. "I always make time for curious students. Has this semester been going well for you?"

"It's okay, but not as fun as last semester since I'm not taking any of your classes." Kyle tried very hard not to smile. He was probably being filmed even now and needed to look good for it.

Professor Collins's cheeks turned crimson. "That's kind of you to say. You were a pleasure to have in class. You're majoring in history, yes?"

"That's right," Kyle said, "but that's not why I'm here."

"What was it you needed to talk about?"

Kyle cleared his throat and made sure his head was held high enough for any cameras to get a decent view of his face. "I just heard of a mysterious artifact that nobody can explain."

Professor Collins raised bushy, gray eyebrows. "Do you have a picture of it?"

"Sorry, I don't. It's supposed to look like a ball of rubber bands, about this big." Kyle used his hands to demonstrate the size. "Apparently it can grant the owner with special powers. It's just a legend, of course." Kyle felt proud of himself for thinking up that last bit.

The professor's eyebrows shot up even further. "Is that so?"

"That's what I heard. But you have to have owned it for twenty-seven years before the special powers kick in."

"Fascinating." Professor Collins leaned forward ever so slightly. "Tell me—which culture is this artifact said to be associated with?"

"Nobody knows, but it's said to have been originally discovered right here in this town, but the people who found it originally lost it and never saw it again. I wondered if you'd heard anything about it."

The professor shook his head almost distractedly. "No, I can't say I have. Are you sure someone wasn't pulling your leg?"

I know someone was pulling my leg, Kyle thought, but he said, "I don't think they were. So, if you don't know anything about it, where should I look?"

"Oh, the library. Definitely the library. There isn't much that books can't tell you. Now is there anything else I can help you with today?"

"No, sir, I think that's it."

Kyle had thought long and hard about how he would proceed after his meeting with Professor Collins. The professor was in on everything, but Kyle had to be able to get the "egg" from him without making it look like Kyle knew the truth—the viewers of this prank show would be more entertained that way.

In the end, he chose to sit on the bench outside the Social Sciences building and pretended to work on assignments until Professor Collins emerged half an hour later, briefcase in hand.

"Have a great evening, Professor!" Kyle called after him.

"You as well, Mr. Burton!" Professor Collins strode past him toward the parking lot. Kyle watched until the man unlocked a white sedan before jamming everything into his backpack and making a mad dash toward the dorm parking lot, where Kyle kept his rattletrap car. He gunned it out onto the street and spotted the sedan waiting at a nearby light with its left blinker on.

Kyle eased into the lane behind the sedan. The chase was on.

Professor Collins's house turned out to be a tiny, yellow-brick ranch with an attached garage. A rusting pickup truck sat on four flat tires beside the somewhat newer Corolla that the man had just driven home from the university.

Kyle drove past the house and parked around the corner on another street, then got out and speed-walked back to the professor's house.

He'd pulled up his hood for dramatic effect. The viewers would love that.

When he reached Professor Collins's property, Kyle checked all around to make sure no neighbors were watching him, then crept into the yard and went around to the back of the house, where a light conveniently glowed in a window.

Kyle hunkered down into a crouch and peered carefully over the sill into the house. Sheer drapes fell past the window, and through the narrow gap between them, Kyle caught sight of a dresser and bed.

While he watched, Professor Collins slid open a closet door and withdrew a box from the top shelf. Sitting atop the rumpled bedclothes, the man pried off the lid and removed a softball-sized sphere that looked so remarkably like a rubber band ball that Kyle had a hard time not bursting into peals of laughter. Whoever had set Kyle up for this whole thing had gotten him good. It was probably Paulo, the little punk.

Professor Collins shook the rubber band ball and held it to his ear. Kyle stifled another giggle. Who would have guessed that his archaeology professor from last semester would be such a skilled actor?

The man shook the ball again. Sniffed it. Breathed on it. Okay, now this was getting creepy.

Kyle huffed an impatient sigh. Part of him just wanted to get this over with by knocking on the man's door and asking him to please just hand over the "egg" so he could claim the $20,000 and get on with his life. Yet it was fun, in a sense, playing along like this. He could step back a moment and pretend he was someone else; a brave hero who would stop at nothing to rescue an innocent egg from the vile fiend who had taken it from its—parents? Guardians? Whoever.

Well, maybe not a hero, exactly. Heroes didn't get paid.

Inside the bedroom, Professor Collins set the object back into the box, but instead of replacing the lid and returning it to the closet, he set it on his bedside table and rubbed his eyes.

Then he rose and walked out of the room, dousing the light.

Kyle's stomach let out a whine—he hadn't eaten his supper. Why hadn't he thought to bring a snack with him? Oh well. He could snack to his heart's content after he'd brought the egg to Tam and Flea.

He wondered what their real, non-reality-show names were.

Fifteen minutes ticked by with agonizing slowness. The professor was probably making dinner for himself right now. This might be Kyle's chance!

He placed his palms against the man's bedroom window, hoping he'd been thoughtful enough to leave it unlatched. He shoved upward, and his heart gave a little leap when it slid up a mere centimeter or two. Sticking his fingers into the gap, he forced the window the rest of the way open and clambered somewhat gracelessly into the bedroom.

Amazing, how there hadn't even been a screen over the window. One would almost think Kyle's entry by that route had been planned for.

Kyle gave himself a few minutes for his eyes to adjust to the shadowy room. A faint glow from beyond the partially-closed bedroom door didn't do much for illumination. Dim forms slowly came into view— the rectangular shadow of a desk, the larger outline of the bed.

He tiptoed around the side of the bed and patted around on the bedside table for the box. Once he located it, he stuck his hand in and closed his fingers around the egg.

Some sort of energy emanated from it, like static electricity, but yet again completely different. He let out a gasp and jerked his hand back before cautiously putting it in again. He withdrew the egg and held it carefully in both hands.

Kyle couldn't quite see it in these shadows, but he could feel it thrumming, pulsing, almost as if it were alive.

At once, a crystal-clear scene took shape in his mind: *a much-younger Professor Collins goes for an evening stroll and spies a strange, round object on the ground. Curious, he stoops to pick it up and gasps when the seemingly inanimate ball hums with life.*

He can't just leave such an extraordinary thing behind. He must take it home to nurture and see what it will do. And when the long years pass and nothing happens, he resigns it to a box in his closet, all but forgotten until a student starts asking him about it.

But that's just a story, nagged a voice in some corner of Kyle's brain. *It's all made up for whatever reality show I've accidentally gotten involved in.*

And yet...and yet...

Kyle shook his head. He needed to hurry and get out of here.

He started back toward the open window and stubbed his shoe hard on one of the bedposts. Before he could even register it, footsteps thudded up the hallway, and Professor Collins flicked the bedroom light on.

He was holding a table knife coated with butter. Some weapon.

"What are you doing?" he demanded, his gaze moving from Kyle to the egg.

Kyle rolled his eyes. "I'm finishing the game, and you know it."

"What game? I'm calling the police."

A flicker of irrational fear flashed through Kyle's veins. "No, you're not."

"I'm not?"

"No, because this is all part of the show. I'm not stupid. I know you,

Tam, and Flea are all in on this. You guys made up the story about the egg and wanted to see if anyone at school would be gullible enough to fall for it."

Professor Collins blinked twice. Man, he was a good actor. It really seemed like he didn't have a clue.

"That's an egg?" the professor asked.

"That's what they tell me. It doesn't really have special powers. I just made that up. Now you're going to let me take this back to Tam and Flea so I can collect my prize money."

"I don't have any idea what you're talking about!" Professor Collins blurted. "I found that thing on the ground in Washington Park decades ago. It was strange enough, I had to keep it. Anyone would have!"

"That's what you're supposed to tell me, but I know it's not true. It's all made up."

"But I was there!"

"You're supposed to say that, too! Now are you going to let me leave with this thing, or are we going to just keep standing here pretending to argue?"

Muscles flexed in the professor's jaw, though it took him a moment to speak. "You're honest-to-God insane."

"Maybe, but I'm leaving now, okay? Bye." Instead of trying to scramble back out the window, Kyle strode past the seemingly bewildered professor into the hallway and left through the front door, egg in hand.

·· ✦ ✳ ✴ ✳ ✦ ··

Kyle rapped on the door of 798 East Walnut Street. Tam opened it, her expression guarded. "Did you retrieve the egg?" she asked in a sort of half-whisper.

Kyle brought his other hand out from behind his back and presented it to her. "Ta-da! Now do I get my money?"

Tam's eyes brimmed with sudden tears as she reached out a trembling hand and picked up the thrumming, rubbery object. "Yes, yes! Please come back inside!"

She led him back into the living area, where Flea was baby-talking to a basket full of rubber band balls of varying colors. He straightened when they entered and ran to Tam the moment he laid eyes on the "egg" that had been in Professor Collins's possession.

"Oh, you did it!" Flea cried. "You really did it! Oh, it's been so long...we would have tried to get it ourselves, but entering the home of another without permission is not in our ways. The repercussions we'd have faced if caught..." He shuddered. "Let me get you your reward!"

He took the metal box of cash out of the filing cabinet again and thrust it into Kyle's hands. "Here, just keep all of it. We won't be needing it now that our family is intact again."

Kyle was sure his eyes were bugging out of his head. "How much is in here all together?"

"Let me think...about fifty thousand? I hope it's enough for all your trouble."

Kyle's heart stuttered. "It's enough."

·· ✦ ✳ ✴ ✳ ✦ ··

Over the next several months, Kyle searched the internet for any mentions of the crazy reality show he'd taken part in but couldn't find anything. He supposed the studio must have canceled it before it ever went on air. It was really a shame. He wondered how he'd looked on all those hidden cameras.

Still, the prize money was nice, and ought to cover his expenses for a while. Or he could go out and buy himself a better car, or some new blazers, or something. He hadn't made up his mind yet.

Fifteen years later, when college lay far behind him and life had turned into an endless cycle of paychecks and bills, Kyle retrieved a stack of mail from the mailbox. Junk mail, more junk mail—what was this?

He frowned at a lavender-colored envelope that had been made out to KYLE BURRTON but had no return address, mailing address, or postage on it. Tearing it open before he went back into the house, he withdrew a lavender sheet of paper and read:

Dearest Kyle Burrton—

We thought you should know that the egg you rescued for us, as well as all the others, has finally hatched. All babies are happy and healthy! We have four boys and four girls. The egg you saved turned out to be a girl. We named her after you!

As you may have guessed, we returned home not long after we were reunited with baby Kyle's egg. Our friends and families missed us, and we were tired of looking at your same blue sky day after day. No offense, but do you know how boring a blue sky is?

We passed by the Great Nebula again on our way to drop off this note. We've enclosed a picture of it and one of our baby Kyle. We thought you would appreciate that!

Anyway, have a fabulous day!

Sincerely, Tamalarynda and Flearizor

His skin prickling, Kyle reached back into the envelope and pulled out the two photographs.

The first showed an amazing pinkish cloud floating in space surrounded by glimmering stars; a beautiful sight even for someone not that interested in astronomy.

Kyle gaped at the second picture, which showed...dear God, what the hell was that thing? The lovechild of Cthulhu and a supermarket lobster? The photograph didn't look faked, and yet...

He turned his head up toward the sky and caught a glimpse of something shiny and spherical hovering perhaps two thousand feet above him, shrinking gradually as it dwindled into the upper distance.

He looked back down at the tentacled, chitinous thing in the photograph, swallowed the fearful knot that had formed in his throat, and hurried back into the house.

THE FAMILY
NAME

THE FAMILY NAME WAS ROSEWOOD, and it was good.

Edwin Rosewood had inherited it from his father, Corbin, and Corbin inherited from his father before him, and so on, all the way back through history until its origins were lost beneath the weight of the ages.

Edwin shared that fine surname with his younger brothers, Byron, Sherman, and Nathan. The four brothers were proud, and if ever for a minute they forgot that pride, their father would invite the four of them into his vast study to remind them of it, while their mother and sister busied themselves elsewhere doing Edwin knew not what.

"Your teacher tells me some troubling news, Byron," Corbin said one Saturday afternoon while pacing back and forth in front of the tall rows of bookcases along the study's north wall, his hands clasped firmly behind his back. He wore a tailored gray suit with a black necktie—Edwin rarely saw him in anything else.

The four boys stood in a row. Byron stared at the floor, unable to meet their father's gaze. Not wanting to appear weak like his brother, Edwin watched Corbin with his back straight, not daring to blink.

When Byron said nothing, Corbin went on. "I hear that you complained to a classmate that your last name sounds too much like a flower, and you wish you could change it."

"But 'rose' is a flower," Byron said, barely louder than a whisper. "Flowers are stupid."

Corbin stopped pacing. He bored into the younger boy with his gray-eyed gaze and said, "For generations, the Rosewood name has garnered respect. Our family has produced senators, CEOs, and judges. *Nothing* about our noble name is stupid." Corbin paused. "As punishment, you will write me an essay on why a family's name is a vital part of its legacy and turn it in to me by the end of the day today, or there's no entertainment for the rest of the week. Do I make myself clear?"

"Yes, sir," Byron sniffled.

"Look at me and say it again."

Byron seemed to strain to lift his gaze. Edwin bit down on a laugh. At eleven, Byron was just a year younger than him, but with as upset as he looked right now, he might have been a little baby.

Byron wavered on his feet. "Yes, sir."

"Good." Corbin clapped his hands together. "The rest of you take warning. I might not be as generous if I hear of this happening again."

The group disbanded, and Edwin went up to his room to work on some of the assignments his teacher had given him the previous day.

He would never disrespect the Rosewood name.

He would make his father proud.

On Monday morning, Edwin walked three blocks to Madison

Academy, the private school he'd attended since he was in kindergarten. In his freshly-pressed uniform shirt, blazer, and slacks, he made his way to his classroom on the second floor and took a seat next to his friend Alonzo Garcia, another fine young man with a fine family name.

Alonzo rested his head on his hands and glared at the top of his desk.

"What's the matter with you?" Edwin asked. Class had not yet begun, so he and the other students were permitted to speak freely.

Alonzo sighed. "My dad gave me the talk last night."

"Which talk?"

"The one about having to find a good wife so I can have good sons to carry on the family name." He completed the sentence with a dramatic eye roll.

"What's so bad about that?"

Alonzo looked at him as if he had lost his mind. "Look around the room, will you? The only girls I know are Lilly and Sue, and I don't even like them."

The two girls in the class of twenty-four students sat together in the back. Edwin glanced back just in time to see them throwing Alonzo dirty looks.

"There's other girls," Edwin said, lowering his voice to a whisper.

"Where?"

"There's Tonya in the seventh grade."

"And Tori and Cathy in the fifth. No thanks."

Just then, Mr. Watson, the teacher, called the classroom to order, and Edwin forgot about Alonzo's problem until recess, when he regrouped with Alonzo outside by the soccer field.

"You still look awful mad," Edwin said.

"I am mad." Alonzo plopped in the grass as some younger boys kicked a ball past him. "I mean, if there were girls I liked, maybe I wouldn't be. But I don't know if I even *like* girls."

"My dad would say that's scandalous." Edwin thought of the time his father wouldn't stop ranting about a colleague who'd been caught having an intimate moment with a male coworker during their lunch break. Corbin's face had been redder than a beet as he paced his office, informing his sons that if they ever so much *thought* about doing such a thing, he'd beat them so hard they wouldn't know what hit them.

"Dads can be the worst."

"Not my dad. I want to be just like him someday."

Alonzo made a face, and the two were silent for a minute.

"There's always my sister," Edwin said.

"Isn't she only seven?"

"That's only five years different from you. My dad is twelve years older than my mom. He said he really liked both the girls in his class, but his two best friends got to them first."

"Ugh." Alonzo yanked a piece of grass out of the ground and tore it to shreds. "Who would you marry?"

Edwin cast his gaze across the soccer field. The dozen girls who attended their school huddled on benches on the other side, talking and laughing while the countless boys raced up and down the field trying to get the ball into the goals. "I kind of like Lilly," he said as he watched the girl whisper something in Sue's ear.

"Why?" Alonzo asked, aghast.

"She's pretty."

"She's nasty. I saw her picking her nose and wiping it under her desk."

Edwin shrugged. "She works hard, and is stronger than the other girls. I think she'd make a good wife."

"It's a shame there aren't more girls to choose from."

Edwin laughed. "Why would there need to be more girls?"

"Tell me how many people are in our school."

"Two hundred, maybe?" As Edwin said this, he looked back to the girls on the benches. The twelve would grow up to make fine wives for twelve lucky men, and each would bear her husband as many sons as he asked for. That's what Edwin's mother had done. She'd even thought that Edwin's little sister was going to be a boy until she was born—apparently there had been some error on the sonogram that created the confusion.

"Two hundred students," Alonzo said. "And I don't like any of the girls here."

"There's other schools."

"My cousin goes to Wallace High. He says there's a *thousand* students, and only twenty girls. He thought about asking another boy out on a date just because he's so lonely."

Edwin laughed. "But you can't have sons with another man. That's silly."

"I know. The only point of getting married at all is to 'carry on the family name.' That's what my dad says."

"Mine too," Edwin said.

"Same here," said their classmate Alexander, plopping into the grass beside them. "My dad says I have to work hard to make another generation of Ellises." He lowered his voice to a whisper. "And Lilly's going to be mine, so you back off."

Angered, Edwin leapt to his feet. "But Lilly's the only one I like. You can't have her."

"Want to bet?" Alexander rose with the abruptness he'd arrived, strode around the edge of the soccer field, and went right up to Lilly and started talking to her. Edwin couldn't tell what he said at that distance, but it made him angry to see Lilly laugh.

After struggling to get comfortable beneath his blankets that night, Edwin fell into a troubled sleep, where he dreamed he arrived at school only to find that half his classmates were girls. Deeply uncomfortable by the fact there were so many people in the room who could not carry on their family name, Edwin rushed out of the room to the next one down the hallway and discovered the same: the fifth grade class consisted of twelve boys and twelve girls.

He checked each classroom in the entire school. In all, there were a hundred girls—enough for every boy to marry.

Edwin woke in a cold sweat and tried to process the nightmare. It would destroy the fabric of society, having so few men to carry on the family name. Why, the Rosewoods might die out in a few generations if that were the case—they would still have descendants, but they would be carrying on someone else's family name, not the proud name of Edwin's ancestors.

Shaking and wondering what his father would say if Edwin ever told him about the nightmare version of reality he'd imagined in his sleep, he rose and made his way toward the kitchen to get a glass of water.

Along the way, he passed his parent's bedroom, the door of which sat ajar an inch or two.

From inside, Edwin could hear the faint sound of crying.

Against his better judgment, he leaned in close and listened.

"For God's sake, Caroline, you act like you haven't done it before," his father growled. "Why don't you get over yourself and make the goddamn appointment?"

"Three times," Edwin's mother whimpered. "Three times you've made me do this already. I don't think I can do it again."

"It's not even alive yet. What does it matter?"

"I can feel her kicking me. Here, feel it yourself."

There came a brief pause. "You're bloated from dinner, that's all," Corbin said. "If you don't make the appointment tomorrow, I'll make it for you."

"Corbin, please…"

"There is no way I'm mucking up my bloodlines with another *girl*. It was bad enough when Elizabeth came out all wrong. God, can you imagine what imbecile might marry her someday? I want my grandsons to be Rosewoods, not Smiths or Garcias. I should have smothered her with a pillow before we left the hospital to spare me the future humiliation."

Edwin frowned as his mother made a retching sound.

He stepped away from the door and tiptoed the rest of the way into the kitchen to get his drink.

LARRY

IT ISN'T ALWAYS EASY HAVING an imaginary friend.

Since I live alone, I consider Larry an otherworldly roommate. He gives advice, comments on the weather, and tidies whenever he's in the mood for it. Honestly, he'd make the perfect boyfriend, if I was into guys who wore white togas and pink bunny slippers every single day of the year.

I may call Larry imaginary, but he's as real as I am. I know I'm not crazy, either. My mother had me tested after I used a blowtorch to cut a hole in the living room wall at the age of ten, but I'd really just been trying to open up a portal to a parallel universe. The doctors told her I was "precocious," but sane.

My theories about Larry's origins abound. One I've narrowed it down to is that Larry must be some sort of angel, or he came from that parallel universe I tried to find when I was ten. If angels exist—and they must, for Larry is here, isn't he?—then they hail from a higher dimension than we do. For whatever reason, Larry has descended into our mere three-dimensional space to befriend me. Or annoy me, or whatever. All I know is he's here now, only I can see him, and if he hadn't come here, I'd be dead.

Larry didn't enter my life when I was a child, as you'd think would be typical. My mother says I had an imaginary friend named Biff until the age of three. Biff, I'm told, was a purple narwhal with blue eyes and a rainbow horn that glowed in the dark.

I don't remember Biff.

After Biff faded into childhood obscurity, I grew up, started college, dropped out once I realized I was a danger to myself and everybody else in the science building, and got a job as a delivery driver for MeeMaw's Pizza. I mostly delivered to kids on the campus, trying not to envy their perfect little lives as they studied to be the next Marie Curie or Nikola Tesla, or whoever. *They* probably never started a four-alarm fire in the first-floor chemistry lab, but I digress.

One night, I trudged out the back of MeeMaw's Pizza with an armful of pizza boxes, my feet aching and my stomach growling from the majestic aromas wafting from my cargo. I unlocked my old beater Toyota, set the boxes in their insulated case on the passenger seat, and started the engine.

"I wouldn't go to the dorms on Henshaw Street tonight, if I were you," said a voice.

I peed a little. I'm not even kidding. Sitting in the passenger seat where I'd just set tonight's deliveries was a man in a toga. Muscles bulged in his arms, and he had faintly Mediterranean features but had spoken with an English accent. Somehow, he was sitting *in* the space that the pizza occupied, as if he had no substance to his body.

I yanked my keys out of the ignition and unleashed my pepper spray keychain right into his face. The spray passed through him and misted harmlessly against the inside of the passenger window.

He blinked a few times and smiled, undeterred by the assault. Coughing and hacking, I fumbled for the door handle and found it locked.

I knew then I was going to die. I'm five-foot two and weigh about a hundred and ten pounds. This guy could have made mincemeat out of me and not even broken a sweat.

"What do you want?" I asked, trying to sound tougher than I was, which was hard to do when my throat rasped from the lingering spray in the air. I wanted to cry, to scream, to run, but he'd done something to my locks, and I couldn't get out.

"I want you to not go to the dorms on Henshaw Street tonight," he said again, politely. "It just isn't a good idea right now."

I gestured vaguely at the pizza he was sitting in. "You do realize that's where all of this is headed, right? If I don't deliver, I'll lose my job."

"You'll lose a lot more than that if you go to Henshaw Street." The man stuck out his hand. "I'm Larry, by the way. It's nice to meet you."

I just stared at him. It didn't look like he'd stashed any weapons inside his toga, but I wasn't about to go sticking my hand into his. There was a *man* in a *toga* inside my car, sitting in my pizza boxes like they didn't even share the same dimensional plane. I spotted the bunny slippers then, and started to cry.

"What's the matter?" Larry asked, sounding full of genuine concern. "Nothing bad has happened to you yet."

But the tears streamed from my face unchecked. "I...I...Jeremy Wickert does LSD between shifts. He must have slipped some to me, I got high, and now I'm screwed."

A crease appeared between Larry's dark eyebrows. "Why would he do that?"

"How the hell should I know? It's the only explanation for…for this." I dragged in a breath. The weird thing was, I'd been high before, and right now I felt totally lucid.

I tried my door again and still couldn't get out. Gritting my teeth, I turned back to Larry the Toga Guy and said, "If you don't want me to make my delivery, will you at least let me get out of the car?"

His expression grew somber. "I just want to you understand the gravity of the situation. I've been sent to warn you, and I want you to know I'm serious."

"Sent by who? What are you warning me about?"

"I haven't been told the specifics, but your mother has been very worried about you, so I came to help."

"You know my *mother*? She sent you to stop me from making my delivery?"

"I have never met your mother. Please, Molly, this is for your own good."

The sound of my own name sent chills down my spine. I almost asked him how he knew it, but he could have just gotten it from one of my coworkers inside. Or, you know, he could have just been a figment of the potential LSD.

"Keeping my job is for my own good," I said, then stabbed my key back into the ignition and turned it.

The engine wouldn't turn over.

I tried the door handle a third time. Still locked. "Let me out of my car!" I cried, balling my hands into fists.

Larry glanced to the ceiling and nodded his head in rhythm as if counting off silent beats. Twenty seconds later, he said, "Very well. You may get out."

I shoved the car door open without any trouble. I looked over to Larry, only to find he'd disappeared. Heck, I thought, he'd probably never even been there.

I went to start the engine again. It refused to do anything cars were supposed to do, so I pretended I wasn't having a psychotic breakdown and plucked the insulated carrying case full of pizza off the passenger seat.

If I couldn't drive to the dorms on Henshaw Street, I could walk there instead and keep my job.

The thought that I could have borrowed a coworker's car didn't even cross my mind—luckily for me.

I was working up quite a sweat by the time I made it down the four blocks separating Henshaw Street from MeeMaw's Pizza. As I hung a right on the sidewalk and moved toward the crosswalk that would have brought me over to the dorms, I heard the bone-chilling sound of screaming.

I halted in my tracks and watched, dumbly, as a gaggle of freshmen spilled from the nearest dorm building—the one to which I was making my delivery. One of them clutched a bleeding arm, and the wail of approaching sirens filled the air. Law enforcement vehicles screeched to a stop at either end of the block to barricade it, and one officer urged me to get back before I got hurt.

Long story short, one of the freshmen girls flipped her lid studying for exams and went on a stabbing spree. Nobody died, but her actions sent four people to the hospital.

If my car had started just fine, I would have been there making the delivery right when it happened. I might not have been so lucky.

"Thanks, Larry," I whispered, and shivered.

I didn't see Larry for a while after that. At first I thought he was being shy, but then I thought maybe he wanted to give me a little space since I'd basically freaked out when I met him. See, I'd decided he had to be real. Turns out Jeremy Wickert, purveyor of LSD, had been fired unbeknownst to me two days earlier, so he and his drugs were off the hook.

Larry came back, out of the blue, a few weeks later. At the time, I was sharing a crappy ground-floor apartment with two other dropouts from the university, Greg and Amy, both of whom had been off at their respective crappy jobs during Larry's appearance.

I was lounging in the recliner with a can of Red Bull and one of my old chemistry books, leafing through the tattered and slightly-scorched pages, when an English-accented voice said, "Pleasant day, isn't it, Molly?"

I spluttered on my energy drink for a second or two. Larry, replete with toga and bunny slippers, stood at the living room window, peering out at the scenic parking lot view with his hands clasped behind him.

"You saved my life," I choked once I could breathe halfway properly again.

He turned and smiled. "Yes."

"Well, um, thanks." I sat up straighter, feeling my blood run cold. "What's going to happen to me now?"

Larry tilted his head slightly to one side. "What do you mean?"

"You showed up in my car and stopped me from getting stabbed at the dorms. Why are you here now? Is our roof about to fall in?" I glanced up warily at the ceiling.

"Oh, no, it's nothing like that at all. It's just that…" He waved his arms to indicate the room, which had been decorated in the Lazy American Twentysomething style, consisting of numerous empty bottles, cans, wrappers, and mounds of unwashed laundry none of us had taken down to the onsite laundromat yet.

I narrowed my eyes. "It's just that what?"

"You need help, Molly. Your mother is very worried about you."

"You said that before."

"It's true. You don't want her to worry, now, do you?"

"I guess not." I couldn't fathom what a messy apartment had to do with my mother's wellbeing, so I said, "What do you propose to do?"

"I can help you keep this place clean. Your roommates will appreciate it, making them less likely to throw you out."

I laughed. "They helped make the mess. Why should I take the blame for it?"

Larry just shrugged. Together, he and I gathered up the cans and bottles, washed them, and took them down to the recycling bins next to the dumpsters at the edge of the parking lot, and during the short time I wiped down the kitchen counters, Larry somehow managed to vacuum the floor, fluff the throw pillows, wash out the stains on the rug, and dust all hard surfaces.

When Greg and Amy filed into the apartment late that night, their mouths fell open in wonder.

"Hey, thanks for tidying, Molly!" Amy said, running a finger across the top of the end table and examining it for dust. "I guess we'll keep you around after all!"

It felt like worms wriggled beneath my skin as she uttered those words. "It wasn't just me," I said. "My imaginary friend helped. It was his idea."

"Good for him," Greg said. "It's about time you did your part around here."

He winked, but I said, "Meaning what, exactly?"

My roommates exchanged a glance, suddenly appearing uncomfortable. "Nothing," Greg said quickly. "It's just that we work a whole lot more than you do, and, well, never mind."

I could hear the words behind his words, though they hadn't been spoken. Greg and Amy thought I was useless, and had probably discussed ditching me for a more helpful roommate. Or they'd wanted to get rid of me and turn the apartment into their little love nest, and changed their minds once they'd realized I could be their sort-of live-in maid.

Thanks again, Larry. Now I know how people see me.

On one of my days off from MeeMaw's Pizza, Larry appeared on the other side of the kitchen table as I was sipping my morning coffee and working my way through a book of sudoku puzzles my mother had given me for a recent birthday. I jumped only a little this time when I realized I wasn't alone.

"Hi," I said, feeling more at ease in his presence than on the first two occasions. He'd already proven his use, and I figured that my fortunes were about to improve once again under his influence.

He dipped his head in acknowledgment. "Hello."

I laid my puzzle book down and regarded him. "So, what is it this time?"

His mouth quirked into a smile. "Does it have to be anything?"

"You haven't hung out with me just for kicks yet. That means you're here for something again."

"Ah. Well, yes."

I tensed, waiting for the big reveal.

"You would be well-advised," Larry said, "to quit your job at MeeMaw's Pizza."

"You're kidding me. I've been making good tip money these past few weeks!"

"Don't even go in for your next shift. Call them today and tell them you quit, no questions asked. It's for your own good."

"You realize that if I bail on my job, Greg and Amy are going to put me out on the street."

"How is your mother doing, Molly?"

Jarred by the change in subject, I said, "She's doing great. She's glad I'm finally able to put extra money away from my tips—which I won't have anymore if I quit."

Larry gave me a look that in time I came to know as The Look.

I thought about his warning not to deliver to Henshaw Street, and his serendipitous apartment cleanup.

Hating myself for it, I said, "Okay. I'll call and tell them I'm quitting. I just hope you know what you're doing."

Larry smiled in an air of forced innocence.

So, I called them. My astonished boss offered to bump up my pay, to give me more hours if that's what I needed, and it took every fiber of my will to refuse.

That night when Amy came home from her new, neat little office job, she said they were hiring for a secretarial position that paid double what I'd been making at MeeMaw's Pizza, and would I be interested in applying for it?

Later that night, MeeMaw's Pizza caught fire and burned to the ground. Arson had been ruled out; it was an old building, and the wiring had finally called it quits. It would take them months to rebuild.

Thank you a third time, Larry.

So, that's how it's been. Larry pops into my life, he dishes out sage advice, my life improves as a result of it. I saved up enough money from my new job to get myself a condo, and I live alone, save for when Larry visits, which is often. He doesn't always come with portents of disaster; sometimes he just comes to hang out and talk, take out the recycling, and listen to the opera station on the satellite radio, though he's never very open about himself or where he came from. Maybe it's part of the imaginary friend code, not being allowed to tell.

I learned that only I can see Larry, which is disappointing. He showed up once when my mother was visiting and stood in the corner beaming the entire time while Mom and I chatted and laughed over bowls of Indian carryout.

"I'm so happy you've been able to turn your life around these past few years," Mom said to me one day while we were out shopping. "I was so worried about you when you blew up the chemistry lab and got thrown out of the program—"

"Dropped out," I said hastily. "I dropped out."

"Whatever you want to call it. I was worried sick you'd never amount to anything, and here you are, with your own place and everything."

"You can thank my imaginary friend for it," I said. "His name is Larry, and he wears a toga and bunny slippers."

My mother threw her head back and laughed—a magical sound that made me smile. "With an imagination like yours, you ought to start writing books!"

"And take away all the credit from Larry?" I grinned at her, and she grinned back, and I thought that my life had ended up being pretty much perfect.

I've been thinking, though. If my mother was so worried about me, did she herself conjure Larry into my life? Did her worry call down a higher being to guide me, or did her worry manifest itself into some quantum construct to do the same?

Either way—thank you, Mom.

It was the darnedest thing, though. Once we'd left the mall and crossed the parking lot back toward the car, I caught sight of something colorful in my peripheral vision.

When I turned, I spotted Larry standing in an empty parking spot between a minivan and a Kia Soul. Next to him stood a purple narwhal with blue eyes and a rainbow horn, and both of them were smiling.

THIRTEEN

1993

THE BAR

8:05 PM

IT WASN'T OFTEN THAT MARSHA Marquez had to travel alone, but when she did, she gravitated to the nearest bar each evening so she wouldn't feel the crushing weight of solitude, knowing that her closest friends were hundreds of miles away and unable to chat unless she spent half her travel money at the hotel payphone.

Besides, Hotel Stormcove's two payphones were both currently out of order. "The phone company's sending someone out next week," the yawning front desk clerk had said after tearing her gaze away from a tattered word-find book. It seemed a godawful inconvenience for the guests, but what would complaining do?

Marsha sat at the polished wood counter in the hotel's on-site bar, gazing at the myriad glimmering bottles on display behind it while she nursed a whiskey sour. A single television off in the corner played some sporting event that had gotten a few of the bar's patrons riled up, and she was starting to wish that her whiskey sour had the magical ability to drown out their noise.

At least this place had its own bar, unlike some of the sleazier motels she'd stayed at during her business-related travels. It saved her from having to trudge in high heels through the rain that had been drenching the coast all day.

She twitched as a man sidled up to the counter and took the stool right next to hers. She discreetly scooted her stool a few inches in the other direction to allow herself some space.

"I'll have a Manhattan, please," the man said to the bartender.

The newcomer had graying hair and wore a deep blue business suit that looked more expensive than Marsha's entire wardrobe. The pretentious sort, it seemed, if she were to judge from the tailored shape of the suit, his gold cufflinks, and callus-free hands. He was probably fifteen years older than she was, maybe twenty, but still handsome in a movie star sort of way, which of course added to the whole ensemble.

As the bartender began to assemble the man's beverage, Marsha said, "You just get in?"

Mr. Pretentious turned toward her and gave her a smile that was actually kind of friendly. "I checked in this afternoon," he said, looking surprised that she'd spoken to him. "Let me tell you, I've never been happier to get off a plane."

"Rough flight?"

"There were screaming kids *everywhere*. What about you?"

Marsha took a sip of her whiskey sour. "I've been here four days. I drove in from Cincinnati for the big trade show. My boss is paying for all of it." She glanced at her drink. "Well, not this."

The man laughed and held out a hand. "I'm Everett, by the way."

She gave his hand a hearty shake. "Marsha Marquez. I hope you got a better room than I did. The brochures brag about the amazing cove views, but all my room has is a breathtaking view of the dumpsters out back."

"Oh, that's too bad. From my room, I can see all the way out to the ocean."

"Which room is that?"

"1310."

"You're kidding."

He raised his eyebrows. "Why would I kid?"

"There *is* no thirteenth floor in this building. They did it for superstitious people who freak out about that kind of thing, so it goes from Floor 12 straight to Floor 14. I know, because my room is on the fourteenth floor, and I see the discrepancy every time I go up the stairs."

"You don't take the elevator?"

"I have a desk job. I take my exercise however I can."

"If you don't believe me about the number, it's on my room key." He fished in his jacket pocket and withdrew a key which, true to his word, dangled from a keychain bearing the aforementioned number. "Why would anyone be afraid of the number thirteen?"

"Why do they think breaking a mirror gives you seven years of bad luck?"

Everett gave her a blank stare.

"You haven't heard of that one, either?" This guy must have grown up under a pretentious rock.

"Perhaps it's a regional thing?" He sipped at the Manhattan the bartender passed to him. "You said you're from Cincinnati."

"It's more than just Cincinnati that thinks thirteen is unlucky. I've been to hotels all over the country, and very few of the tall ones have a thirteenth floor."

"They go from 12 to 14, you mean."

"That's right."

"Fascinating." Everett's eyes went out of focus as he took another drink. "You know, I've always heard that six is an unlucky number. There isn't a sixth-floor button in the elevator here, and fear of the number six is why hardly anyone schedules weddings for June."

That made Marsha cross her arms. "Is making up facts for the sake of argument some new way of picking up women? Loads of people get married in June. I work for a wedding planner; I'm in town for the big bridal expo."

A crease appeared in Everett's forehead. "I'm not trying to come on to you. I'm genuinely curious as to why you think thirteen is some omen of bad luck, and six is just a number, when for my entire life I've heard just the opposite."

"Six *is* just a number." Marsha looked to the bartender, who was meticulously straightening the bottles on the shelf behind the counter. "Right?"

"I'm not superstitious, ma'am," the bartender said, looking up from his task. "If you ask me, all numbers are just numbers." He shrugged. "If you two can't figure out who's right and who's wrong, go find out. I'll keep an eye on your drinks."

"Shouldn't you know which numbers are in the elevator and stairwell?" Marsha asked. "You work here."

"Yes. In this bar, on the first floor. I've never even been in the elevator."

Marsha glanced at Everett. "All right. Let's go look at the numbers to see who's right. But if you try to touch me, I'll karate chop your ass into kingdom come."

"Fair enough," Everett said stiffly.

They exited the bar together. Marsha wondered if Everett had drunk so much already that common facts had gotten all jumbled up inside his head like the scattered pieces of a jigsaw puzzle.

But his keychain had "1310" printed on it.

So he'd brought his own keychain and put it on his room key.

But what would be the point?

They arrived at the bank of elevators. Marsha hit the call button, stepped back, and gave Everett a prideful look, knowing she would soon be proven right.

The nearest elevator dinged, and the doors slid open.

"After you," Marsha said, and Everett stepped inside.

She joined him, cautiously.

"See?" Everett said, pointing at the rows of buttons. "One, two, three, four, five, seven. And here's number thirteen."

Marsha gaped at the numbers, then shook her head as she realized the buttons in here had simply been mislabeled. She slapped the 12, and the doors slid shut. "All right," she said. "Now I'll show you the stairwell."

They glided smoothly up to the twelfth floor, stepped into the carpeted hallway, then moved to the door marked "Stairwell" and pushed their way through it. A large "12" was emblazoned on the wall just inside the door.

"I'm telling you I walk past this every day," Marsha said, moving toward the steps.

Everett followed her up one flight. Marsha drew up short as she spotted the large "13" on the wall where she knew darn well a "14" was supposed to be.

Everett's mouth formed a condescending smirk. "You were saying?"

She stared at the number in exasperation and floundered for words. "I—I don't believe this! Someone's repainted the number!" Marsha burst through the door into the corridor, fully intending to go directly to her room to prove they were actually on Floor 14, but she was distracted by the gleaming evening sunlight spilling through the window at the far end of the hallway. Her feet drew her forward until she reached the floor-to-ceiling glass. The sun hung low in the sky above the green hills farther inland, and not a single cloud dotted the azure heavens.

"Is there another problem?" Everett asked.

"It's been pouring all day today." She gestured at the sky. "This can't be right."

He glared at her. "It's been sunny since I got off the plane, but maybe I'm just *imagining things*. I'm going back down to my Manhattan."

With a huff, he boarded the elevator, and the doors whooshed shut. Marsha watched gulls swoop through the clear evening air for a few seconds before returning dazedly to the stairwell.

Inside, on the wall, the number 14 stood out, bold and clear as day.

She descended the steps, passed the number 12, and got off on that floor. Sheets of rain sluiced against the window at the end of the hallway, so strong it sounded like hail.

She called the elevator. The doors opened, and she stepped on. The button for Floor 6 sat right between the buttons for Floors 5 and 7, just like it was supposed to.

There was no button for Floor 13.

When Marsha made it back to the bar on the first floor, Everett wasn't there, nor was his half-consumed Manhattan. She picked up her whiskey sour, started to take a sip, then shook her head.

"Everything all right, ma'am?" the bartender asked.

She almost—*almost*—asked if he had seen Everett come back down here and finish his beverage, then decided against it, as she wasn't entirely sure she wanted to know.

"It's been a long day," Marsha said, shoving the glass away from her so hard that some of the remaining whiskey sour sloshed over the top onto the counter. "I'm going to bed."

INHERITANCE

THE FUNERAL HAD SEEMED TO last for years. Gretchen recalled it as a series of tragic snapshots: rows of mourners in their Sunday best sitting in polished wood church pews while Cousin Charlie performed the eulogy, a somber procession out to the cemetery damp with morning dew, the priest reciting prayers in his white vestments beside the grave.

Gretchen sat in the attic bedroom of her Aunt Rosita's house now, watching raindrops trickle down the panes of spotted glass. Why hadn't she come to visit more often these past few years? Grandma Sherry, her father's mother, had spoiled Gretchen with treats while growing up, and had taught her how to play both the piano and the violin. They'd shared secrets and private jokes, and never would again.

When Gretchen had gotten a new marketing job in Cleveland and moved away five years ago, Grandma Sherry had given her a bone-crushing squeeze and said, "You're going to have the best life, sweetie."

Gretchen had laughed and said, "Well, I certainly hope so!"

A knowing glint appeared in Grandma Sherry's green eyes. "I'm not wishing you the best life, Gretchen. I'm telling you you're going to have the best life. Trust me." She crossed her heart with one finger.

Tears ran freely down Gretchen's cheeks as she remembered the woman who'd meant so much to her. If only she could talk to her again…

Footsteps ascending the attic stairs drew her attention away from the window, and there came a soft knock at the door. "Gretchen? Can I come in?"

"Sure." Gretchen wiped her eyes on her sleeve, and her cousin Emily stepped into the room holding a cardboard box with the words "For Gretchen" printed on the side in violet permanent marker.

Violet had been Grandma Sherry's favorite color.

"Grandma wanted me to give this to you," Emily said, spitting a strand of copper hair out of her mouth since her hands were too preoccupied. "Where do you want me to put it?"

"On the bed is fine. What is it?"

Emily plopped the box down atop the old quilt. "I didn't look. Stuff she thought you'd like, I guess. I got one, too."

"What did you get?"

"A couple of rolling pins and some antique pie plates. I'm going to bake some dessert and eat myself sick in her memory."

Gretchen couldn't help but crack a smile. "I can help. I'm here for another week."

"Sounds like a plan. I can start ransacking Mom's kitchen for ingredients."

Emily started toward the door, but Gretchen said, "Wait. You can stay here while I open it."

"I'm going to cry again, aren't I?"

"Yep, but at least you won't be alone."

Gretchen sat down on the edge of the bed, and Emily did the same. Gretchen pried the cardboard flaps up and peered inside, smiling at the little snow globe she used to play with at her grandmother's house every Christmas. She picked it up, shook it, and watched the snow cascade over the tiny house inside of it. Then she set it aside and continued to dig through her inheritance.

Some things Gretchen recognized, like a rhinestone necklace and a book of poems. In the bottom of the box, however, lay a rectangular velvet case Gretchen couldn't remember seeing at her grandmother's house before.

"What's that?" Emily asked, leaning in for a closer look.

"I don't know." Gretchen flipped up the velvet lid to reveal a shiny blue pen lying inside of it, along with a folded note. The note had been written in Grandma Sherry's handwriting and said, "You'll understand someday."

"Why would she leave me a pen?" Gretchen asked. She picked the pen up. Since it was made of metal, it had a bit of weight to it, but it couldn't have been worth any great fortune. Was the pen supposed to mean something to her? Maybe it was meant to go to one of her other cousins, instead, like Charlie, who'd always dreamed of being a writer.

"You'll understand someday," Emily said in an ethereal tone, waggling her fingers. "Come on, let's go make some pie."

·· ✦ ✳ ✦ ✳ ✦ ··

The drive back to Cleveland was long and wet—it was storming again, and Gretchen started to wish she could hop on a plane and fly to some dry place full of sunshine and seagulls.

She wouldn't be happy in a place like that, though, because Grandma Sherry wouldn't be there to share it with her.

Could she ever be happy again?

After unpacking at her condo, Gretchen took the things from her grandmother and laid them out in a row on her coffee table, smiling at the memories they evoked—save for the pen, which meant nothing specific to her, since she'd never seen her grandmother use it.

She dug through her purse and found a crinkly notepad, then clicked the pen and scribbled some circles onto the first blank page.

The pen worked. She wondered how old it was.

Gretchen had never been much of a writer, but she remembered that Grandma Sherry had sent her a writing journal covered in metallic jellyfish and octopuses for one of her more recent birthdays. She located it in one of her desk drawers and took it and the pen to her couch, where she held the pen poised above a lined page. Gretchen thought for a few moments, and wrote.

I wish I could see you again, Grandma. I wish I could thank you for the things you gave me, too, but this will have to do.

Writing out her thoughts might help her cope with her grief, she supposed. Tears stung her eyes, and she wiped them on her sleeve.

Gretchen touched the pen to the page to write some more, then let out a startled cry when ink bled out of the pen tip. It formed into words that scrawled themselves across the page of their own accord.

What's happening? Who is this?

Her heart galloped. She blinked, and the words remained on the page beneath her own, as fixed in place as any ordinary ink.

She recognized the narrow, looping penmanship immediately.

Hand shaking, she wrote, *This is Gretchen Wyler. How can you be writing in my journal?*

Nothing happened at first, but after a lengthy pause, more ink leaked from the pen and shaped itself into words. *This is Sherry Wyler. How can you be writing on my shopping list?*

Afraid that she might be losing her grip on reality, Gretchen wrote, *Is this a haunted pen?*

Haunted? came the reply. *I'm no ghost. I was just getting ready to head to the supermarket, when your words butted in. And who's Gretchen? I don't know anybody named Gretchen. Maybe* you're *the ghost here.*

Gretchen stared at the new words that had appeared. Were they really there at all? For now, she would assume they were. She'd never been taken on flights of fancy.

How old are you? Gretchen wrote. *I was born in 1985.*

More ink bled out the end of the pen. *1985? You're kidding me! It's 1982 right now. Are you writing to me from the future?*

I guess so, Gretchen wrote, and marveled at the mystery of it all.

To her surprise, she didn't feel as sad as she had when she'd first sat down on the couch.

Gretchen had thought about mentioning the strange pen to her father to see if he'd known anything about it, but decided against it. Besides, the pen had been meant for her, not him. If Grandma Sherry had gifted her with a pen that held magical powers, maybe nobody else was supposed to know about it.

When she returned home from work the next day, Gretchen kicked off her flats and immediately snatched the pen and journal off the coffee table.

Hello, Sherry? Are you there?

What? Yes, I'm here. How can you be writing to me? Do they make time-traveling pens in the future?

Not that I've heard of, Gretchen wrote. *Is it still 1982 where you are?*

Yes, last I checked. Are you one of my descendants? Wait! Don't tell me...you're one of Michael's future kids!

Gretchen couldn't help but smile. *Not Michael's. James's.*

James is going to have a little girl? Oh, this is exciting! What does the pen that you're using look like? Is it a space-age pen? I've always loved those sci-fi movies.

It's just a blue pen that came in a velvet case. You gave it to me.

Now that's funny, said the words on the journal page. *I'm writing with a blue pen. It's made out of metal, and I just so happen to have a velvet case, but it was for a silver bracelet my husband bought for me. I always kept the case because it was so pretty. It's the right size for this pen, so maybe I'll start storing it in there.*

Do you think it's the same pen? Gretchen asked.

Who knows? It never seemed magical to me before. I bought it here in town. Nothing irregular about it until it started leaking ink and making words out of it without my help.

Gretchen sat back, hearing the words inside her head in her grandmother's own voice. Grandma Sherry would have been so young in 1982; only in her early forties.

Do I have a good life? the ink asked, after a pause.

Gretchen thought about the loss of her grandfather nine years ago, and how Grandma Sherry had sunk into a depression so deep that the family worried she'd never come out of it.

She thought of Grandma Sherry bouncing her baby great-grandchildren on her knee, and singing them nursery rhymes.

She thought of music lessons and mouthwatering pies topped with whipped cream.

Yes, Gretchen wrote. *You're going to have the best life.*

Oh, good! I'm looking forward to it.

Gretchen's schedule was too full for her to write in the journal every day, though she looked forward to those moments with a burning ferocity she would never be able to explain to anyone else. Sometimes she'd open a fresh page to see cheerful greetings scrawled on it in her grandmother's writing, and she'd tell the young Grandma Sherry about her day and what her plans were for the coming week. In turn, Grandma Sherry would update her on the things her relatives were doing, and Gretchen would chuckle as she imagined her young father and mother planning their wedding—a hectic affair, by the sound of things.

It's 1983 now, her grandmother wrote. *Only a couple more years until I get to meet you. Should I tell your parents to name you Gretchen?*

No! Gretchen wrote back so quickly, a cramp formed in her hand. *Don't do anything to influence things. Things should just pass as they're meant to, don't you think?*

That sounds very wise to me. My lips are sealed.

The pen did not run out of ink as the years passed. The sting of Grandma Sherry's passing lessened with time, helped, of course, by these secret communications, which Gretchen refused to ever share with anyone, for fear of what people might think. She knew she was not writing Grandma Sherry's words; that somehow this pen possessed a sort of magic, connecting grandmother and grandchild from across the decades.

One day the ink spelled out excited words to report Gretchen's own birth.

Gretchen, you're such a beautiful baby. You didn't tell me you would be born with a cleft lip! You're simply gorgeous, though, and I wouldn't want you to be any other way.

Tears cascaded down Gretchen's cheeks as she rubbed at the faint scar between her nose and upper lip—the scar she never even thought about since it had been with her for as long as she remembered, as ordinary to her as her eyes or her ears or her hair.

She received periodic updates telling her that she'd learned to crawl, and walk, and say no. In turn, Gretchen reported to Grandma Sherry that she was now seeing a man named Omar, and that Omar had proposed, and that they were getting married in May, and that they were buying a house soon out in the suburbs, because there would be more room for them to raise a family.

She told her grandmother how she and Omar were adopting a little boy. She told her that the adoption had fallen through, and teardrops fell to the page of her current journal while Omar sat in the other room talking in low tones to his sorrowful yet understanding parents, who assured him that everything would work out in the end, somehow, some way.

Page after page filled with Gretchen's accounts of their second adoption attempt, and through the magic pen, Grandma Sherry congratulated her upon the adoption of a little girl they named Marian.

I wish I could meet Omar and Marian, Grandma Sherry said, *but I fear I'd have to live to a mighty ripe old age to do that.*

Thankfully, Grandma Sherry never asked questions about herself, though Gretchen always assured her that things had gone well for her. The act of writing became such a joy for Gretchen that she craved it much in the way that one lost in the desert craves water and shade, and she never stopped using her magic pen, not even when her hair turned gray and her three children moved across the country with their families, leaving Gretchen and Omar alone with each other.

I'm old now, Grandma Sherry's words said to her one day. *I don't think I have much longer. It's been a while since I've seen you in my time, dear, but I'm sure you know how that goes, with Marian and your boys off having their own adventures now.*

Sorry about that, Gretchen wrote, her arthritis making her joints ache. *I should have stayed so I could keep you company in person.*

Nonsense! You did what you had to do. I'm leaving you this pen, by the way. You told me years ago that I gave it to you. Might as well put it in with the other things I know you'll want. I'll stick a note with it, in case that helps. And you know what? I have an idea for you. When I'm gone here, in my time, I won't be able to write to you anymore. Why don't you give this pen to someone else? It can be to whoever you want. But maybe the pen will decide for you.

Gretchen and Grandma Sherry wrote to each other a few more times after that, but then the pen fell silent.

The final words that Grandma Sherry had ever written to her were,

I need to go close my eyes for a while; it's been a long day. Perhaps I should hide this journal somewhere, so nobody ever sees it. Love you.

Omar kept asking Gretchen what was wrong, and she longed to tell him the truth, but only said, "It's just time. There's just been too much of it…and I miss my grandma."

He put his arms around her and gave her a squeeze. "I wish I'd known her. She always sounded like one hell of a woman."

Gretchen laughed and said, "Now that, she was."

Gretchen sat on her back patio one day with a fresh journal, gripping her magic pen while Marian's two girls tossed a frisbee back and forth to each other.

The pen had been silent for a month, but Gretchen kept it busy.

It's true how they say time is like a great cog, turning and turning and turning, she wrote, keeping one eye on her grandchildren, who were in town visiting for the week. *What ends begins again, and we can't really stay sad about it when there's so much to be happy about. I love Omar and our kids and their kids, and as much as I miss the past before all of them came into my life, I would never want it back. I love what I have, and even though it hasn't always been easy, this has indeed been the best life.*

She paused to think of what to add next, and to her startlement, new words not her own formed beneath the paragraph she'd just written.

I miss you so much, Gran-Gran. Mom says you'll always be close to me, unseen, but right now you feel so far away.

Her skin turned to gooseflesh as she lifted her gaze to her

granddaughter Stephanie, who had just lobbed the frisbee at her sister's head.

Stephanie was the only one who ever called her *Gran-Gran*. The writing even resembled Stephanie's, only it was more refined, as if penned by an adult.

I'm here, now, Gretchen wrote, lips forming into an understanding smile. *And for as long as I can, I will be.*

THE LAST TO
PASS

THE ALLEYWAYS WERE DARK THIS time of night, but Tisha didn't mind the shadows.

She didn't mind much of anything anymore, and hadn't for so long that she scarcely remembered what it meant to care. What, after all, was there to fear? Pain? Poverty? Heartbreak? She'd known those things, and a thousand others, and grown bored of them like old shirts gone through the wash a hundred times. Nowadays, boredom was the only thing she knew, and while she didn't cherish it, it had become a companion as permanent as her own flesh.

The memory of music from the nightclub echoed inside her head as she meandered through the dark toward her apartment. In the morning, she would rise and walk the ten blocks to the office where she kept the books for a firm that manufactured tires, and she would do the same thing the next day, and the next day, and the next day until she deteriorated into utter insanity.

Tisha rounded a corner onto a sidewalk, crossed a street, and entered another alleyway just as dark as the first one. Trash bins were often kept in this alley, and she stepped carefully to avoid walking straight into one.

Five meters in, Tisha heard a clang and stopped short. "Hello?" she called out, seeing no movement in the shadows. "Is someone here?"

No reply came, so shrugging, Tisha continued onward. Her apartment lay just one block past the alleyway, and she could already hear her bed calling to her like an old friend.

Before she could emerge from the other end of the alley, a silhouette stepped in front of her, blocking her way. From the curvaceous shape of it, she could tell it was a tall woman.

"Excuse me," Tisha said, trying to step past her.

The figure didn't move and said nothing. A noise behind her made Tisha whirl and see another silhouette blocking the only other way out of the alley.

She turned back to the first silhouette. Her heart began to thump a little faster—this was the most interesting thing that had happened to her in years. "Are you trying to scare me?" she asked.

They said nothing.

"If it's money you want, you can have it. I'm not poor."

"We don't want your money," the woman said in a low voice.

"Then what? Are you going to kidnap me and sell me into slavery? It might make a neat chapter in my memoir."

The woman took one step closer to her. "You don't need to worry about what we want."

"I don't—"

The person behind her seized her, and the next thing she knew, something sharp was being jammed into her arm. A needle? What in the world was this about? What did they think they were—

A blinding light made Tisha's eyes snap open. A quick assessment of her surroundings revealed that she had been strapped to some sort of table, and that a longer table along the wall to her left contained racks of glass vials and bottles of chemicals whose names Tisha couldn't pronounce.

A tall woman stepped into view—very likely the one from the alley. She had long hair tied in a ponytail that spilled over her left shoulder and wore a soft gray lab coat over a casual shirt and slacks.

Tisha's pulse was definitely beating faster now.

The woman stared down at her, her face grim. "You're awake. Good. It's better for you to understand what's happening."

Tisha recalled an ancient myth about people kidnapping other people and harvesting their organs to sell on the black market. "You know I'll just grow another liver if you cut mine out of me," Tisha said, her voice trembling. "I really don't see the point of this."

The woman's mouth twitched. "We've volunteered you to take part in an experiment. Consider it a blessing."

Tisha twisted to try to free herself from the bindings that strapped her to the table. "What's the experiment?" she asked when she realized her efforts were fruitless. "Can't you get any willing volunteers? I know plenty of people who'd pay money for scientists to tinker around with them if it would give them all something to do."

"Unfortunately," the woman said, "the classified nature of our experiment prevents us from gathering willing participants."

"But this is illegal!"

Instead of trying to defend her position, Tisha's captor went to the table along the wall. Tisha could hear clinking sounds as the woman rearranged some of the bottles, and the next thing Tisha knew, the woman was holding a syringe full of a faintly blue liquid.

Tisha's eyes widened. "What is that?"

"Hopefully, our salvation."

Tisha remained helpless as the woman jammed the needle into her left arm and depressed the plunger. Instead of the fire Tisha expected to flood her veins, she felt a sudden sluggishness, and the room grew dimmer around her. In her mind, she saw herself as a child running after her dog, Vega, on the Titania Plains down past the southern edge of the Lilac Mountains—a place she'd not even thought of in more years than she could count.

Why was she thinking of this now? What was happening to her?

"Help," Tisha tried to whisper, but her mouth wouldn't move, and as she tried but failed to draw in a breath, she finally understood that after five thousand, five hundred and seventy-eight years, she'd reached the end.

"We're losing power."

"Are you *kidding* me?" Francis tapped frantically at the instrument panel and swore when most of the indicator lights turned from blue to red. "Clary told me she fixed everything the last time we had it in the shop!"

"Calm down," Tanvi ordered, stomping away from her swivel chair and yanking open one of the metal covers on the wall protecting some of the ship's more sensitive circuitry. She prodded a gloved finger at one of the wires, which was now smoking. The acrid scent of it made Francis wrinkle his nose.

She slapped the door shut. "We'll need to make an emergency

landing again. Hopefully wherever we end up is nicer than that planet full of carnivorous grass we landed on last month. This scar isn't going away for years." She grinned as she flexed her recently-healed bicep, on which a red, eight-inch furrow was clearly visible.

Francis shivered, wishing he could feel as tough as Tanvi always seemed to be. The last time, it had taken two weeks for them to be rescued and towed back to the distribution center on Jarlexium, and he was still having nightmares about it—of all the equipment they'd had on board in case of emergency, none of it happened to be a lawnmower. "Why can't people just order things from their own planets?"

"Because we would be out of a job if they did." Tanvi flipped some switches on the instrument panel, then pulled up a glowing, three-dimensional map that hovered in the air in front of her. Their destination, a lonely little planet called Hugh, appeared as a winking green speck, while their current location showed up in red, three parsecs away.

Too far.

Tanvi zoomed the map in on their current position, and several system names appeared next to their respective stars. "Start looking these places up while I make sure our backup drive has enough juice."

Francis nodded, trying not to tremble too much. If the ship lost complete power out here in the void, it wouldn't stop dead like a broken automobile. The lack of friction here in space would be a clear demonstration of Newton's First Law of Motion: an object in motion will stay in motion.

Forever and ever and ever.

He and Tanvi would freeze to death barreling toward infinity.

He'd face the carnivorous grass sans lawnmower any day than have to deal with that.

Francis picked up a data pad, squinted at the first system name he saw on the hovering map, and typed it into the search bar. "The Eridani System," he read aloud while Tanvi tinkered with more wiring. "Population: four million. Primary species is…I don't know how to pronounce it. Ek-to-stine?"

"We can't stop there. The Ektostine breathe sulfuric acid vapors; we'd be dead in about two seconds." Something fell to the floor with a clang and rolled off into a corner. "We have backup power. Good."

Francis hurried to the next system. "The Pryok System, population 10 billion. Primary species is—"

"Arristans." Tanvi plopped back into her chair. "They eat humans for breakfast and wear our femurs for jewelry. Next!"

Francis's heart was climbing into his throat, for even though they had backup power, he could still feel sand sliding through a metaphorical hourglass grain by steady grain. "The Shuula System," he stammered. "Population is two billion." He paused, feeling a relieved smile creeping across his face. "They're human."

"Perfect. Setting a course now."

·· ✦ ✳ ✦ ✳ ✦ ··

The blue-green orb that was Shuula loomed large in the viewport like a textured marble. Three tiny moons hovered near it, and Francis snapped a couple of pictures on his data pad and uploaded them to his Skywire account. *Not gonna die today!* read the caption he'd typed, and two people had liked the post by the time they were making landfall near a city on the coast of one of the bigger landmasses.

"There doesn't seem to be a lot of space traffic around here," Tanvi mused as she opened a frequency to make contact with any nearby ports. "Delivery Ship *Augustus* requesting permission to land," she said into the comm.

"It says on here that nobody has heard from these people in about five thousand years," Francis said, holding up his data pad. "That's when the last census was taken."

"Great, so they could all be dead."

Francis prayed otherwise—but at least on this planet, the foliage was unlikely to eat them.

Tanvi circled the ship lower. One of the screens on the instrument panel indicated that their backup power was now down to five percent. Nobody replied to Tanvi's request, and Francis imagined comm centers staffed by ghosts.

A minute later, she banged her fist on her leg in frustration. "That's it. I'm going to find us a nice field and touch down there before we do a nosedive into packed earth."

The city loomed closer in the viewport. It didn't look like ruins. A grassy space appeared among some of the buildings—probably a park, or something—and Tanvi angled them toward it as the backup power trickled down to four percent.

Francis made the sign of the cross, as he did every time they were about to land, or take off, or pass near a neutron star or pulsar. One could never be too careful about these things.

They landed gently on the lawn with nary a hiccup. Tanvi shut off all systems once they'd settled, and Francis breathed a heavy sigh.

Tanvi swiveled toward him and smiled. "You okay, newbie?"

"This isn't how I expected my training to go. I thought this was supposed to be a boring job."

She laughed. "Working for Gobi Express is the least-boring thing that's ever happened to me. Remind me to tell you about the time I delivered a package to a couple of Loolians who tried to turn me into their love slave." She straightened her long, black ponytail and smoothed out a wrinkle in her jumpsuit. "All right, Francis. Let's go see if anyone on this planet knows how to fix a ship."

The first thing Francis noticed upon exiting the ship was the silence. Back home, he was used to the ambient sounds of traffic, aircraft, and the general hustle and bustle of humanity, but here, he heard the wind, a distant, arrhythmic metallic clanking, and an eerie melody played on an instrument he couldn't identify.

It made him think of Sunday afternoons when most of the shops were closed in Greenport, and most folks were passed out in their lawn hammocks with coolers full of honey lager beside them.

Perhaps a part of him was starting to feel homesick after so many weeks out among the stars.

"Well, *somebody's* here," Tanvi said, blinking up at the gleaming skyscrapers surrounding the greenspace they'd landed in. "Unless songs on Shuula like to play themselves."

"Great, Tanvi, now I'm going to have nightmares again."

Tanvi let out a chuckle. "Just think of the stories you'll tell your kids someday. They'll think you were so brave, fighting off invisible musicians so soon after taking on a bunch of man-eating plants."

Not feeling brave at all, Francis turned slowly in a circle, taking in more of their surroundings. The grass in the greenspace had been recently cut, and the azure sky overhead didn't even look polluted. At least these people, wherever they were, had that going for them.

"Maybe we should go that way," Francis said, pointing toward a park bench in the distance.

"Why that way?"

"Because I'm learning to make independent decisions in uncertain situations."

"Kid, you let me pick on you too much. All right, we'll go that way. I hope to God they've got some good mechanics around here, because I'm not waiting another two weeks for someone to come rescue us."

They set off in the direction Francis had chosen. Both he and Tanvi were armed, just in case trouble arose, but their weapons remained holstered, and they wouldn't draw them unless a verifiable danger presented itself. Company policy.

When they reached the park bench, Francis pointed to an engraving on the back. The letters were shaped a bit different from the ones he was used to reading, but he could make out the gist of it. "In memory of Luella Shayne Grissom," he read aloud. "The last to pass." He looked to Tanvi, who'd stopped when he had. "What do you think that means?"

"It means these people still speak a dialect similar to ours. Makes our translators not have to work so hard." She tapped the side of her head, where her translation device would have been implanted. All employees of Gobi Express were required to receive the implant once hired, so there would be no issues in communicating with their customers.

Francis let his gaze slide away from the bench, and they continued toward the eerie music, which stopped abruptly as they rounded a corner onto a street where a woman walked a shaggy dog on a lead on the opposite sidewalk. Despite the fair weather and the fact she was outside walking what was likely her best friend, the look on her face was sullen, and she kept her gaze fixed on the ground.

No traffic clogged the street, which appeared freshly-paved. Skyscrapers towered over both sides of the street, and plain shopfronts decorated their ground floors.

"Food and Coffee," read a sign over one storefront. "Haircuts," read another.

"I think I might know why it seems a little weird here," Francis said as he spotted another storefront sign that read, "Liquor."

"What's that?" Tanvi asked, squinting upward as she took in the sights.

"The people here don't have any imagination. That's why the only thing in the park was a bench, and why the stores on this street make me want to fall asleep looking at them."

"That's an interesting assessment to make about an entire culture, given that we've only seen half a kilometer of it. And that music was imaginative."

Francis shrugged. "Maybe. But mostly it sounded sad."

"I never pegged you as someone who pays attention to aesthetics."

"I studied art in college." Francis felt his face flush. "The department head told me his guinea pig could draw better than me."

"Sorry to hear that." Tanvi planted her hands on her hips as she continued to survey the area. "I wanted to be a psychologist, but apparently you have to be nice."

Movement up above caught Francis's eye, and in horror, he watched as a figure plummeted from a window ten or twelve stories up. He clapped a hand over his mouth to stifle a shriek, and Tanvi stared in open-mouthed shock as the figure hit the ground right where the woman and her dog had passed a minute earlier.

The figure lay still. Since there were still no cars on the street, Francis and Tanvi hurried across and approached the figure, Francis dreading what they might see in closer detail.

Francis was surprised that the man who'd fallen didn't look at all pulverized from the forty-meter drop. He wore a plain white shirt and gray slacks, and as Francis took a few steps closer, the man's eyes fluttered open and fixed on him.

"What are you looking at?" the man snarled. He pulled himself into sitting position and then got to his feet. He looked about forty years old and didn't have a scratch or a bruise on him.

"You just fell out of a building." It seemed a silly thing to say, because surely the man had noticed.

The man brushed some dirt off his sleeves. "I jumped out. You act like you haven't seen anyone do it before."

Francis looked to Tanvi, whose expression became a cross between bewilderment and incredulity. "Is this a normal pastime on Shuula?" Tanvi asked, her voice taking on a higher-pitched tone.

The man's eyebrows knit together. "You're from off-world?"

"We had engine trouble. Do you know any mechanics who might be able to help?"

"Not who could help with a spaceship. We don't get much traffic from off-world. Last visitors I remember came fifty-something years ago—or maybe it's been a hundred now—it all blurs together. It made the news, though. Sometimes I forget there's other people out there, living their own lives." He tilted his head toward the sky, blinked, and shook his head.

"Do your people not travel off-world?" Francis asked, marveling that anyone would choose to stay put when an entire universe lay at their fingertips.

The man laughed, without humor. "What's the point?"

He started to walk away, but Tanvi said, "Do you know anyone who might be able to help us find a mechanic?"

"Ask Gordie at Food and Coffee. She knows everybody, and I'm not even kidding."

Then the man was gone, striding away from them as if nothing at all peculiar had just happened.

"He remembers something from a hundred years ago?" Francis still tried to process the fact he'd just seen the man fall from a height that would have turned any other person into a bloody pulp.

"I caught that, too," Tanvi said. "I think this place just got interesting."

Together, they turned and walked through the front door of Food and Coffee.

Though he was young, Francis had visited many a coffee shop during his travels, and virtually all of them possessed a warm, community sort of vibe of people coming together to celebrate caffeine and camaraderie.

Inside Food and Coffee, rows of tables and chairs sat along the two walls perpendicular to the street, and an aisle between them led up to the counter. At the table closest to them, a woman about Francis's age gripped a blank notebook and pen. She touched the pen to the page, pulled it back, started to write again, and threw both pen and notebook to the table, narrowly missing her empty mug.

"I give up!" she shrieked, scooting her chair back with an ugly grating sound. "I've literally run out of ideas!"

She stormed from the shop. None of the four other patrons or the employees behind the counter batted an eye. An older woman on the opposite side of the room stared blankly off into the distance while a mug steamed in front of her, a middle-aged couple murmured softly to each other a few tables down from her, and a solitary man with a beard leaned against a wall, sound asleep.

Francis followed Tanvi to the counter, more than a little unnerved.

"Good afternoon," said a glum barista standing behind a register. Her limp hair was dyed purple, but instead of making her look peppy, it just made Francis imagine a sad person trying to come up with some way to spice up her otherwise colorless life.

"Good afternoon," Francis said with a smile. "We were wondering if a Gordie is here?"

The barista pointed listlessly at the older woman close to the entrance. "That's her."

Exchanging a glance, Francis and Tanvi retraced their steps through the coffee shop and stopped beside the woman's table.

"You're Gordie?" Tanvi asked, and the woman swiveled her head toward them.

"That's right." Gordie looked them up and down. Her glum face slowly morphed into a smile. "And you're new in town."

"You really do know everyone," Francis said, amazed.

"Heh. Well. When you've been around as long as I have, you tend to make acquaintances." She tossed her gray, wavy hair over one shoulder and propped an elbow on the table. "What can I help you two with?"

Francis dragged out a chair across from Gordie and sat in it, and

Tanvi followed suit. "We're delivery drivers for Gobi Express on our way to Hugh," Tanvi said. "We have a whole cargo hold full of packages, but we ran into some technical trouble. We were hoping you'd know a mechanic who knows ships inside and out, because it will save us a ton of time."

"I'm afraid we don't deal too much in space travel these days," Gordie said, sounding chagrined. "There's a mining operation on Ullul—that's our largest moon—and as far as I can think of, they're the only outfit who's still running spacecraft. We haven't even launched a satellite in a thousand years."

"But why?" Francis blurted. "Don't any of you want to leave?"

Gordie gave him a soft smile that made him think of his grandmother, dead and gone these long years now. "You don't know much about Shuula, do you?"

"The files I read say that nobody has made contact with your planet in five thousand years, but the man who jumped out the window a few minutes ago said he remembers 'visitors' who came fifty or a hundred years ago."

Gordie nodded thoughtfully. "That sounds like Mr. Onklin, and it was three hundred and seven years ago that we last took note of a foreign craft. Once their ship was repaired, we requested that they not tell anybody about us. We like to keep our privacy."

"But that man couldn't have been more than fifty years old," Tanvi said. "How could he remember something that happened three centuries ago?"

"History books?" Francis said, but Gordie shook her head.

"If only. When I'm finished with my coffee, I can take you to the place where the mining operation manufactures their transport ships. With luck, your ship's systems will have a similar configuration as theirs."

Gordie accompanied Francis and Tanvi on a monorail that shuttled them a hundred and fifty kilometers north to a city whose name Francis had forgotten already.

"I've already notified Grant Fournier, one of the maintenance crew at Ullul Enterprises, that we're on our way," Gordie said, making herself comfortable in her window seat. "You have the schematics of your ship with you?"

"I downloaded it into here before we met up at the station," Tanvi said, holding up her data pad. Both she and Francis had packed their suitcases with overnight essentials, just in case this took longer than expected.

"You understand it is unlikely he will be able to help you," Gordie said.

Francis watched out the window as the lifeless city center gave way to lifeless suburbs full of square, white houses that all looked the same. "It's worth a try, though, right?"

"Those words have been used to justify far too many unwise decisions." Gordie spoke without mirth. "But if it will save you two weeks of waiting for your employer to send out a repair crew, then yes, I think it is worth a try."

At one point in their journey, the monorail stopped at another station, and a couple boarded in silence and took seats toward the front of the car. They both looked like someone had cancelled every holiday for the next hundred years.

Francis cleared his throat. "I don't mean to sound rude," he said in a low voice, "but did something bad happen here recently? Everyone seems so sad."

Gordie's jovial expression sobered. "Something very bad happened, but not recently, though sometimes it feels like yesterday. We don't like to talk about it." She turned her gaze out the window. "We'll be in Chagtha soon. It was a booming seaport after Shuula was first settled, but of course that was before my time."

Francis looked to Tanvi, who shrugged, looking as bewildered as he felt. He discreetly woke his data pad from sleep mode and did another quick search for Shuula. He clicked on the topmost result.

Shuula was first settled 45,000 years ago, chosen by humans due to its similar size and composition to Earth, the original human home world. The Shuula culture is secretive with outsiders and ceased all communications with neighboring systems roughly 5,000 years ago. It was initially thought that some disaster had wiped out either the Shuulans' communications network or the Shuulans themselves; however, several scouting missions from Ling, the nearest human colony to Shuula, noted that the Shuulans were alive and well—they just wouldn't talk.

Of all the millions of planets they could have made an emergency landing on, they'd had to pick the most antisocial one in the galaxy, hadn't they?

The sun hovered low in the sky by the time they made it to their destination. Gordie ushered Francis and Tanvi off the monorail ahead of her, and they walked on foot for three blocks until they reached a row of town homes with slate-colored brick walls and white trim.

"We're not going to Mr. Fournier's shop?" Tanvi asked.

"He didn't go in because he didn't have anything to fix today. Until now." Gordie rapped on the door of Number 17, and a fiftyish man in coveralls opened it.

"It's good to see you, Gordie," the man said, smiling the sad smile Francis had come to expect from these people. "These are the aliens I'm supposed to help?"

"We're humans, just like you!" Francis retorted, briefly forgetting his manners.

Grant Fournier squinted at him with hazel eyes. "You're not from this planet, are you? That makes you alien. Come in, all of you. When I heard Gordie was coming, I made a feast fit for a President."

Francis and Tanvi followed the Shuulans into a warm living area populated with plush furniture and throw pillows—not exactly the type of place he expected a mechanic to call home. A square table in the open area between the living room and kitchen had been heaped with steaming trays of food that Francis couldn't identify, but it smelled as good as anything you could eat in the finest establishment on Jarlexium.

"Go ahead and help yourselves," Grant said, moving toward the table. "It isn't often I have guests of such high esteem, but don't expect me to wait on you like some servant." His expression was deadpan, but he winked.

"I don't like being waited on, anyway," Gordie said, occupying one of the chairs. "It makes me feel useless, like some piece in a museum."

She spooned an orange glob of something onto her plate. Shrugging, Francis did the same. It looked like a cross between marmalade and mochi and smelled like grapefruit.

"What exactly is it that you do here, Gordie?" Tanvi asked, loading up a plate of her own.

"Grant already said. I'm the President."

"Of what?"

Gordie looked to Grant and raised her eyebrows, and Grant let out a low guffaw.

"Of Shuula," Gordie said.

Francis, who had been about to spoon one of the mysterious orange globs into his mouth, dropped his utensil with a clatter. "The whole planet?"

"The whole planet," Gordie confirmed. "Before you start groveling in my presence, I should let you know it's not as prestigious as you might think. We aren't at war with anyone, and the most interesting thing I've done this year is attend the christening of a cruise ship down in Hallmundland. The drinks were free."

Francis could only imagine how lively a cruise might be in these parts. "But shouldn't you have security with you?" he asked. "Where we come from, no president could go out for coffee on their own without some extremist trying to assassinate them."

"If only we had a few extremists here," Gordie murmured. "It might alleviate the boredom."

Grant, looking suddenly uncomfortable, cleared his throat and looked to Tanvi. "So. Tell me about your ship."

"It's a Dorian Model 5500," Tanvi said. "Not that that will mean anything to you. Gobi Express, our employer, uses them for most deliveries due to their large cargo holds. Francis and I are delivery drivers. I have some mechanical knowledge, but not enough to fix the power drain that forced us to land here." She tapped at the screen of her data pad, which she'd laid beside her plate, and a three-dimensional image of the ship appeared in the air above it. "I'm fairly certain the ship needs a new battery. If you have a way to rig it up enough to get to our destination and then back to the distribution center, we would be immensely grateful."

"Can you pull up an image of the battery?" Grant asked, curiosity blazing in his eyes.

Tanvi tapped at the screen again, and a rectangular shape with holographic wires coming out of it appeared midair. "Does this look like anything you have here on Shuula?"

Grant's eyebrows knit together. "Yes, and no. I'll have to come out and take a look in person tomorrow. If you three don't want to ride back down to the capital tonight, you're more than welcome to my spare rooms upstairs. It's been so long since I've had overnight guests, I've forgotten what it's like."

"Don't you have any family?" Francis asked.

Grant smirked. "Of course I've got family. We got sick of each other. After this long, who wouldn't?"

As Francis lay in bed that night, twirling his St. Christopher medal in his fingers, he couldn't stop thinking.

When their meal with Grant and Gordie had concluded, he and Tanvi had gone for a walk around Grant's neighborhood for lack of anything better to do to pass the time. They'd watched as a woman plummeted from the top floor of another townhome a few blocks away and landed, unharmed, on a garbage can, spilling its contents across the sidewalk; and they'd wandered through an entertainment district where a few nightclubs advertised such amusements as "Stripping" and "Dance Music."

"Maybe false advertising is against the law here," Tanvi had said, but it didn't sit right with Francis at all. Something felt off about this place. It was more than just differing cultures, as Francis had visited several planets since leaving the university, and as different as each had been from the other, they'd all exuded some degree of vivacity.

Shuula just seemed dead, like all its inhabitants had given up and started going through the motions.

He replayed everything he'd seen from the moment they'd left the ship: the denizens of the café, their fellow passengers on the monorail, the indolent couples he'd seen hanging around the entertainment district, who'd apparently tired of the "Stripping" and "Dance Music" and found it more bearable to mope outside in the fresh air.

None of them were children, he realized with a start. Everyone he'd seen had been his age or older. There had been no teenagers, no toddlers, no screaming babies wanting a bottle.

"Something very bad happened," Gordie had said to him.

Had a disease ravaged the young?

In his mind, he watched the man jump out of the skyscraper window and land unbroken on solid concrete.

Maybe all the children had died—or maybe they had all grown up.

Something sterilized them, maybe? And they're sad their race won't go on?

His heart skipped a beat as he realized that perhaps something in the very air here had caused such sterilization. And maybe they remained on their planet because they didn't want to spread the disease across the stars.

Then they wouldn't want to help fix the ship, a voice chided in his head. *They'd say you have to stay here forever and ever to keep the disease contained.*

Francis ground his teeth together in frustration. He'd been good at solving riddles as a child, but the answer to this one eluded him, like smoke in the wind.

"I hate to say it, but I'm afraid I can't help you," Grant said, looking up from the large battery that he and Tanvi had pried out of the ship's drive as soon as they'd made it back to the capital in the morning. "I'm not even sure what material this is."

Francis watched as Tanvi sighed. "All right. I'll alert the company that we need help."

She clomped from the room in her heavy work boots, leaving Francis and Grant alone with each other.

"Why the long face?" Grant asked him.

Francis felt his cheeks heat up. "People just seem so sad here, and I think it's starting to rub off on me." Already that day he'd suffered through another melancholic monorail voyage, and he'd endured lunch at an equally-dismal diner where red-eyed patrons gazed past their meals with the vitality of drugged tree sloths.

Lunch had been on Grant, though, and it had tasted half-decent despite its peculiar spongy texture, so Francis couldn't really complain.

Grant gave a little sniff as he straightened. "They're sad because they've forgotten how to be happy." He paused. "What's something you like to do? Like a hobby?"

"I like to travel. That's why I applied to work at Gobi Express."

Grant nodded. "Okay. Now suppose you travel and travel and travel until you've seen all the places you can possibly see a thousand different times. Would you still be happy?"

Francis couldn't help but laugh. "It would take an eternity for me to do that."

"Suppose you did have an eternity."

"Hmm." Would he still be happy given those circumstances? Francis took a moment to reflect on that. He'd marveled the first time he'd lain eyes on the triple sunset on Kingston B, but would it still hold its beauty a thousand times later? And the largest known waterfall in the Milky Way, a two-mile-high monstrosity on Garcia, had taken his breath away, though he supposed it might lose some of its majesty eventually if he saw it too much.

"I don't know," Francis said. "I might get bored, wanting to see new things."

"And there you have it!" Grant brushed his hands together. He looked to the ceiling of the ship. "You don't know what I would give to get off this rock and out of this system for good, but it's against the law—and even if it wasn't, I couldn't bring myself to do it. Not unless…but that's not going to happen. How old are you, Francis?"

Francis blinked in surprise. "Twenty-three standard years. Why?"

"Oh, what a thing it would be to be twenty-three again." Grant's smile turned wistful. "When you get to leave here, there's one thing I want you to remember: cherish what you have, and tell your family and friends you love them. I guess that's two things, then."

Tanvi reentered the room before a bewildered Francis could conjure a reply. "They're sending out a new ship so we can finish our deliveries while they tow this derelict hunk of junk back to the distribution center," she said. "They'll be here in twelve days, so it looks like we get to do some more sightseeing in the meantime."

"Sounds like fun," Francis said, but he was afraid of just what sights they might see.

Gordie, in her benevolence, gave Francis and Tanvi some currency and a place to stay so they wouldn't have to live in the ship the whole time they were on Shuula. "Go on, go out and do the things young people do," Gordie said that evening after they'd dined in her apartment. "Don't let an old woman like me keep you."

"You're too kind," Francis said, fingering the wad of cash she'd handed him. He almost couldn't believe it. Who used cash anymore? It was like something you might see in a cave painting—he'd only ever heard mention of it in his university history classes. "Tanvi, if you don't mind, I'd like to head out alone."

Tanvi waved a hand at him. "Fine, I'm sick of looking at you, anyway." She winked. "Maybe you'll meet some nice Shuulan girl out there."

"Maybe," he said, though he didn't believe it.

When he stepped outside, he smiled to himself. It wasn't Shuulan girls that were on his mind. The mystery of this place burned inside him like a bed of hot coals, and Grant's words to him earlier had given him something of a clue.

Francis intended to confirm his hunch.

He set out into the evening sunshine and down the sidewalk running past the row of nearly-identical apartments. Not too many people seemed to be out and about, so he supposed most people might still be at work, or they were holed up inside their homes, too indolent to bother going outside to enjoy the fine weather.

It felt good to stretch his legs—you didn't get a whole lot of exercise being cooped up in a delivery ship for weeks at a time—and before he realized it, he'd arrived in one of the suburban areas where the squarish houses all looked the same, as if the architect had come down with a bad case of limited imagination. His own neighborhood back on Jarlexium contained a motley assortment of homes with landscaped gardens full of lawn furniture, fire pits, and children's playsets, giving each property its own unique character.

He strode the length of Seventh Street, as the sign had called it. The only person in sight trudged from their parked vehicle to their front door, paying him no heed. While some lawns bore gnarled shrubs and a few exotic-looking flowers to distinguish them from the neighbors, he saw no sign of children at any of them—no monkey bars or swing sets, no unattended tricycles with wheels spinning in the air—adding more weight to his theory that there *weren't* any children.

Francis rounded a corner and almost collided with a dark-haired woman carrying a canvas sack bulging with pamphlets.

"Sorry!" Francis exclaimed, stepping aside to get out of her way. "I didn't see you there!"

"That's okay," the woman said in a dull tone. Her gray eyes held no emotion, as if she were an automaton. "Here. You can have one of these, since you're right here." She thrust a pamphlet into his hand. No doubt it was some political tract, so Francis jammed it into his pocket without reading it.

"Thanks," Francis said. "You have a good evening."

Instead of moving onward, she cocked an eyebrow at him. "Why is it good?"

"Why isn't it good? It's a beautiful day to be alive." It was something his grandmother had always said to him, and he wasn't entirely sure why he'd thought to say it now.

She pursed her lips at him. "I felt that way too, about two million days ago. Are you one of those joy-heads I hear about in the news?"

Francis tried hard to keep a straight face. "Joy-head?"

"You know, joy? The drug they've been passing around over in Swampsburg? It makes people insane with happiness, and then they lose control of their bodily functions and have to be shut up in an institution. It's a horrible drain on our tax dollars, though I can't really blame any of them for wanting a way out."

"I'm definitely not a joy-head," Francis said, trying but failing to mentally calculate how many years that two million days added up to be. "I just like being happy."

"Well, good for you. And have a *good* evening." She walked away from him, her shoes echoing against the sidewalk in the still air.

Curiosity getting the better of him now, Francis pulled the pamphlet out of his pocket and read:

ARE YOU TIRED OF LIVING?

IF SO, YOU ARE INVITED TO A MEETING AT THE OCEANSIDE CENTER ON SATURDAY, THE TENTH OF DECTOBUARY, AT FOURTEEN O'CLOCK, TO DISCUSS THE DEVELOPMENT OF A CURE FOR LIFE. REFRESHMENTS WILL BE PROVIDED.

A cure for life? What did that mean?

Francis felt as though someone had just punched him in the gut as he remembered seeing the man and then the woman falling from great heights without trouble. *Nobody* could have survived falls like those, not even if they'd given themselves bio-upgrades like the soldiers back on Jarlexium.

It could mean only one thing.

The Shuulans had cured death, and now some of them wanted to fix it.

Tanvi looked up from the pamphlet. "This is crazy."

"It makes sense though, right?" Francis's heart was still hammering after his lengthy jog back to Gordie's place. "We both saw people jumping out of windows, and nothing happened to them. And the woman passing these out said she felt happy to be alive two million days ago. That's got to be thousands of years."

Tanvi appeared uneasy as she glanced to the closed door separating them from Gordie, who had gone to bed early. "I don't know how long a Shuulan year is, but that many days is something around 5,400 standard years."

"That's horrible." Francis felt the room sway, so he sat down on a maroon ottoman and took some slow breaths. "Those people who jumped out of the windows must have been trying to see if the death cure finally wore off."

"Or they were just bored." Tanvi's face was ashen. "I know if I got to be over five thousand years old, I'd be looking for new thrills anywhere

I could get them. It's probably their version of riding a roller coaster."

They fell into a contemplative silence for a minute. Francis broke it by saying, "I don't think they have children."

"I imagine they wouldn't want to. Can you imagine how fast a planet would overpopulate if people were being born all the time but never died?"

"They could have moved to a different planet."

"But they don't go anywhere, remember?" Tanvi bit her lip, then said again, "This is crazy."

"It is crazy," Gordie said from behind them.

Francis turned and saw Gordie standing just outside her bedroom door, which was now open, wearing a violet, flannel-like set of pajamas.

"I'm not used to guests, so I couldn't sleep," Gordie said apologetically. "I couldn't help but overhear you."

"Are we right, then?" Francis asked.

Gordie bowed her head in a gesture of resignation. "It wasn't something I wanted to burden you with. It's considered an embarrassment among our people, and most of us don't even talk about it, like ignoring it and going on with our lives will just make it go away." She crossed the room and sat at one end of her maroon sofa, her long, gray hair spilling over her shoulders. "Unfortunately, all we *do* is go on with our lives—on and on and on with them."

"I'm sorry," Francis said.

Gordie shrugged. "Being sorry about it won't help anything. I don't believe anything will."

"Can we be nosy and ask how this all happened?" Tanvi asked.

"Only if you promise not to share a word of this with anyone once you leave our planet."

"We won't tell, will we, Francis?"

Francis shook his head, and a lump of emotion lodged in his throat.

"Very well," Gordie said. "I don't expect you to really keep any promises, but it removes the liability from me by asking it of you." She paused, as if collecting assorted memories from dusty corners of her mind. "When I was sixty years old, a bioterrorist from the then-country of Tyne in our western hemisphere developed a pathogen that dissolved the human body over the course of several days if someone inhaled it. It was a cruelty that killed well over a million people by the time the terrorist was caught and executed. Scientists had to work frantically to develop an antidote against it, and some genius in the scientific community decided that not only should they develop a cure for the pathogen; they could cure everything else while they were at it."

"So they developed a super cure," Francis said.

"It took several years, but yes. Millions more people died while it was being developed, but by the time it was ready, citizens the world over lined up to receive their dose. It was a dark age, then—people huddled in bunkers underground to avoid inhaling the pathogen, and all interplanetary travel was banned so we could keep the pathogen contained to Shuula.

"Nobody really knew the full capabilities of what the cure could do—it was supposed to kill the pathogen the moment it entered our bodies, and it was believed to eliminate all cancers and degenerative diseases. Wounds would even heal faster." Gordie's eyes filled with regret. "And then people stopped dying. Within just a few years, enough babies had been born to replace all those who had died from the pathogen. Governments all over the world made sterilization mandatory. Even for the children." Gordie wiped a tear from her eye. "The pathogen was destroyed, as had been intended, and we had everything to live for. But our babies grew up—and then there were no more babies. I haven't seen a child in more than five thousand years. And I hate that."

Francis thought of his little cousins back home who made each family get-together a form of entertainment with their antics. He imagined them growing up into studious adults, and frowned.

Though he was not a father, he could see how the absence of all children might dim an entire civilization's collective psyche.

"You don't realize how many things change when there are no children, and when no one dies," Gordie said after a long pause. "Schoolteachers were soon out of jobs, as well as daycares. There was no longer a need for doctors or morticians. There were so many people whose passions became irrelevant, and they became lost."

"Were you one of them?" Tanvi asked quietly.

"I taught Year One in school for forty years. Once the children had all grown up, I taught in a university for a while, but it wasn't the same as seeing innocent young faces in the classroom every morning, teaching them their alphabet. I left academia and took up politics, and here I am today."

Francis held up the flyer the woman on the sidewalk had given him. "Do you know anything about this?"

Her forehead creasing, Gordie took the paper and read it, then passed it back to him. "Several attempts have been made to return our humanity to us, and none of them have worked. Not to mention there are some blessed individuals who have loved every moment of the past five thousand years and wouldn't bat an eye at the thought of living for five thousand more. They say it's their right to live as long as they want to."

"Why don't you want anyone to leave Shuula?" Francis asked.

"Because people from across the galaxy would come to us begging for immortality. The entire universe cannot live as we do. It would be the downfall of everything." Gordie made a vague gesture toward the entrance to her apartment. "Just take a look out there and see all those souls who've given up. They're like breathing corpses. Would you want that for the people of your own planet?"

"No," Francis said softly.

Tanvi said, "What will happen if you really do live forever? Your sun will burn out and destroy your planet eventually."

Gordie's face became grave. "Then my kin and I will float in the void forever with only our thoughts to keep us company."

The mental image of frozen yet living bodies drifting through space filled Francis with such a visceral sense of horror that he rose, shaking, and said, "I need to use your bathroom."

He hurried out of the living area and into Gordie's bathroom, locking the door behind him. He stared at his pale reflection in the mirror, paler than normal now that he'd heard Gordie's tale. The freckles on his cheeks stood out like a reverse constellation. Bracing his hands on each side of the marble sink, Francis breathed in, then breathed out, as his therapist had told him to do before he went into his job interview with Gobi Express.

He looked back up at his reflection and set his jaw. He may have been a failed artist and a trainee delivery driver with few marketable skills, which made him something of a nobody in the eyes of most people, but in spite of that, he wanted to help Gordie and her people.

What that might mean, he didn't know. He was no scientist who could tinker around with compounds capable of changing the world, but he did have a heart, and somehow he felt that heart was what some of these people needed.

At once, he knew what he had to do.

He would go to that meeting at The Oceanside Center on the tenth of Dectobuary, then figure out the rest from there.

The tenth of Dectobuary turned out to be the very next day. When Francis announced his intentions that morning over breakfast, Tanvi shook her head and said, "I'm not going with you to listen to a room full of people talk about dying."

"You make it sound so grim."

Her expression tightened. "My uncle took his own life three years ago. Forgive me if I'd rather spend my day elsewhere."

"The people who attend meetings like these aren't suicidal," Gordie said, returning to the table with a pitcher of juice. "They simply demand the right to live as we were meant to: finitely."

Francis scooped a blob of oatmeal onto his spoon. Before popping it into his mouth, he said, "There's one thing you haven't told us about your planet's situation."

Gordie's eyebrows raised. "What is that?"

"Your entire population is immortal. That's a lot of people. Not all of them are going to be good. What happens when one of them turns bad? You can't kill a tyrant who tries to mess up everything you've worked for."

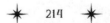

"No, we can't." A sardonic gleam appeared in the woman's eyes. "But even the tyrants grow bored and languid when they cannot kill, and the fear of a literal eternity behind bars keeps a lot of the would-be criminals in line."

"It sounds like the perfect justice system," Tanvi mused. "Punish the crooks with unending life instead of executing them."

Tanvi's words still echoed inside of Francis's head hours later when he followed Gordie's directions to The Oceanside Center, which turned out to be a conference hall of sorts less than a kilometer from the beach—he could see the lapping blue waves between trees and buildings off to the west.

He followed a throng of people through the center's front doors and into an auditorium already filled with at least a hundred people. Not many spoke, so the place was filled with an eerie silence interspersed with the sounds of breathing and shuffling feet. The people were all adults, of course, but looked like they ranged in age from twenty-five to eighty. It was hard to believe they were all more than five thousand years old.

If nothing changed here on Shuula, they would still look exactly the same even after their sun eventually gave up the ghost and roasted the planet in its death throes.

Francis didn't really want to think about that, so he turned his attention to the stage, where a plain white podium had been erected. He sat only five rows back, so he would have a fairly good view of the speaker, whenever they emerged.

Fifteen minutes later, a bronze-skinned man and a tall, pale woman in a lab coat ascended the few short steps onto the stage and scanned the audience, who had now fallen so utterly silent that Francis could hear his own heartbeat.

The man moved behind the podium and cleared his throat. "Thank you all for coming, my friends," he said in a baritone voice. "It's our hope that this is an evening that everyone here will always remember." He paused as he stared out at the gathered crowd. "For those of you who don't know us, I am Dr. Hollis Finn, and this is my colleague, Dr. Yin Grange. We are both based out of the University of Russelo Sound, and like you, we have lived for more than five millennia.

"Our longevity is unnatural and has hampered any sort of progress our race might have been able to make in that time frame. With new births come new innovations, yet we all live virtually the same as we did before this *mistake* cost us our humanity."

There came a few murmurs of affirmation. Francis risked glancing behind him and saw rows and rows of dead-eyed people who probably came here tonight only because it gave them something different to do.

"Many of us," Dr. Finn said, "have been seeking a cure for our longevity. It has not been easy, and has often been met with opposition." He smirked. "But look at all of you. You seem dead already. I think some of you would hardly notice at this point if your heart ceased to beat."

Someone toward the back of the room shouted, "Our longevity would be more bearable if we were allowed to leave Shuula like we used to!"

"What happens if a cure is found?" someone else yelled from off to the left. "Do we shrivel and die of disease?"

Dr. Finn gave a thin smile. "Not exactly." A glint appeared in his eyes that made Francis feel a sudden discomfort. "And we have no business reconnecting with our galactic neighbors in our current state. If anyone out there were to find out what we've done to ourselves, we'd be invaded in a wink, and the nuisance would be unbearable."

"I could use an unbearable nuisance or two right now," someone muttered loudly enough for most of the room to hear.

"Forgive me for saying so," said Dr. Finn, "but an invasion is not an acceptable solution for chronic tedium." The man's gaze swept the room, and for one terrifying instant, Francis thought Dr. Finn was looking right at him, as if he *knew* an alien was present in the crowd, listening to words that had never been meant for him.

"But I digress! In actuality," Dr. Finn continued, "the manner of your death is partly up to you. Dr. Grange?"

His tall associate, the woman in the lab coat, disappeared off to the right-hand side of the stage and returned wheeling a gurney on which lay a human-shaped figure shrouded in a white sheet. Dr. Grange parked the gurney in the center of the stage right by the podium and took one step backward, a smirk on her face.

Francis's skin had gone clammy. He and others near him craned to get a better look, even though he wasn't sure he really wanted to see what lay beneath that shroud.

"This is a momentous day, my friends," Dr. Finn said, his voice booming loudly through the chamber. "This is the day we finally get things right."

Dr. Grange yanked the sheet off the gurney. A young woman—who wasn't young at all, Francis knew—lay still as a corpse, her skin a pale, grayish tone. Long, brown hair spilled about her shoulders, and she wore a tight-fitting top and leggings.

"We have been testing cures all this past year," Dr. Finn said. "Not one of them worked. Until now."

Someone gasped. "Tisha? Is that Tisha Warris?"

A man in the front row stood, clapping a hand to his mouth. "It is Tisha! She's been missing for days!"

As the murmurs in the room grew louder and more panicked, Dr. Finn pulled a stoppered vial from his pocket and held it up for all to see. "This woman gave her life for our cause. Contained here in this vial is the very serum that killed her. I'm giving each of you the opportunity to partake of it if you choose."

The man in the front clambered up onto the stage, grabbed the late Tisha by the shoulders, and gave her a violent shake. "Tisha! Wake up!"

Tisha's head flopped around as if she were nothing more than a life-sized doll.

"Tisha isn't going to wake up," Dr. Finn said.

The man shot him a scathing glare that Francis was glad he wasn't the recipient of. "Tisha never would have consented to an experiment like this." His voice cracked. "She's my sister. I know everything about her."

Dr. Finn's eyes narrowed. "What exactly are you trying to accuse me of?"

"You abducted her, or tricked her, or something!"

"You have no proof of that."

"Knowing my sister would never do this is proof enough for me!"

The man lunged at Dr. Finn, who dodged him with the grace of a dancer, keeping the vial close to his chest so he wouldn't drop it. Two burly, uniformed men appeared onstage and grabbed Tisha's brother, then escorted him out of the auditorium to the accompaniment of his wails.

The sound of his grief chilled Francis to his marrow.

Several other members of the audience had gotten to their feet and were glaring at Dr. Finn with loathing in their eyes. The tension in the air had become so thick, Francis felt like he inhaled it every time he drew in a breath.

Dr. Finn chuckled. "Why the angry faces? You know this is what you all want, deep inside. You're tired of living. I can see it in your eyes. In fact, this might be the most alive some of you have felt in centuries, knowing that the contents of this vial could end your life in moments." He gave the vial a little shake for emphasis. "Dr. Grange, will you please bring in the cart?"

The tall woman in the lab coat dipped her head, exited stage left, and returned pushing a wheeled cart bearing several racks of stoppered vials just like the one in Dr. Finn's hand. A collection of syringes lay next to them.

Francis could feel himself sweating.

"I have twenty-five vials of serum right here, ready and waiting for whoever would like to take it," said Dr. Finn. "Death should occur between one to two minutes after injection. You may receive the injection here, by my hand or by Dr. Grange's, or you may take it home to administer it to yourself at whichever time you choose. The choice is yours."

Nobody moved. It felt as though the whole room was holding its breath.

Dr. Finn's face flushed as he scanned the ranks of gathered Shuulans. "Really? None of you are brave enough to do it? I didn't think my race was so cowardly." He stepped to the edge of the stage and glared down at a young-looking blonde woman in the front row. "You, for example. Why do you want to keep living like this?"

"I—I grow flowers," she said in a small voice. "In a greenhouse."

Scorn wrote itself across Dr. Finn's face. "Flowers."

"They're beautiful. I—I sell them."

"People still buy flowers?"

"A few do. Enough to keep me in business these five thousand years."

Dr. Finn puffed out his chest. "If you love your plants so much, why did you come to this presentation?"

"My hair appointment got canceled, and I didn't have anything else to do."

Jerking his head toward the man seated next to the gardener, Dr. Finn said, "What about you? What makes your life so good that you have to keep on living it?"

The man grabbed the gardener's hand. "Yuli is my wife. We've been married for three hundred and two years. It took us a long time to find each other, and now I can't imagine being away from her."

"And how many wives did you have before you met Yuli?" Dr. Finn sneered.

"Four. The first one died in the plague. The other three got bored and left me. But not Yuli."

"This is ridiculous." Dr. Finn glared at the crowd. "I've worked hard on this serum, and now I find out that none of you here want to use it. Poor Tisha died for nothing."

Francis realized he was trembling with barely-controlled rage. He considered himself a mellow guy, not easily given over to extreme emotions, but Dr. Finn was taking this way too far.

He remembered a time in elementary school when he watched a bully terrorize a pair of younger students into handing over their credit chips, which had been loaded with enough money to pay for their lunches for the whole rest of the school year. Francis, who hadn't been much bigger than the bullied students, had done nothing, since his family had not been rich and he didn't want to lose his own credit chip—he never would have heard the end of it at home.

Now, though, was different.

Francis stood up. "You need to leave these people alone."

Dr. Finn's gray-brown eyebrows rose. "Who are you to dictate what I can and cannot do?"

Francis held his head high even though he felt like curling up into a little ball in some obscure corner where no one would notice him. "My ship was having engine trouble, so we had to make an emergency landing on your planet. I guess you could call me an alien. I'm not immortal like all of you. If I don't have any accidents, I'll live to about a hundred and fifty, and then I'll die." He swallowed. "It was wrong to cure death, but it's wrong to bully these people into killing themselves. You aren't a god. You have no right to manipulate them."

Dr. Finn's cheeks darkened to a shade of crimson. "You are truly an alien?"

"That's right. I'm from Jarlexium, and I work as a delivery driver for Gobi Express."

Though Francis felt the gesture unnecessary, Dr. Finn pointed at him and shouted, "Seize him before he gets back to his ship and tells the whole galaxy about us!"

Most present appeared too stunned to make a move, but another set of security guards appeared in one of the doorways leading out of the auditorium and began their soldierly march directly toward him.

Oh, dear.

Francis's mind raced to come up with his next move. If he were escorted out of here, they would probably throw him into some high-security prison, and Tanvi would never know where he'd gone and have to leave Shuula behind without him when the replacement ship arrived.

Or they'd kill him. No doubt some of these Shuulans were bloodthirsty freaks who would delight in committing murder for the first time in five millennia.

The security guards drew nearer. Dr. Finn remained onstage, looking both enraged at his people's lack of enthusiasm and Francis's defiance, and pleased at the conflict—a terrifying combination that Francis was unlikely to ever forget.

Francis tried to think of what the heroes did in the comic books he'd read as a teenager and couldn't remember one single thing under this kind of pressure, so he did the only thing he could think of: he vaulted like an awkward Olympian over the few rows of seats separating him from Dr. Finn, threw himself onto the stage, and swiped the racks of vials off of the cart.

He knew that Dr. Finn would very likely have more of this serum back in his lab, and if he didn't, he'd at least have the formula written down so he could make another batch when the first one ran out. But removing this abomination from the auditorium would show Dr. Finn that bullying would not be accepted here and hopefully inspire more of these Shuulans to stand up for themselves.

Francis made a beeline toward the steps at the end of the stage farthest from the approaching security guards. He'd almost made it to the first step when a hand seized his shoulder, and in his surprise at having been caught, one of the racks of vials fell from his arms and shattered on the floor.

The deadly liquid trickled out onto the glossy hardwood, and at once, a faint, greenish mist began to rise into the air as the liquid evaporated. It smelled like burning tar.

"You're a fool," Dr. Finn hissed, letting go of his shoulder.

Dr. Grange covered her mouth with her lab coat and fled as if the devil were after her.

Francis stared at the evaporating mess. He looked back to Dr. Finn, then to the Shuulans sitting nearby in stunned silence.

"Are the fumes...deadly?" Francis asked in a whisper. The security guards had ceased their approach and were looking uncertain. A few Shuulans had risen and were making a hasty departure without looking back.

"Any part of the serum is deadly," Dr. Finn spat, then laughed. "A full injection kills almost instantly, but breathing it in will just delay the process." He clapped Francis on the back. "The serum that made us immortal caused our cells to continuously regenerate, and this serum switches off that ability. Getting a few good whiffs of this should make us start aging again, perhaps slowly, perhaps fast. Congratulations, boy. You've just helped me accomplish what I set out to do."

In the front row, Yuli the gardener and her husband gazed sadly at the body of Tisha Warris while still holding hands. A few others remained seated while the rest made for the exits.

"Will all of them die?" Francis asked hoarsely.

"We'll have to wait and see, won't we?" Dr. Finn's eyes glimmered. "But this little mishap has given me an idea. Instead of having people volunteer to be injected, I can just release the serum into the water supply and make this whole process that much easier. Then we can reverse everyone's sterility so we can start reproducing again, and this planet can get back to the way it was meant to be."

"What gives you the right to do this?"

Some of the spark faded from Dr. Finn's eyes. Lowering his voice so no one but Francis could hear, he said, "I invented the serum that stopped us from dying in the first place. I've had to live most of my life as a different man so no one would know it was me and retaliate, and now, thanks to your help, I can finally make things right."

Francis didn't talk much for the next few days even though Tanvi kept trying to wheedle information out of him every five minutes. News of a cure for life had spread like a wildfire, and Gordie walked around her apartment with a smile that Francis couldn't quite understand.

"Why are you so happy?" Francis asked the evening before the replacement ship arrived from Gobi Express.

"Because if we're all going to start dying, people will get their sterility fixed, if they can. There will be babies again, and children. I can retire from politics and start teaching again. I've missed it so much." Her cheeks practically glowed with enthusiasm. "And we can rejoin the universe without the worry of spreading our mistakes to others. Maybe if I live long enough, I can hitch a ride on a ship and come visit you two on Jarlexium. We can make it a party."

"I'd love that," Tanvi said. "You've been very kind to us."

"I'm always willing to help a stranded alien in need." Gordie winked and looked to Francis. "Why the long face? Any party that involves me is guaranteed to be a blast. You should have seen me in my university days—but then again, maybe you shouldn't have."

Francis tried to smile, but he only felt hollow, like an empty husk.

The gorgeous blackness of space was visible in the viewport in the replacement ship as they hurtled toward the planet Hugh, where they should have landed nearly two weeks ago.

Tanvi sidled up to Francis as he gazed out into the void, twirling his St. Christopher medal around in his fingers. "It's just us now," she said. "So spill the beans."

Francis couldn't look at her. He took a deep breath and said, "I tried to stop that scientist from bullying people into dying. He wanted people to inject themselves with serum. It would have killed them immediately."

"*You* tried to stop him?"

"I haven't always stood up for what's right. And I tried to do the right thing, broke some vials of serum while trying to do it, and found out that the fumes will kill people too, only a lot slower. Everyone who was in that auditorium is going to grow old and die, and Dr. Finn, the man who made the serum, said he's going to dump more serum into the water supply so people drink it. I gave him the idea, Tanvi. Accidentally."

He turned to look at her. She was pursing her lips.

"What?" he asked.

"The guy is a scientist. He would have thought of that eventually."

"But I'm the one who made him think of it now. I feel like a murderer."

"Look how happy Gordie was, though, knowing she'd get to teach

kids again in a few years. If you ask me, I'd say everything is going to work out for those people just fine in the end."

Francis remained silent for a time. He thought of the dreary city streets and the somber shop signs and the plain tract housing that were the contemporary artifacts of a people who ought to have been buried five millennia earlier, and then he imagined scores of laughing, giggling children skipping through the park and singing and throwing balls and falling and scraping their knees and their parents bending over them to give them kisses to make it all better.

Before he knew it, Francis was smiling.

He said, at length, "I think maybe you're right."

THE HOUSE WITH AN INSIDE BUT NO OUTSIDE

"WHEN I WAS A LITTLE girl," Grandma said, "there was a house in the woods that no one could see."

Kenzie sat on the floor at Grandma's feet with her cousins Elijah and Cory, staring at the older woman with rapt attention, as they always did whenever she told them stories.

"Was it invisible?" Kenzie asked, imagining how hard it would be to find the door to get inside. "Or camo...what's the word?"

"Camouflaged," Elijah said smugly, puffing his chest out for emphasis.

"Neither," Grandma said with a crafty look in her eyes. "The reason nobody could see it was because...it didn't have an outside."

"*What*?" Kenzie gasped. Cory giggled at her outburst, and Kenzie threw him a dirty look.

Grandma nodded. "That's right. The house had an inside, all right, with a big, stone fireplace and cozy chairs and shelves of books and long windows that let you see right out into the woods surrounding it. It always smelled of woodsmoke and freshly-baked bread. But the moment you stepped out the door into the shade of the trees and turned around, you couldn't see the house at all. If you walked through the place where you knew the house to be, you wouldn't even run into anything."

"Because it didn't have an outside," Cory murmured in seeming contemplation.

"But Grandma, how did you find the house in the first place?" Kenzie asked.

"Ah. Well." Grandma paused, as if trying to remember. "The first time I found the house, I was playing all by myself down in the woods and kept thinking about how good it would be to have some hot bread fresh out of the oven. Then I smelled it, and I followed the smell with my nose. The next thing I knew, I was inside the house, and a girl just about my age was setting a loaf pan on a potholder on the counter. She told me her name was Esther, and she lived in the house with her grandma and pet cat. The cat's name was…Sam. Sam the Cat. He was gray, with lots of stripes. His nose twitched like he wanted to eat the bread, too."

Kenzie's stomach growled. In the kitchen, her mother was busy making spaghetti and meatballs for all of them, but it didn't seem like it would come soon enough. "Did they let *you* eat the bread?" she asked.

"Oh, yes, of course. And it was dee-licious!"

"Are you telling your tall tales again, Mom?" Kenzie's mother called from the kitchen.

Grandma placed a hand on her heart. "There's nothing tall about them!" She looked to Elijah and winked, and Elijah gave her a sly smile like he knew some secret that Kenzie and Cory didn't. "Anyway," Grandma went on, "I visited Esther and her grandma and Sam nearly every day that summer, and every day, they had fresh bread. Sometimes Esther would come outside so we could go look for fossils in the creek together, or we'd pick wildflowers and weave them into crowns so we could pretend we were the princesses of the forest."

Grandma fell silent, and her eyebrows knit together.

"What is it?" Kenzie asked. "Do you miss Esther?"

"No—I mean, yes—I mean..." Grandma shook her head and smiled. "My mind sometimes likes to get away from me. My own mother used to scold me for having my head in the clouds all the time. She'd tell me if I wasn't careful, I'd float up into the atmosphere all the way into outer space, and then she'd never be able to find me again."

Kenzie felt a little sad, at that. She imagined herself drifting into the sky, while her mother ran around frantically below her, begging for her to come back.

"Why was the house invisible?" Cory asked.

"It wasn't invisible," Elijah said, rolling his eyes. "She said it just didn't have an outside."

"They used magic to build it, of course," Grandma said. "They didn't want nosy people stopping by to sell them vacuum cleaners or new windows. I just happened to be lucky to find the house. Esther told me I must have been a very special girl to find my way inside."

It was hard, trying to imagine Grandma as a little girl like Kenzie. She strained her mind to the limit to place Grandma's bright, hazel eyes into a child's face. Maybe Grandma had looked like Kenzie herself. Yes, that was probably the easiest way to imagine her.

After dinner, Kenzie's dad and Uncle Harry planted themselves in front of the television to watch a boxing match while her mother, Grandma, and Aunt Kim sat around the long, oval table, chatting.

Kenzie liked it when her dad watched boxing, because if he had the news on instead, all the people talked about was a Water Gate, which sounded like a pretty thing but seemed to make a lot of people angry.

Elijah and Cory wrestled on the floor, fighting over who got to play with which action figure. Kenzie ignored the two of them and went into the kitchen to pour herself a glass of apple juice.

She could hear her mother talking from out in the dining room.

"It's one thing to make up stories to tell the kids, but it's another thing to tell them like they really happened to you."

"Oh, Suzanne, I'm just having fun with them. You should have heard some of the yarns my grandmother told me. For years, she had me convinced they'd all found me inside the wreckage of a crashed spaceship in the field across the street from their house."

Aunt Kim laughed. "I remember you telling us about that one. No wonder I turned out the way I did, with all that Martian blood inside me."

Kenzie finished filling her cup. She put the bottle of juice back into the fridge and continued listening.

"We've been trying to teach Kenzie the difference between truth and fiction," Kenzie's mom went on. Even though nobody could see her from her position in the kitchen, Kenzie blushed. "Her teacher told me she's been making up stories in class to impress the other students. Last week she told everyone her father had been eaten by a shark."

Aunt Kim let out a peal of laughter. "Dave, have you ever even put a toe in the ocean?"

"Nope!" Kenzie's dad called from the living room. "And now I'm not gonna!"

"You should be proud that Kenzie has such an imagination," Grandma said.

"And I am!" said Kenzie's mom. "But sometimes I worry it's going to get her into trouble."

After school the next day, Kenzie got off the bus and let herself into the house. Both of her parents were still at work, so she set her backpack and lunchbox down and wandered from room to room, trying to figure out what to do to keep busy. TV just didn't sound very fun right now, and she wasn't in the mood for drawing, so she ventured outside onto the stone patio behind the house and stared at the edge of the woods, thinking about Grandma's story.

These weren't the same woods Grandma had played in as a little girl. Grandma had grown up in a faraway place called Vermont, where there were mountains and lots of maple syrup. There weren't any mountains here, just little hills in some places, but Kenzie's backyard didn't even have those.

Just woods.

But woods could be fun. Grandma had more or less said so.

Kenzie strode toward the edge of the trees, and within seconds she was walking in their shade. The wind made a soothing noise as it rustled through their boughs, and at last, Kenzie flopped down on a bed of dried pine needles and lay on her back to stare up at the sunlight filtering down between thousands of ever-swaying leaves.

She imagined she was resting after a long journey on foot through treacherous terrain. Her horse must have given up on the trip and run away, leaving her to face the wild alone. She didn't even have any food with her! Would she starve out here? No, she would have to just forage for food like the cavemen did a billion years ago.

Kenzie stood and scanned the area for berry vines and other food sources. As she inhaled the scents of the forest, she caught a whiff of… spaghetti and meatballs?

Following the unexpected scent, Kenzie stepped over tree roots and past the rotting remains of an ancient fence.

Suddenly she stood inside a house, as if she'd been teleported there. To her left lay an immense stone hearth, a fire blazing inside. A little dark-haired girl sat on the floor petting a stripy, gray cat.

Kenzie blinked. "Are you Esther?" she asked, remembering Grandma's story.

The girl lifted her head and giggled. "No. That's my grandma's name."

"Then who are you? I thought a little girl named Esther lived here."

"I did," said an older woman, entering the room. "And then I grew up!" She frowned for so long that at first Kenzie thought she would send her away, but then she said, "I'm making spaghetti. You can stay and have some, if you'd like."

"I can *stay*?"

"I don't see why not. It's not every day that somebody barges in and finds us." The old woman's mouth twitched into a smile. She had long, white hair tied back into a braid and wore a white apron over a flowery dress, not unlike Kenzie's own grandmother.

"I'm Izzy," the girl said, then pointed at the cat, who had rolled onto his back for a tummy rub. "And this is Whiskers."

Kenzie sat down to pet the cat's belly. His fur was soft beneath her fingers, and it made her wish her parents would let her get a cat of her own. "Not Sam?" she asked.

"This is Sam's great-great-great-great-great-great grandson," Izzy's grandma said. "Whiskers comes from a long line of noble cats. He loves being scratched between the ears, too."

Kenzie scratched Whiskers's head. The cat purred as if he had never been more relaxed in his life.

It soon came time to eat. Grandma Esther set out plates on the table, and Kenzie and Izzy loaded them up with as much spaghetti and meatballs as would fit on them. There was even garlic bread—one of Kenzie's favorites.

"I never knew there was a house back here," Kenzie said between bites. "And I've lived here my whole life."

"We tend to keep quiet," Grandma Esther said, smiling. Whiskers the Cat had climbed up into her lap at the table, a proud look on his furry face. "There's no point in bothering the neighbors when we don't have to."

"We never talk to our neighbors," Kenzie said. "Mom and Dad say the Edwards are dizzybodies, and the Molinas are snobs." Kenzie wasn't entirely sure what either of those things meant, but she knew they weren't good.

"It's a good thing we're neither." Grandma Esther winked. "I like to think of myself as the Queen of Hospitality. In fact, I am!"

"Is that like a kingdom?"

"A queendom!" the old lady exclaimed, making Whiskers bolt out of the room. "And you, Kenzie, are our honored guest."

Kenzie liked the turn this was taking. Not only was she getting a free dinner to stave off starvation, but she was in the presence of nobility, no less!

Her gaze drifted to the grandfather clock ticking contentedly in the corner, and Kenzie gave a start. She may have been young, but she'd known how to read a clock since she was four.

"What is it?" Izzy asked.

"It's…it's six o'clock," Kenzie said. "My parents will be home soon. They'll wonder where I've gone." She looked at her plate and realized it was empty. Would her parents be angry if she was too full for supper?

"It's been lovely having you here," Grandma Esther said, then paused, pressing the tip of one finger against her left temple. "Tomorrow's your birthday, isn't it?"

"That's right!" Kenzie grinned, because she'd briefly forgotten. "I'm turning six."

"Well, I've got just the perfect present for a six-year-old." The woman rose and left the room, returning minutes later with a box wrapped in bright red paper. "Go ahead, open it!"

Kenzie took the box and ripped the paper off to see that underneath, the box was an ordinary brown one made of thick cardboard. She lifted off the lid and gasped.

Inside lay a silver and diamond tiara, fit for a princess—no, an empress!

She lifted it out with trembling hands and placed it upon her head. There weren't any mirrors nearby, but she imagined the tiara glimmered in the light like stars.

"Thank you," she said. "This is the best birthday present ever."

"You're very welcome," Grandma Esther said. "It fits you perfectly."

"I need to go now, though," Kenzie said, moving toward the door. "Can I come back?"

"Anytime you like! All you have to do is come look for us, and you'll find us."

Grandma Esther and Izzy both gave her a hug and showed Kenzie to the door. She stepped out into the forest and heard the door click shut behind her. When she turned around, there was no sign of a house anywhere, only trees, but that was to be expected.

"Kenzie?"

She opened her eyes, feeling disoriented as she focused on her mother's worried face. It took her a moment to realize she was lying on her back on the forest floor. Pine needles clung to her shirt as she sat up. She patted her head for her tiara and felt nothing but hair.

The tiara wasn't on the ground, either. Her heart ached as she realized she must have dropped it somewhere after leaving Izzy's house.

"What time is it?" Kenzie asked.

"It's almost six—when I realized you weren't in the house when I got home, I came out here looking for you. You had me scared there for a minute."

"I'm sorry, Mom. I was visiting Izzy and Grandma Esther in the house without an outside. We had spaghetti, and they gave me a beautiful tiara for my birthday." Kenzie glanced at the ground again. "But I think I lost it."

Kenzie's mother gave her a look of exhaustion, then smiled. "We'll have to find you a new one, then. Now come in and wash up, and I can get dinner started."

Though Kenzie's mother had kept her word by finding her a new tiara in the discount bin at the supermarket two days later, Kenzie was determined to locate the one she'd misplaced, seeing as it had been a gift from the people in the house without an outside. Presents were supposed to be special, and losing special things was enough to make anybody sad, especially the people who'd given them to you.

On another afternoon after Kenzie got off the bus and before her parents returned home from work, Kenzie ventured forth into the woods by herself in spite of her mother's insistence not to and began to scan the ground for signs of something silver and glimmery. Something sparkling in the sunlight for a moment near the base of a pine tree caught her eye, but it was only a candy wrapper, blown there by the wind. Kenzie picked it up and put it into her pocket to throw away later, then continued onward.

She had traveled much farther than on that first day when she plopped down onto a bed of evergreen needles and put her chin on her hand to think of where else the tiara might have gotten to. Could some other little girl have been playing out here, found it, and kept it for herself? It wasn't impossible; there were a few other children on Kenzie's street, although she'd never seen them venturing near the woods before. Perhaps leaves had blown over it, or maybe an animal had even taken it to decorate its nest.

Giggling at the mere thought of a fancy racoon in a crown, Kenzie stood, brushed the needles off her pants, and turned back toward home, but nearly squealed when she saw Izzy, the girl from the house without an outside, standing ten feet away from her, holding out a tiara for Kenzie to take.

"Looking for this?" Izzy asked.

Kenzie took it from her and set it atop her head, feeling as regal as a fairy princess. She twirled in place and imagined herself standing in a vast ballroom filled with ladies in long dresses and men in suit jackets with gold buttons, all watching her.

"Thank you," Kenzie said to her. "Where did you find it?"

"On the ground near our house," Izzy said, putting her hands into her pockets. "Grandma Esther found it yesterday and cleaned the mud off. You weren't supposed to lose it, silly."

Kenzie's cheeks burned suddenly as she stared at her feet. "It was an accident."

"It's okay. One time I lost my favorite doll, and it took me weeks to find her."

"Where was she?" Kenzie asked.

"In a box of Whiskers' toys. He was hiding it from me. Want to come home with me and play with him?"

"Sure!" Kenzie beamed, and skipped along behind Izzy until they'd magically appeared in the house without an outside. Whiskers, the tabby, sat on the floor in front of the hearth grooming one of his feet while Grandma Esther sat at the table playing cards with an old man who smiled at Kenzie and waved.

"Kenzie, this is Grandpa Freddie," Izzy said, indicating the man. "Grandpa Freddie, this is Kenzie. She lives in the house just outside the woods."

Grandpa Freddie frowned at Kenzie a moment and said, "Ah."

Not knowing what "ah" was supposed to mean in this instance, Kenzie said, "My parents are Suzanne and Dave Fairweather. Do you know them?"

The old man chewed on his lip. "It might be I've heard of them. They're not our type, are they?" He glanced to Grandma Esther with raised eyebrows, which were bushy and reminded Kenzie of gray caterpillars.

"I don't think so, no," Grandma Esther said, a note of sadness in her voice. She laid her cards face down on the table and turned toward Kenzie while Izzy enticed Whiskers with a piece of string she'd withdrawn from her pocket. "Kenzie dear, do your parents know you're here?"

Kenzie shook her head. "They're at work. I was supposed to stay in the house, but I wanted to find my tiara." She absently patted the top of her head to assure herself the tiara was still there. Her chest tightened as she realized she would have to hide it when she got home—if she didn't, her parents would know she'd snuck out of the house again, and they would take away her picture books and her crayons as punishment, which they'd done once before when she wouldn't eat her spinach.

"I see," Grandma Esther said softly, appearing contemplative. "I feared this sort of thing might be the case when you…well, never mind about that. It's happened so many other times, too. Oh, dear. Why does this always happen to us?"

"Because it's how it happens," said Grandpa Freddie. "Just like with your parents, and their parents." He paused. "Best ride things out to the end, like usual."

Grandma Esther sighed. "You're right, of course. And to think having a house without an outside was meant to keep *out* trouble!" She turned back to Kenzie and gave her a weary smile. "Is there anything I can get you, sweetie?"

Kenzie, who had begun to feel baffled by the exchange between Izzy's grandparents, shook her head. "I just want to play with Whiskers," she said. "If that's okay."

"Only as long as Whiskers is willing," Grandma Esther said with a wink.

And willing, Whiskers was. Izzy and Kenzie took turns racing up and down the staircase trailing the piece of string so the cat could chase it, and when the tabby wore out, the two of them sat on Izzy's bedroom floor scratching him behind the ears. Kenzie wished she could ask her parents to get a cat of their own, but they would just say no because that's what parents did.

"Where are your parents?" Kenzie asked once Whiskers had hopped up on the bed to wash himself again—apparently playing with string tended to get one dirty.

Izzy shrugged. "I don't really know. They're busy and gone a lot. Right now I think they might be off in the Shadowed Lands fighting off the Seven-Eyed Terror of Undoon."

"What's *that*?"

"A monster with a bunch of tentacles. Sometimes it slips into this realm invisible and takes children from their beds. My parents talked about ways they could trick it." Izzy paused. "Or maybe they did that already, and now they're visiting my cousins in the Willow Court. Sometimes I get things mixed up. What do your parents do?"

"My mom works at a dry cleaner," Kenzie said. "And my dad is a bank teller."

"What's a bank teller?"

"He works at a bank and tells people how much money they have. He tells my mom that we don't have enough of it."

Izzy's nose wrinkled. "What's so important about money?"

Kenzie thought about it, but she didn't know.

Kenzie's mother found the tiara.

"What's this?" she asked, coming out of Kenzie's room after bringing in a stack of clean laundry. She held up the tiara, which glinted in the glare of the living room light.

Kenzie could feel herself blushing. She'd hid the tiara in her sock drawer, which seemed an awfully silly place now that she thought about it. "Izzy and Grandma Esther gave it to me," she said.

Her mother's frown deepened. "Where did you really get it? It's made of real metal." She rapped on it with her fingernails as if to test its solidity.

"I told you, it was Izzy and Grandma Esther. They live in the house with an inside but no outside."

"We need to have a little talk about that," her mother said, then gestured for Kenzie to sit on the couch.

Kenzie obeyed, bracing herself for the confiscation of her books and art supplies.

Her mother sat down next to her but did not relinquish her hold on the tiara. "Honey, there is no such thing as a house that doesn't have an outside. That's just a story your grandma made up to entertain you and your cousins. It's what she does."

"But I was there. They have a cat, and a fireplace, and a grandpa, too."

"You were using your imagination. There is no house out in those woods, invisible or otherwise. The woods extend about twenty acres and end over on Park Road. It's just trees. So I'll have to ask you again—where did you get the tiara?"

"It was a present from—"

"Izzy and Grandma Esther. So you've said. Now you need to tell me the truth."

Kenzie stared helplessly up at her mother. What did she want her to say? Kenzie *was* telling the truth, and saying anything else would be a lie.

"They did give it to me," Kenzie said. "Then I lost it. Then they found it for me."

Her mother opened her mouth and closed it. Then her face paled and she said, "You're sure they're real people?"

"Yes! And they live in the house with an inside but no outside! I'm telling the truth, Mama!"

Kenzie had the sensation of shrinking as her mother rose from the couch with the air of a towering storm cloud. "You stay in here," her mother said coldly. "If you so much as leave the house before I get back, you'll be grounded until you're forty."

Her mother still didn't let go of the tiara as she stormed out the back door. Kenzie went to the wide window looking out onto the backyard and watched her mother disappear into the trees, no doubt trying to find the magical house herself. Hopefully Grandma Esther and Grandpa Freddie would be nice to her even though she was in a bad mood. Maybe they'd even give her some fresh bread or spaghetti.

Perhaps fifteen minutes later, Kenzie's mother reappeared from among the trees, disheveled and still gripping the tiara that was causing Kenzie so much grief. When she came through the back door and set the tiara on the counter she said, "It's just like I thought—no houses out there, not even a tent. Whoever you met out there either lives in one of the houses over on Park Road, or they were a couple of creeps just passing through."

Kenzie frowned. "Creeps?"

"People who might want to hurt little children. Sometimes they give kids gifts to get them to trust them."

Kenzie couldn't imagine Grandma Esther or Izzy hurting even the tiniest fly, and though she'd only met Grandpa Freddie the one time, it seemed wrong he'd want to hurt anyone, either. "But why would they do that?" she asked.

"Because people can be cruel. I don't want you to go out there again. I'll see if either your father or I can arrange to get off work early on the days you have school, so you aren't left alone. God knows we can't afford a cut in hours, but we'll do whatever we can to keep you safe. Okay?"

"Okay, Mama." Yet already, Kenzie felt sad, as if a burning bright light above her had gone out for good.

$$\cdot \cdot \ast \ast \ast \ast \ast \cdot \cdot$$

The next Monday when Kenzie emerged from the bus of chattering children, she spotted her mother's pale blue sedan in the driveway and skipped up to the front door, trying not to feel disappointed that she wouldn't be able to sneak out into the woods to play with Izzy and Whiskers again.

Inside, the house smelled of chocolate chip cookies, and Kenzie gasped with delight when she entered the kitchen and saw dozens of them cooling on trays. Not only that, but a new coloring book and set of colored pencils sat on the table. This was almost like a dream come true!

Her mother entered the room while Kenzie scribbled furiously with a violet pencil on the first page of the coloring book—a page showing a scene of a butterfly perched on a daisy—and she sat down across from her at the table.

"How was school today?" she asked.

Kenzie looked up from her page. "Sammie said at recess that she and her parents are going to Mars on summer break."

Her mother's mouth twitched. "And do you believe that?"

Kenzie scrunched her forehead up in thought as she replayed the memory of her classmate discussing plans of going to the nearest spaceport and meeting all the Martians who'd greet them when they arrived on the red planet. It had all sounded very exciting, but something in Sammie's words just hadn't rung true. "I think she was just telling a story," Kenzie admitted. "Like when I told them all Daddy got eaten by a shark."

"So you know you were telling a story then."

"It was a funny story, though, wasn't it? No sharks would ever try to eat Daddy; he'd taste terrible."

"I'm sure he would." Her mother smiled faintly. "Now are you ready to admit that going inside a house with an inside and no outside is a story, too?"

"Oh, no. I was really there, Mama. If I'd had a camera, I could have taken pictures to show you."

Instead of arguing, her mother rose and plucked two cookies off of one of the cooling racks, then gave one to Kenzie and bit into the other one herself. "Here's what I think really happened, Kenzie. You probably found the tiara on the ground out there and had a dream that people in an invisible house gave it to you, because Grandma had just been telling you all that silly story. I've been asking around at the neighbors, and nobody has seen an old woman and a little girl sneaking around out there. I don't think they're real, either."

Kenzie finished chewing up a bite of her own cookie and swallowed. She wanted to argue, to tell her mother it was mean to say that real, flesh and blood people were just dreams, but Suzanne Fairweather could be as stubborn as a team of angry mules (according to Grandma, that was), and was not likely to budge on what she thought.

Over the course of the next few weeks, Kenzie got nearly no moments alone. Sometimes Daddy was home when Kenzie got off the bus, and sometimes it was Mama, and sometimes Grandma had driven all the way over from Middletown to keep an eye on her if Kenzie's parents had to stay and work extra.

Grandma would tell her stories, as usual, but she never mentioned the house with an inside but no outside again.

Despite her lack of alone time when she could wander and roam, Kenzie began to love the afternoons with her parents. Daddy would take her down to the park and push her on the swings, or try to teach her the names of the birds they'd see pecking the ground near the picnic shelter, and Mama would ooh and ahh over Kenzie's drawings and read to her from a huge book of fairy tales, because Grandma had recommended it.

In time, she began to think of Izzy and Grandma Esther and Whiskers less and less, until she'd nearly forgotten them altogether.

It had been months since Grandma told the story of the house with an inside but no outside. Kenzie emerged from the bus once more and saw an empty driveway in front of her house.

A sticky note had been adhered to the front door. It read:

Kenzie—neither your father or I are able to get off work early today, and Grandma is at an appointment, so you will be alone until 4:30. DO NOT GO OUTSIDE BY YOURSELF. —Mom

Kenzie was getting better at sounding out words, and it only took her a few tries to get the full meaning of the note. A small pang of sadness filled her, knowing she wouldn't have any company for a while, but she shrugged her small shoulders and went into the house.

She set her lunchbox and backpack down in the kitchen and made herself a snack of peanut butter and celery, which she ate sitting at the kitchen table while staring out the back window toward the woods.

What should she do in the meantime? Read one of the new books Grandma had sent over for her? No, the weather was much too nice for that today—the sun gleamed brightly overhead, and dandelions were peeking from the ground as the first signs of spring. Even the bare trees in the woods were starting to show hints of green. As Grandma often said, staying inside on a day like this would be a crime.

Her mother didn't want her going outside, but if she didn't stay out there long, her mother never needed to know, did she?

Grinning to herself, Kenzie skipped out the back door and breathed in the fresh spring air. Birds chirped in the trees at the edge of the woods, and Kenzie stepped closer to them, trying to remember all the bird names her daddy had taught her. She saw a dove, and a blue jay, and a cardinal, and…

She soon found herself enveloped by woods. A chipmunk scurried through the underbrush with its tail held high, and Kenzie bolted after it with a giggle but suddenly found herself inside a cozy living area with a hearth and rustic furniture.

At first she felt dizzy like she'd just gotten off of one of the rides at the carnival, but then realized exactly where it was she'd found herself. It was Izzy and Grandma Esther's house! She couldn't believe she'd forgotten about it.

"Is anybody here?" she called out, for she saw no one, not even the cat.

She heard the sound of footsteps, and then Izzy entered the room wearing a red summer dress and matching ribbons in her hair. "Kenzie!" she said. "I didn't think you'd be coming back."

Grandma Esther came into the room behind her, Whiskers twining around her ankles. "Goodness, Kenzie, you've caught us just in time! We were all about to move on."

"What do you mean?" Kenzie asked, looking from one of them to the other.

"You didn't think houses with insides and no outsides just stay in one place forever, did you?" Grandma Esther asked with a twinkle in her eye. "The signs have all been there for a while; now we'll just have to see where we end up next."

"You don't know where you're going?"

"We never really do." The old woman sighed. "It's always an adventure, you know, being the Queen of Hospitality. We turn up in a new place, and without fail someone like you wanders in needing love and attention. Would you like a cookie, dear?"

"Sure," Kenzie said. "And thanks."

She followed Grandma Esther into the kitchen, and the woman handed her a frosted cookie from a jar. "I'm afraid you can't stay here for more than a few minutes," she went on. "It's been a pleasure having you here, Kenzie Fairweather, but it's time we all moved on."

Whiskers bumped up against Kenzie's legs. She scooped him into her arms and scratched his head while he purred. Her eyes burned as tears formed in the corners of them, and the cookie nearly stuck in her throat. "Won't I be able to come back here again?" Kenzie asked.

"Most likely not," Grandma Esther said with a note of sadness. "That's just the way of things."

"I'll try not to forget you," Kenzie said as Whiskers leapt from her arms.

"We won't forget you either, dear."

Then, without warning, Kenzie was standing in the middle of the woods holding a half-eaten cookie with a clump of cat hair stuck to one side of it.

The house with an inside and no outside was gone.

Holding back tears, she left the woods and went back into her own house to wait for her parents to get home—and when they did, Kenzie's tears flowed unchecked down her face.

"What's happened, sweetie?" her mother asked, sitting beside her on the couch and giving her a squeeze.

"They're gone." Kenzie sniffled. Her eyes and throat ached from crying. "Izzy and Grandma Esther, and Whiskers, too."

Kenzie's father, who stood in the doorway looking uncertain, exchanged a glance with her mother. "I've been thinking," he said. "Maybe it's high time we got ourselves a cat of our own. Might be good at taking care of mice."

Kenzie could feel her tears subside, as if her father had just uttered magic words. "Do you really mean it?"

"Of course I do!" He sat down on the couch beside them and ruffled Kenzie's hair with one hand. "We can go to the pound tomorrow and see what they've got. We can even name one 'Whiskers,' if that's what you want."

"Can he be gray and stripy?"

"Absolutely."

Kenzie thought it sounded like the best idea in the world. She bounded off the couch into her room, saying, "I need to make him a bed, and give him toys to play with!" She turned to see both of her parents eyeing her from her bedroom doorway, and she felt a surge of delight to see them both smiling at her. "You two are the best parents in the world!"

"Grandma, can you tell us a story?" asked little Amelia, the daughter of Kenzie Fairweather Riley's second son, James.

The child's eyes were so bright and eager that despite Kenzie's overwhelming fatigue, she couldn't help but appease her.

Kenzie rocked back in her chair and looked up at the ceiling. "Let me think," she said, her voice creaking from years of use leading the weekly story times at the local library. She'd read thousands of books to children over four decades of volunteering, yet right now she couldn't think of a plot to a single one of them off the top of her head.

She strained her thoughts back through the years and, giving up, decided to make something up on the fly.

"Once upon a time," Kenzie said, "there was a house in the woods that no one could see."

STORY NOTES

LETTER FROM GLOMSUET

I have the tendency to get carried away while Googling things, which then causes me to fall into peculiar corners of the internet I never would have stumbled into otherwise.

I will never forget the day I discovered the Flat Earthers who, like their name suggests, believe that the Earth is shaped like a pancake. (Perhaps they read too many *Discworld* novels?)

Then I wondered what might happen if a Flat Earther got abducted by aliens.

I might have had too much fun writing this story.

THE MAN OF HER DREAMS

I can't tell you how many evenings my dear friend Jennifer and I spent getting wasted on the couch while watching movies and campy episodes of classic *Doctor Who*. (Those of you who know a bit about me might remember that I, too, am named Jennifer in that mysterious place called The Real World. No, my friend Jennifer is not some alternate part of my psyche. Parents in the 1980s just didn't know what else to name their children.)

There is a certain actor whom my friend held (holds?) in high esteem, who is brilliant at acting but is something of a shitty human being. Jennifer once made the comment that she thought that she and that actor "could have made it work" if she had been born several decades earlier and actually met him.

She still doesn't know I've written this story.

JAY

Have you ever wondered what might happen if Jesus showed up at church? Me too.

DAILY LOG FROM OUTPOST #602

Sometimes if I'm not sure what to write about, I use a random word generator online to compile a short list of words that I can incorporate into a brand-new story. The ten words that got incorporated into the first draft of this story were "ear," "abnormal," "duck," "use," "glorious," "cakes," "elbow," "sloppy," "utter," "shrug," "house," and "color."

"Duck" got edited out during rewrites, but it did influence the nature of the species that invades the base. *Quack quack.*

NO GOOD REASON

I've met a plethora of interesting people during my tenure as a published author. People come up to my table at book signings and tell me fascinating tales of how they've been inside Area 51, how they've been turned into lizard people, how the government has been harassing them by transmitting a constant high-pitched whine into their heads, and so on.

Perhaps it's the nature of what I write that attracts this crowd?

One man I met was perplexed because all his life, people have attacked him for no reason. Since I *am* an author, I turned it into a story, but I do hope that man finds some peace, since the fellow in my story didn't.

HOW TO MAKE MONEY FAST

When I attended Northern Kentucky University what feels like a thousand years ago now, strange things were constantly happening on the campus plaza, from peaceful protests by men dressed as Santa Claus to performance art classes traipsing around in spacesuits. Were any of the people out there actually aliens in disguise? I honestly wouldn't be surprised.

THE FAMILY NAME

I've never understood the preference for sons over daughters in some cultures. It makes no sense, really.

LARRY

"Larry" came about when I learned of an anthology seeking submissions featuring imaginary friends. My story didn't quite make the cut, but it was weird enough that I slapped it into this collection instead.

THIRTEEN

This story originally appeared in *Five Minutes at Hotel Stormcove*, an anthology of stories published by Atthis Arts that each take place over the course of five minutes at the titular place of lodging. When I read in the anthology guidelines that Hotel Stormcove has no thirteenth floor, it got me wondering...

INHERITANCE

Like the previous story, this one also originally appeared in an Atthis Arts anthology. *Community of Magic Pens* was about—you guessed it—stories involving magic pens. This pen was the most magical I could think of.

THE LAST TO PASS

Immortality sounds like nothing but fun and games until you sit back and ponder all of the potential consequences.

THE HOUSE WITH AN INSIDE BUT NO OUTSIDE

People might be surprised to learn that I did, in fact, have a normal childhood.

Whether or not this means I was a normal *child* is another question entirely.

And now, just for fun...

When I was in high school, I wrote a short poem called New Frontier. It sat in a notebook for the better part of two decades...until now! Consider it a prize for reaching the end of this book.

NEW FRONTIER

Always turning
Always spinning
Never losing
Never winning
Born in cloud and
Dies in fire
Watch the flames of
Stars rise higher
Endless voids of
Outer space are
Too much for the
Human race but
Someday we just
Might get there but
Maybe we will
Just not care.

ABOUT THE
AUTHOR

J. S. BAILEY is the author of eight novels and numerous short stories. She works at an independent bookstore in Cincinnati and lives nearby with her husband and daughter. She enjoys walking in the woods and daydreaming about her next book. Stay up to date on Bailey news by visiting her website and following her on social media.

www.jsbaileywrites.com
Facebook.com/jsbaileywrites
Instagram.com/jsbailey_author
Twitter.com/jsbailey_author
Goodreads.com/jsbailey